THE YORK MINSTER KILLINGS

WES MARKIN

Boldwood

First published in Great Britain in 2026 by Boldwood Books Ltd.

Copyright © Wes Markin, 2026

Cover Design by Head Design Ltd.

Cover Images: Alamy and iStock

The moral right of Wes Markin to be identified as the author of this work has been asserted in accordance with the Copyright, Designs and Patents Act 1988.

Every effort has been made to obtain the necessary permissions with reference to copyright material, both illustrative and quoted. We apologise for any omissions in this respect and will be pleased to make the appropriate acknowledgements in any future edition.

A CIP catalogue record for this book is available from the British Library.

Paperback ISBN 978-1-80656-173-5

Large Print ISBN 978-1-80656-159-9

Hardback ISBN 978-1-80656-152-0

Trade Paperback ISBN 978-1-80656-162-9

Ebook ISBN 978-1-80656-161-2

Kindle ISBN 978-1-80656-171-1

Audio CD ISBN 978-1-80656-178-0

MP3 CD ISBN 978-1-80656-182-7

Digital audio download ISBN 978-1-80656-164-3

This book is printed on certified sustainable paper. Boldwood Books is dedicated to putting sustainability at the heart of our business. For more information please visit https://www.boldwoodbooks.com/about-us/sustainability/

Boldwood Books Ltd, 23 Bowerdean Street, London, SW6 3TN

www.boldwoodbooks.com

To Andy's Man Club – it's good to talk.

PROLOGUE

In the shadow of York Minster another stone hit him.

He gritted his teeth against the pain. The bullies laughed.

He waited for it to stop, to go quiet, and then opened his eyes.

They were leaving.

He didn't get to his feet just yet, content to stare at the Gothic towers spearing into a blood-red sky.

Was this a dream or was this real?

Did it matter?

Maybe not – the bullies were real. Always had been.

Always would be.

Crows circled now.

A few at first, though they quickly multiplied. Suddenly, there were hundreds, descending from the Minster's towers like a black avalanche.

Always.

He closed his eyes, willing them to leave, but when he opened them again, they were all around him. Hopping.

Cocking heads. Penetrating with eyes locked somewhere between life and death.

He thought of his Irish gran; dead almost five years. The only person who ever really seemed to have time for him.

Who fought his corner.

She once told him a story of battlefield crows. 'The ones that would choose who lived, and who died.'

There was the Morrigan, though he'd thought it sounded more like 'Morgan' when he was younger. 'A queen who became a crow.'

Or maybe she was always a crow?

It had been many years since she'd told him the story, and he'd read a great deal since then.

Three crows came close.

Three sisters?

The first pecked at his hands where the stones had cut. The second at his cheek where tears mixed with blood. The third watched. But that was so much worse.

Those that watch. That allow this. That somehow relish this.

'Washer at the ford,' his gran's voice echoed. 'She washes the blood from your clothes before you die.'

But there was no water.

Then there were more beaks and feathers.

Brothers and sisters.

A thousand tiny wounds opening across his skin.

But it didn't hurt any more.

There was only release.

Yes... he lay, still encouraging them.

Peck deeper.

Find the poison in my veins.

The fever in my brain.

Make me clean. Make me empty.

Take away the grief in my heart...

* * *

'It's a good heart,' DI Paul Riddick said.

'Can you please not talk for another moment, Paul?' Dr Mitchell said.

'Strong,' Riddick said, ignoring the command. 'I mean, I'd know, wouldn't I?'

'Please, Paul...' Jerome, the assisting nurse, added.

The cardiologist withdrew the biopsy forceps from the catheter threaded through his jugular.

Riddick sighed, as he always did during these quarterly endomyocardial biopsies, over the peculiar sensation, which he assumed to be psychological.

Ice water trickling backward through his bloodstream towards his transplanted heart.

A gauze pad was pressed firmly against the puncture site in his neck. 'All done,' Mitchell said.

'Rejection results in forty-eight hours?' Riddick said with a raised eyebrow.

Mitchell smiled. 'Have I become that predictable?'

'Well, maybe we can start cutting it down to twice a year or even once a year?' Riddick asked. 'Like I said, it's a good heart...'

'Sorry, Paul, not yet. I'm sure it is a good heart, but we follow the procedures for a reason.'

Procedures, Riddick thought. *Speak to most people and they will tell you that I've always had a problem with procedures.* He thought it best to keep this to himself.

Riddick nodded, acknowledging that Mitchell was right. After all, it'd only been just over a year since the esteemed heart surgeon, Dr Gresham, had given him this second chance at life with this good heart. Although, a notable mention should go to the poor twenty-four-year-old motorcyclist from Leeds who'd supplied it.

'I know it's difficult,' Mitchell said. 'But so far so good... Let's not put it into jeopardy.'

'I agree,' Riddick said, despite the inner turmoil he felt over the frequent tests, as well as the medication schedules.

It was a good job he had his smartphone to keep him on track – he wondered how people used to manage their medication regimes.

Tacrolimus with breakfast to suppress his immune system, prednisolone with lunch despite the weight gain it caused, omeprazole before bed to protect his stomach from the cocktail of other medications slowly poisoning him to keep him alive.

'Any chest pain, shortness of breath, unusual fatigue, or bleeding from the site, call immediately,' Mitchell said. 'So, it goes without saying that there is no heavy lifting for twenty-four hours.' Just before he turned to leave the room, Mitchell turned back. 'Oh, and I strongly advise you to take the rest of the day off... maybe tomorrow too.'

Riddick smiled and said, 'Bye, Doc.'

Mitchell sighed, interpreting that smile for exactly what it meant.

Time off?

Are you mad?

1

He didn't even make it to the car before the option of the rest of the day off disappeared in a puff of smoke.

One of his mobile phones rang. And not his personal one.

He tried to stem the surge of adrenaline, for obvious health reasons, but this was a tall order, especially when the only person who contacted him on this mobile was his informant, who was not due to check in for another couple of days.

Jamie Morrison.

Nineteen-year-old Jamie was a small-time dealer from Tang Hall with fingernails bitten down to an eye-watering degree. Jamie was certainly no rock – in fact, he was as shaky as they came – but he remained Riddick's best source of intelligence on the recent spate of commercial burglaries plaguing York's city centre.

Also, the paranoid ones always came good – it made them more observant. If they could get away with jumping at every shadow and staying alive, then they were absolute gold dust.

The fact that the phone was ringing right now suggested one of two things. Hopefully, something was about to happen that he had the inside scoop on. Or, probably more likely, he'd been spotted jumping at shadows and was in mortal danger.

Riddick was about to answer the phone when a few nurses came close, and he was subject to their conversation about long shifts, so he waited a moment to answer. When the sound of the nurses was behind him, and all he could hear was the traffic humming along the ring road close to York Hospital, he contacted Jamie.

'Jamie?'

The voice that came through was high-pitched and breathless. 'Thank God you picked up.'

Riddick tried his best to not jump immediately to the most negative conclusion – after all, Jamie nearly always sounded like this anyway. 'Go on, Jamie.'

'They know... they bloody know!'

Riddick felt the icy February wind, closed his eyes, and rubbed his temples with his available hand. The news was bad. Still... rein it in... calm it down. 'Okay, Jamie. Slow down. Deep breaths. Who knows what?'

'Danny Hurren.'

Riddick winced. It was going from bad to worse. Still... 'How did you find this out?'

'He's been asking questions about who I've been talking to. I'm buggered. I'm absolutely fu—'

'Jamie,' Riddick said, moving away from the hospital entrance, seeking privacy near the car park's edge. 'You don't know he discovered anything. Who gave you this information?'

'Christ... Shit... I've got to run...'

'Jamie... tell me where you are and what's happening?'

'A black BMW, been following me since I left the betting shop.'

'Are you sure? You've been jumpy lately...' Well, always, but...

'No, it's them. I recognise the driver – it's one of Hurren's boys. Big lad with the scar through his eyebrow.'

Riddick's stomach dropped. This wasn't paranoia – this was real. Jamie in genuine danger, and Riddick potentially too far away to help.

'I've got to go,' Jamie said.

'Where are you?'

'Tang Hall Explore Library. The car park.'

'Go into the library... Stay visible...'

The line was already dead.

Riddick jogged to his car.

No heavy lifting for twenty-four hours.

He suddenly felt like he had a twenty-kilo dumbbell in each hand.

2

It was a cold February morning and the heater in Graham Blank's 2008 Ford Focus was broken.

Still, it didn't stop the sweat pooling in the small of his back and the steering wheel slipping under his wet palms.

The traffic jam hadn't moved in twenty-three minutes.

He stared at his dashboard, trying to concentrate despite his vision swimming in and out of focus. One hundred and eighty thousand miles on the clock.

The time caught his eye next.

Missing Lucy's hospital appointment now seemed a foregone conclusion. She was due at 10 a.m. and he'd not even picked her up. The way it was going, it'd already be ten by the time he did.

He looked back up. The windscreen was fogging from the heat of his fever. He coughed and hit the steering wheel.

Bollocks!

He rolled his head, trying to ease the tension in his neck. He swallowed; his throat burned and he closed his eyes.

Stay calm. Stay focused. Everything depends on that ten o'clock appointment. Everything.

You can still do it.

He cracked the window, allowing the glass to clear, and then looked around.

Who was he kidding?

York's Viking Festival had turned Hull Road into a car park. Tourist coaches lined up like siege engines along the Heslington Road junction, disgorging crowds in plastic horned helmets and fake fur cloaks. Red and white banners fluttered from every lamppost: *Jorvik Viking Festival – Experience the Past!*

York University's accommodation blocks rose like concrete monuments. Students walked freely along the pavements, carrying coffee cups. Laughing.

Look at them living their lives while I stay trapped in this metal box. While the whole world around me shrinks to—

A coughing fit seized him.

He spat crap out the window.

His eyes went back to the LED dashboard.

I'm like a fly around lights…

Nine fifteen.

I've no fucking chance.

He needed to call his ex-wife's mother, Samantha. Warn her that she needed to get Lucy to the hospital in a taxi before it was too late. He grabbed his phone from the other seat. Three per cent battery remaining.

'Piece of shit.'

It beeped its disgusted reply. A warning that the battery was now 2 per cent. A notification showed a missed voicemail. He needed the battery for Samantha, but what if Samantha had phoned him already…

What if Lucy had phoned him?

The message incensed him. Not because it wasn't from either of them, but because it was so damned antagonistic.

'You have missed your 9 a.m. appointment at Jobcentre Plus, York. This is your third consecutive missed appointment. A sanction decision will be made within seven to fourteen working days. Your Universal Credit payments may be reduced during the sanction period.'

Shit! He'd forgotten! Again.

Third consecutive missed appointment meant automatic sanctions.

The 'may' was bollocks. He was certain to lose over ten pounds a day.

'Stone the fucking crows,' he said.

For Graham Blanks, things were going from bad to worse.

3

Three months into his deployment with York's Intelligence Analysis Unit, Riddick was finally starting to feel useful again.

The workload was manageable, but since it was practically a desk job, it was difficult at first. Gone were the adrenaline-filled days of chasing suspects up flights of stairs.

However, it was at least keeping his brain active. The only alternative really was daytime TV or early retirement and then work doing God knows what. And it was much easier to stay on the straight and narrow this way. No temptations, and limited opportunities for maverick behaviours which had cost him so dearly in the past.

This moment, this high-speed race towards Tang Hall Explore Library, was an anomaly.

Riddick wouldn't go so far as to say he was enjoying it – after all, a man's life was on the line – but he couldn't deny that he was suddenly feeling alive again.

And his heart was thrashing in his chest.

Or, rather, the motorcyclist's heart.

He tried calling the other member of the Intelligence

Analysis team while driving. They didn't answer. He recalled last night's leaving event organised for DC Michael Webb who was taking a secondment to Counterterrorism in some other part of the country. They were probably nursing a hangover. Riddick had been happy to give the morning hospital appointment as his excuse, as well as the need for someone to be on hand to welcome Webb's replacement. Plus, he didn't go to bars or pubs any more for obvious reasons. It was rather insensitive of them to arrange the farewell in such a location. The fact that he was a recovering alcoholic was no secret.

From Jamie's call, it did sound like their operation was about to go up in flames.

They'd been tracking Danny Hurren's crew for months, building a case around what had started as petty shop burglaries but showed signs of escalating into something far more serious. Also, if Jamie's cover was blown, he may need witness protection. That required authorisation from above, safe houses arranged through proper channels – it was a lot of faff. The situation was going to get messy.

He tried Jamie again. Straight to voicemail. He resisted the urge to tell him to get inside the library and act like he was reading. If Jamie was collared by Hurren, he may end up hearing Riddick's message, thus confirming Jamie's betrayal, and possibly condemning him to... well... who knows? It certainly wouldn't be pretty whatever the outcome.

The route from York Hospital to Tang Hall would normally take him down Hull Road, but he was aware of the Viking Festival chaos choking the main arteries. Three months of surveillance work had given him intimate knowledge of these alternative approaches: the network of residential roads, the mix of social housing and newer developments that comprised this corner of York. He took the A1237 outer ring road, then cut in via the A1079 – a longer route but one that avoided the tourist gridlock.

The adrenaline was now making his chest feel tighter. He tried to ignore it. If he worried, it would only intensify. Also, the immunosuppressants made everything feel slightly disconnected, as if he were operating his body remotely, so he had to work at keeping his mind on the task at hand – getting to Jamie and getting him out of danger.

Each turn of his head to check traffic sent a sharp burst of pain where the pressure bandage was – but he welcomed it. It gave him a sudden flash of clarity.

Tang Hall Explore Library sat in the heart of The Centre @ Burnholme, a modern community complex serving as the estate's hub. Even at this time of day it remained busy: mothers with pushchairs navigating the car park, teenagers in school uniforms congregating near the entrance, elderly residents making their way to the community centre's afternoon activities.

He had a quick look around outside, but there was no sign of a black BMW.

He found Jamie in the reference section, reading a mountaineering book with a photograph of Everest dominating the cover, or rather, pretending to.

The thought of this shaky kid taking on one of the world's extreme challenges was ridiculous!

'Mountains,' Riddick said quietly, settling into the chair beside him. 'Looking for somewhere to hide?'

Jamie dropped the book and fixed Riddick with a stare. His eyes were twitching in their sockets. 'There is nowhere to hide,' he hissed.

Riddick took a deep breath. He still couldn't believe that the lad's cover had been blown, but there had been the black BMW apparently, and Hurren's man with the scarred eyebrow. 'How then?'

Jamie dropped his eyes.

Oh dear... what have you been up to, Jamie?

'I was seen talking to...' He turned fully away. '...a plain-clothes officer outside the Co-op last Tuesday.'

A plainclothes officer that wasn't me? Riddick thought. *Now things are becoming clearer!*

'Look, it's a very informal arrangement.'

'Informal arrangement?' Riddick's voice carried an edge. 'Oh good. Better that it's casual, since it's not as if we're dealing with dangerous people, are we?'

'It was just a bit of information for a few extra quid.'

'I'm the only person you speak to. Doing that protects your safety. I protect your safety. You've taken this completely out of my hands.'

Jamie's eyes darted around the empty reference section. 'It wasn't about the burglaries and Hurren, I swear!'

'It doesn't matter if it was about fly fishing! You were seen talking to an officer. Now, if they recognised them...'

'They did...'

'Then the whole thing's buggered.'

'I'm sorry.' There were tears in his eyes. They looked genuine.

'I'm half-tempted to leave you here. Bloody hell. How many officers are you stringing along?'

'Just this one... and... well... occasionally others, when something—'

Riddick held up his hand, silencing him. 'Okay... let's talk about the black BMW. I looked on the way in. I couldn't see any sign.'

Jamie sighed. 'They mustn't have seen me come in here.'

'Okay... so, I've put in a request for help, but all my colleagues are somewhat preoccupied, so I'll run you in. Sounds like the cover's broken anyway. I need to get you safe.'

'Thanks... also... something big is about to go down. Bigger than we anticipated.'

Good news and bad news, all at once. Good that Jamie possibly now had intel worth protecting him for. Bad that whatever was coming would be bigger than they'd prepared for.

'Go on.'

'The shop jobs? They're just distractions.'

Riddick rubbed the scar on his chest through his shirt. 'For what?'

'They're going to do some cash-in-transit van. Danny's brought in a professional crew from outside York. This isn't amateur – we're talking serious money, serious people. Weapons.'

The implications hit Riddick immediately. This was beyond what the Intelligence Analysis Unit could handle alone. Professional armed robbery crews meant major crime unit support, possibly regional organised crime teams. The kind of operation that would be taken out of his hands the moment he reported it.

He looked at Jamie now. *Christ, you really are going to have a target on you then.*

'You're going to need protection. Come on.'

They walked towards the library exit together. Riddick scanned the car park through the glass doors. There were a few vehicles scattered around.

As they stepped outside, Riddick caught movement between the parked cars. A figure in dark tracksuit bottoms and hooded top, moving with the kind of focused purpose that made the scar on his chest irritate him even more.

Shit... 'Jamie, watch—'

But the figure was a decoy. Another figure emerged from behind a white Transit van, right hand concealed, heading straight for Jamie with practised efficiency.

Despite the morning hospital procedure and the drugs in his body, Riddick's reflexes remained sharp enough to push Jamie aside. The knife caught Jamie in the shoulder instead of the chest – a glancing wound that drew blood and a scream of pain. With a thin build and face mostly hidden by the hood, the attacker pulled back for another strike.

'POLICE!' Riddick shouted, pouncing forward, attempting to grab his wrist.

4

Coughing, Graham watched a group of young people in Viking costumes sauntering past him with not a care in the world. Most of them probably relied on the bank of Mum and Dad. He wondered how they would react to sudden financial sanctions.

He waited until his coughing subsided and then he used the last per cent on his phone to contact Samantha.

'Graham?'

'I'm sorry, Samantha. I'm stuck in traffic.'

'Oh, Graham.' Her voice sounded tired and distant. 'You really should—'

'I'm sorry, but these bloody tourists have shut down the entire city. Kids. Too much time on their hands. If you put Lucy in a taxi, I'll pay you back...' *How*, he thought, *I've no idea, but...* 'I promise...'

No reply. His phone had died.

'Fuck. Fuck.' He dropped the device on his lap and smacked the steering wheel with the palms of both hands. 'Fuck!' He smacked the wheel again.

His window was open, and he could see eyes from all directions on him.

He leaned out into the cold air. 'Just clear the fucking road, will you?'

The idiots dressed like folk from a bygone era that really didn't matter one jot to anyone trying to survive in this particular day and age laughed.

Easy for them to laugh.

He raised his middle finger.

One of them raised a plastic drinking horn in mock salute. He hammered the car horn in response.

A larger Viking flinched, but the others merely laughed.

He caught the woman in the Honda next to him glaring at him. He stared back, filled with a determination that this was a contest she wouldn't win. Eventually, she looked away.

Again, he felt nothing.

Wiping sweat from his fevered forehead, he recalled something.

Back when he worked, he used to take a spare battery pack with him.

He checked the glove compartment. It was rather remarkable that it was in there, beneath old car documents, but there it was.

He connected it to his phone. Would it really work after all this time? Would it have a charge?

He stared at the screen, willing it to come on.

A large lorry beeped its horn, making him jump this time. He scowled into the rear-view mirror at the sneering bastard.

He felt an overwhelming urge to leave the car and approach the lorry—

He broke out into another cough.

Jesus, he thought. *I'm getting worse.*

He spat out of the window. The woman in the Honda looked disgusted, but she opted not to fix him in her gaze this time.

He remembered the lorry driver, but decided it wasn't worth the energy, and turned his attention back to his phone.

There was still no life in it.

Balls, he thought, looking out his windscreen again, catching sight of the Minster's twin towers rising above the medieval rooftops like ancient guardians.

'It's like a castle, Daddy!' Lucy's enthusiastic voice was a beautiful memory.

Months before the wheelchair, before the constant pain, and that dialysis schedule.

'Can we go inside...?'

He saw her face now. Beautiful, sweet, full of wonder and hope. Unaware of what was coming. Tubes, grey skin, and that...

It pained him to even think it, but he couldn't stop himself.

Smell...

He slapped his clammy forehead.

That rotten smell...

'Come on, come on,' he muttered, staring down at the phone, willing it to switch on.

The lane alongside him was moving.

Lucky bastards.

The woman in the Honda had gone. A tour bus pulled alongside, windows full of grinning plastic Vikings.

The moving lane had irritated the lorry driver at the rear, who was now beeping wildly.

The device slipped in Graham's sweaty grip. He squeezed it tighter, tendons standing out on the back of his hand like cables.

He looked at himself in the rear-view mirror. He didn't look well. And everything suddenly seemed distant. As if he was underwater, or looking through thick glass.

'Please, Daddy, can we go inside?'

'Not today, Sweetpea.'

Next payday, he'd thought at the time. 'But, one day, I promise, we'll go inside.'

There'd not been that many more paydays. And now he didn't even have his benefits.

Bloodsuckers.

The battery either had no juice, or the connector wire wasn't working. He jiggled the wire, feeling it moving in the port. Maybe if he held it in tightly enough then—

The connector snapped off in the port.

'Fuck...'

He tried to wedge the broken wires back into the charging port, knowing it was useless, knowing nothing would happen. Irrational desperation driving irrational actions.

'Fuck...'

He returned the phone to the passenger seat and proceeded to slap the wheel again.

He subjected the other occupants of the traffic jam to another loud torrent of expletives.

Out of breath, he leaned into his wheel and muttered, 'Useless...'

Useless. Like you. Lou, his ex-wife.

He looked up. Of course, she wasn't there.

'It's not my fault,' he hissed at no one and nothing. 'This world takes... and... that's fine for people who...'

Who have the means to find their way out of the system, Lou said, from nowhere. *Cream always rises to the top. We've heard it a thousand times, Graham. Still doesn't make you useful in any way, does it?*

In the distance, someone in a Viking costume blew a horn. The sound echoed off the medieval buildings, primitive and mocking, like the city itself was laughing at his desperation.

Wheezing and coughing, he groaned and rested his head back on the steering wheel. Time crawled forward. The traffic didn't.

One day, I promise, we'll go inside...

And just like always, Lucy, his darling Sweetpea, was waiting for him along with all the promises he would never keep.

5

In the heat of the moment, Riddick had engaged the attacker with the knife.

It was a mistake.

More than a year of immunosuppressants and limited exercise had sapped muscle mass and dulled his reflexes. He was lucky to avoid a knife wound himself.

Instead, the attacker opted to knock Riddick to the ground before fleeing alongside the other one who had acted as decoy.

Riddick glanced behind him and saw two people assisting Jamie, who was clutching his bleeding shoulder.

If not for Riddick, it would have been a lot worse. He should take that as a win, but the ambush stirred up something deep inside Riddick's gut.

His own knife wound.

The wound that had almost killed him, and had eventually led to an infection that had destroyed his heart.

He got back to his feet and chased the attackers, but it only took fifty metres before his breathing started to labour.

The attackers barely had to break sweat. They were almost

at Hull Road where the busy morning traffic would provide perfect cover for escape. It was a lost cause.

He gritted his teeth, knowing he should accept this and come to a stop...

I'm a lost cause.

The thought repulsed him. He picked up the pace. For a moment, he thought he may just be on to something. Yes, his chest felt increasingly tight, and his left arm began to tingle, but the attackers were no longer growing smaller in the distance. Of course, they were almost on the other side of Hull Road, having darted around slow-moving traffic, but it was something.

Riddick tried to shout after them, but this made him realise he'd no breath left...

Before reaching Hull Road, the chest pain came sharp and insistent.

He saw the two men disappear into the maze of streets on the other side of the main road, before he groaned and doubled over.

You stupid bastard.

He counted his deep breaths, rubbing his chest with his right hand.

When he counted to ten, the pain started to lessen. Thank God.

At twenty breaths, with the sharpness returning to a dull ache, he realised he may have just dodged a bullet.

'Are you all right?'

Riddick straightened slowly, forcing his breathing to steady. Jamie stood three feet away, hand pressed against his bleeding shoulder.

'Aye... better than you, it seems.' Although he probably wasn't. 'You phone for an ambulance?'

'Someone else did. And the police. Both on the way.' Jamie

stepped closer, eyes narrowing. 'You're white as a sheet. You need to sit down—'

'Give over, you're the one pissing blood.' The words came out sharper than he intended. The lad was only trying to help after all. Riddick patted his chest. It was still twinging painfully, but it didn't feel anywhere near as bad. He needed to put this behind him. And fast. 'Listen to me, Jamie. When they get here, you don't mention this...'

'I... but you, you...'

'Nothing about me feeling unwell. Do you hear?'

'But—'

'If you do, we're finished.'

Jamie gulped.

'Precisely. You're better off with me in your corner.'

Jamie nodded. Agreeing, but probably thinking, *Yes, but a dead man in my corner is nothing to shout home about.*

'Let me get you processed properly and your protection sorted. If you put me in a hospital bed, you may get one of my colleagues. Trust me...' He shook his head. 'You don't want one of my colleagues. They're liable to put you on a hook and hang you out to draw out the piranhas again...'

Jamie went even paler. Suddenly, blood loss looked the least of his concerns.

'I won't say nothing.' Jamie's Yorkshire accent thickened. 'You'll get checked over though, yeah? After I'm safe. You look proper rough.'

The pain had settled into a dull ache that Riddick recognised from too many similar episodes. He straightened up. 'Yeah, of course.'

As his breathing continued to steady, and the sounds of sirens grew, his mind drifted – not uncommon in particularly stressful events – to DCI Emma Gardner.

It was so funny how the mind worked.

He'd been trying to block her from his thoughts for months, focusing on recovery, on building something resembling a normal life.

And yet here he was, tight-chested after a warning shot across the bow, and hers was the first voice he wanted to hear. The realisation stung. After everything – the distance she'd demanded, the silence, the brutal way she'd cut him off – she was still the person he reached for when things went wrong.

The ambulance turned into view, blue lights painting the library walls. Jamie waved them down with his good arm, and Riddick pushed himself upright, forcing a composed expression on his face.

He shook Gardner from his head.

There was no point.

She wouldn't speak to him anyway.

She'd made that perfectly clear over twelve months ago.

6

Graham circled the concrete maze.

The car park was three levels of grey monotony, and the sheer number of rental cars bearing Viking Festival stickers was the icing on the cake.

Twenty minutes earlier he'd been trapped on Hull Road, but a reckless U-turn through a petrol station forecourt had freed him from the tourist coaches. The city centre was his only hope now – get a charger, resurrect his phone, call Samantha, and pray there was still time to get Lucy to the hospital somehow.

Graham found a spot for his ageing Focus between a gleaming Audi and a people carrier plastered with Jorvik Experience decals.

A coughing fit crept up on him. Afterwards, he touched the phlegm on the dashboard. When he pulled his finger away, a long green string stretched out. He tried to tell himself it was just a bad cold. It would pass.

His ex-wife, Lou, however, insisted that Graham was falling apart.

The beginning of the end, she echoed from the back of his subconscious.

Dead phone, external battery and buggered wire in hand, he exited the car. His legs felt unsteady. There was a deep ache now. As if the fever was settling into his bones.

He found the machine. Requested an hour. Pushed in his card.

Card not recognised. Please try again.

He tried again, rubbing the magnetic strip on his jacket first.

Card not recognised. Please try again.

His pockets yielded £1.47 in change. The minimum charge was £3.50 for an hour.

He'd just have to be quick.

On the way out, he glimpsed the Georgian facades of Exhibition Square rising beyond the car park's brutal concrete. York Art Gallery; a temple to culture. Everything here spoke of stability, of systems that worked, of people whose bank cards didn't get rejected.

He spotted a yellow wheel clamp already attached to a Ford Mondeo two spaces down. NCP didn't mess about in city centre car parks.

But with only £1.47 to his name, a dead phone and a sick daughter waiting for him to arrive, what choice did he have?

Strange how you always make the wrong one, Lou insisted.

'Piss off.'

Although she was right – and he was now very concerned about being clamped. He half-ran, half-stumbled down the concrete stairs. February air burned his raw throat.

He didn't just need his phone charged, he needed painkillers, too, before the fever brought him down completely.

Exhibition Square opened before him.

It was crammed with tourists wearing ridiculous plastic helmets. A stench of mulled wine made his stomach turn.

Near the art gallery, Graham spotted Minster Gifts.

Did those who visited Yorkshire really think that the over-priced tat was quaint?

Union Jack tea towels and miniature cathedrals!

Still, through the window, he spotted a rotating display of phone accessories.

He was hot already, so walking into the heated shop was like walking into an oven. His vision swam. He steadied himself against a wall looking through a kaleidoscope of ceramic shep-herdesses and I ♥ York keychains.

'Can I help you?'

Graham spotted a man about his age, mid-forties, softer around the middle though. He stood with his *Daily Telegraph* opened up on the counter.

'Phone charger.' Graham's voice came out ragged. He cleared his throat. 'I need a cable... USB to... to micro-USB.'

The man gestured vaguely towards the rotating stand and then went back to his paper.

Now that was service!

'What's your name?' Graham asked.

The shopkeeper looked up. 'Sorry?'

'Your name?'

'Why?'

'Curious.'

'Clive. Not that it matters.' The shopkeeper returned to his paper.

'Doesn't it? In bigger shops, they wear name badges.'

He shrugged without looking up. 'Not that kind of shop.'

'I can see...'

Just get your sodding phone charger, Lou said.

Graham grunted, went over to the rack, found the cable and placed it down on top of the paper.

Clive looked up with a sneer. An expression that suggested 'all right, smartarse.'

'Sorry, were you reading—' Graham broke off to cough. The first one he didn't catch. The second one he managed to get his closed hand there. A good job. It was a wet cough.

'Jesus, man,' Clive said, stepping back.

'Sorry...'

'You look like shit, mate.'

'Thanks for finally acknowledging me.' Graham pointed to a box behind the counter. 'Flu tablets.'

Clive reached for them. 'I think you need your bed as well, mate.' He scanned both items. 'Twelve ninety-nine.'

Rip off.

He kept this thought to himself as he fished out his debit card. He recalled that the machine had been unable to read it before – God, he hoped that it was the machine's problem, rather than the card...

'Fifteen pound minimum,' Clive said.

'Eh?'

'We only accept fifteen pounds on cards.'

'Why?'

'Because they charge us.'

'How much?'

'Don't know – you have to ask my brother, he owns the place.'

Graham tapped his card on the counter, trying to hold in his frustration. 'Look, I have no cash on me and—'

'There's a cashpoint not too far away. I'll hold your items.' He returned to his newspaper.

He thought of the car park, and his daughter's appointment. 'I don't have any time.'

'I'm sorry, rules are rules.' Clive turned the page.

Graham pulled out his NHS lanyard, still in his jacket pocket from his last shift three years ago. 'Please... I'm late... I work for the NHS.'

'So?' He shrugged.

Really? The NHS? Graham thought. *And that's your response?*

'We're up against it. Lots of flu and...'

Clive grinned. 'We get all sorts in here. Firemen, coppers, paramedics – wouldn't have a business if we took everyone's employment into account! Besides, machine won't work on less than fifteen. You could just make it up with something else or go to the cashpoint.'

Graham leaned on the counter, trying to focus, over-whelmed by fever and frustration. 'Okay. Fine.' He reached down and grabbed the first thing he could.

He slammed a Mars bar onto the counter.

'Still under...'

Graham slammed down another.

'Cool.' Clive punched it in, and Graham held his card to the machine.

'Wait a moment... Shit reception... Hang on...' He shook the machine. His eyes wandered to the paper while he waited. The machine beeped. He looked back and raised an eyebrow. 'Rejected.'

'No...'

Clive handed him the receipt to say that the money hadn't gone through.

Bollocks! Maybe the car park machine hadn't been on the blink after all. He knew he was low... but not that low. A payment must have gone out.

'Any point in trying again?' Clive asked.

'Yes...'

He did. Same excruciating wait which Clive filled with a few sentences of his paper, before another rejection.

'You have another card?' Clive asked.

'No.'

Clive sighed.

Graham took the money from his pocket and placed it on the counter.

Clive smirked.

'One pound forty-seven,' Graham said.

'That'll cover one of the Mars bars.'

'I'll write down my address. I'll bring the rest of the money back later.'

'We're in a city centre,' Clive said, the smirk still in place. 'Not your local village. It really just doesn't work like that.'

'Please... Keep the lanyard... Obviously I'll need to get that back.'

Clive looked at the lanyard, three years out of date, although he didn't know that.

'It could have been printed on your computer.'

'If I could afford a computer and printer, I wouldn't need to rip you off ten pounds.'

'Fifteen.' Clive shook his head. 'No... best I can do is keep the products behind here until—'

'Well, that's some help... Not like you're going to sell out of paracetamol, Mars bars and a phone wire.'

'Well, actually, we—'

'Doesn't matter. Look...' Graham took a deep breath. Sweat ran down his face in rivulets. 'Truth is, my daughter's sick. She needs me. I'm late to pick her up for an appointment. I need my phone. The battery.'

'So you lied?'

Graham squeezed his eyes shut. 'Yes, because I'm desperate...'

'Look... no offence, but round here, if it's not the tourists trying to get one over on us, it's the desperate people. There's a lot of both. We have our policies and, well, that's the way it is.'

Graham swallowed. His throat felt like sandpaper. He closed his eyes, gathered what dignity remained.

'I've always helped people. Always. Twenty years in the NHS, making sure people got their appointments, got their treatment. Now I just need a little help. Just this once.'

'Look, mate... you want some advice? You're sweating buckets. Work, your daughter, whatever it is, it should be on the backburner anyway. You need to get yourself to bed... If I were you, I'd head home. If you have a home, because to be honest, we get a lot of that in here, too...'

'I'll pay you back. Tomorrow. With interest. Twenty pounds, please.'

Clive shook his head.

Graham slammed a fist on the counter. 'My daughter... she's eight.'

He heard Lucy's voice in his head. *Can I have two packets please, Daddy?*

'You can leave now, mate,' Clive said.

'She loves strawberry laces,' Graham said.

'Now, please,' Clive insisted.

'I'm sure I bought some here once... with her... before... She's in a wheelchair and she's thin... so thin. Where are your strawberry laces?'

'I'm calling the police.'

Graham struck the counter again. 'Where?'

Clive pulled his phone out of his pocket.

Graham looked along the counter display until he found the laces. He grabbed two packets and stuffed them into his pocket.

Clive shook his head. He started dialling. 'You're a fucking mad—'

Graham picked up the charging cable. 'I'm taking this too.' He turned and walked towards the door.

'The police will get you.'

'I'll be long gone.'

Graham heard Clive scrambling up from his stool.

'Give them back...'

Graham reached for the shop door.

He felt the hand on his shoulder.

Graham spun and shoved the shop owner hard – harder than he'd meant to. Clive stumbled backward, arms windmilling, and crashed into a display of commemorative plates. The rack teetered, seemed to hang in the air for a moment, then came down in an avalanche of ceramic and wire.

Clive didn't look in a hurry to get up from that one, but Graham took no chances. He grabbed the edge of a tall shelving unit stacked with Yorkshire's Finest mugs and yanked. The whole thing toppled forward. Clive had to dive sideways to avoid being crushed, landing hard in the wreckage of plates.

'You can't say I didn't ask nicely,' Graham said, then stepped out into the cold.

A busker near the Theatre Royal steps played something mournful on a violin, the notes drifting across the square like smoke.

Worried about the car clamp, and now the police, he managed a slow jog back to the car park. By the time he reached the second level, he was wheezing.

When he caught his breath, he headed towards his car.

A yellow metal boot clung to his front wheel like a parasite.

___

7

While Jamie was being treated for the knife wound under the watchful gaze of two police constables, Riddick headed back to Fulford Road Police Station.

Two minutes into typing up the Tang Hall Library incident, he paused, groaned and massaged his temples, suddenly filled with irritation. He should have kept a better eye on his informant.

If Riddick had been top of his game, he could have nipped Jamie's greedy behaviour in the bud. It turned out the lad had been selling information to three other officers and it was all rather embarrassing.

Now that Jamie's cover was blown, discovering where Hurren's crew planned to strike these cash-in-transit vehicles was going to be an absolute nightmare.

Maybe I did come back too soon...

His phone buzzed with a reminder.

'Piss off... I know...'

Still, he checked the heart monitor app anyway.

Elevated stress levels, pulse running high. He checked his

medication schedule. It was only five minutes until his next beta blocker anyway, so he threw one back.

His heroics back at the library had left him the worse for wear. Inflaming all those new connections between a replacement heart and his body was very ill advised. He should probably head in for a check-up. But the prospect of another hospital visit, especially in the same day, made his jaw clench.

Over the last year, he'd spent enough time sucking in disinfectant fumes.

Even now, when he smelled the disinfectant in the police station, he couldn't help but see images of himself lying on a hospital bed, his chest cracked open.

He'd been lying when he said the whole incident hadn't put something else firmly on his mind.

A shame, too, really, as he'd been doing so well.

It'd been over twelve months since he'd last spoken to Emma. Not even a text. It wasn't as if he wanted a Christmas card – just some indication she was well would be welcome.

The last time he'd seen her she'd been hunting two of their colleagues' killers.

Chasing ghosts...

She was convinced she knew who they were. Not that there was any evidence.

He'd been too weak to stop her leaving Knaresborough, and recovering from a heart transplant made following her down south a difficult proposition. She'd also ruthlessly demanded that Riddick stayed out of her life and got on with his own.

She was just trying to protect him, of course, but it didn't make it any less brutal.

He reached for his phone.

Twelve months was a long time.

It'd be better to let it lie... But today, well, today, had really stirred things up.

He dialled Gardner.

'Hi, this is Emma. If this is urgent and police-related, please do contact DCI Michael Yorke on this number...' After leaving Yorke's number, she didn't even bother asking for a message.

He groaned, thinking back to the last time he'd seen her. She'd been sitting by his hospital bed, holding his hand, before suddenly breaking away to tell him she was off, and that the possibility of them ever having a relationship was now null and void.

Maybe he should call DCI Michael Yorke, her holier-than-thou mentor who she'd never had a bad word for. The twinkle in her eye every time she'd spoken about him had been nause-ating. Of course, he'd known it was professional respect. Yorke was happily married, and she'd been adamant that it wasn't anything like that. Still, jealousy could rear its head over anything!

He wouldn't have been surprised if Yorke knew where she was and what she was up to. But, if that was the case, he thought with a smirk, Yorke would have been advised, or rather instructed, not to let her off-the-rails former colleague in on anything. That would be for absolute certain.

Sometimes, he thought about Gardner on her crusade. Obsessed, blinkered, chasing ghosts...

But how could he judge? He'd been on enough crusades of his own...

The office door opened.

A woman in her early forties walked in. She looked like Gardner, except she wore her hair back rather than down, and her suit was pressed with military precision. Gardner wasn't always that meticulous with the way she looked.

'Hi, sir, I'm DS Laura Frost.'

DS Laura Frost was new to the intelligence unit and was swapping out with DC Webb – who'd transferred out the previous day, before taking his other colleague out on a raucous leaving do. At least, Riddick assumed it'd been raucous. His other colleague was yet to make an appearance and so was obviously hungover.

'Morning. Just call me Paul though.' He smiled, but it took a lot of energy to do so – he wasn't in the mood.

'Sure,' she said, returning the smile. He noted that her smile also seemed staged.

Who knows? Maybe she was also having a shit day, or maybe they were just made for each other!

'You can take that desk in the corner,' Riddick said. 'Can't guarantee that Mike hasn't left anything rotting in one of the drawers... He could be like that.'

Her fake smile broadened over his forced humour. 'I'll be sure to sterilise...'

'I'll let you get set up...'

She turned sharply, halfway across the office to her new desk. Her ponytail swished. 'I heard about the incident at the library, sir...'

'Paul.'

'Sorry, Paul...'

He nodded. 'What about it?'

'Well, it was rather... dramatic?'

Riddick nodded. 'Unexpected... and irritating. It's left us up a creek without a paddle.'

She continued to the desk but turned back again. This time she perched on the edge of the desk. 'Yes... it wasn't so much that. I wanted to check in with you. It must have been... terrifying? With the knife. Quite brave of you.'

'Reckless even?'

She grinned. This smile felt more real. 'I didn't mean that.'

Didn't you? Riddick thought. *I think you did... but you'd be right.*

'So.' She raised an eyebrow. 'Are you okay?'

'Yes... and, in fairness, it's nice of you to ask.' He nodded at the third desk in the office. 'My other colleague hasn't bothered to ask. Too busy nursing a hangover I expect.'

He turned back to his screen to continue his report. 'Just need to get this report down while it's still fresh.'

'You threw yourself at an armed attacker... and then chased them afterwards...'

Bloody hell, Riddick thought. *She isn't going to let this go. She doesn't just look like Emma!*

'Aye,' Riddick said. 'Done now... Didn't catch them, prefer not to go over it.'

'Very brave,' she said.

'You've said that already.'

'Dramatic...'

He fixed her with a stare. 'And that too... Shall we get to the point? Maybe try a different word...' He regretted his biting sarcasm immediately. He barely knew her.

'Cinematic?' she offered.

'Cinematic?' He scrunched his face up. Then, he snorted and laughed. 'You taking the piss?'

She went around the other side of the desk and looked at him again. 'It's just, considering your recent medical condition, it was probably not wise. Not wise at all.'

He closed his eyes. That was all he needed. A babysitter. 'Have they put you here to keep an eye on me?'

'No... not at all. I had to read the risk assessment though. If we work as a team then...'

'Look, thanks for the concern, but I need to crack on... really...'

'Okay... I'll just be getting myself oriented. This is all quite different from the Midlands. Much more...' She glanced around the office like she was surveying an old room in a manor house. 'Rustic.'

Riddick's phone rang.

'DI Riddick.'

'It's PC Harrison, sir. About the CCTV from the library incident?'

'Great. Go on.'

'It isn't good news, I'm afraid. Both attackers kept their hoods up. Faces angled away from the cameras.'

'What about the BMW?'

'False plates. Professional job. We're checking ANPR cameras on the surrounding roads, but...' Harrison let the sentence hang.

'Thanks. Keep me posted.'

He ended the call.

'Everything all right, sir?'

'Aye. And it's Paul!'

'Sorry, Paul. You look quite pale.'

He looked at her. 'Just tired.'

'Okay, if you need to rest, I can pick up some slack.'

'Just leave it.' The words come out harsher than intended, echoing in the small room. Her expression shifted for the first time since she'd come in, a flash of something genuine – hurt? anger? – before the mask slipped back into place. 'Sorry.'

'Don't be. You've had a trying day. I'm just trying to help. And being too eager.'

You can say that again, he thought.

She approached the door and turned. 'You don't want a fuss. Very Yorkshire of you.'

She left, closing the door behind her.

He didn't know whether to laugh or cry over that particular interaction. His mind returned to Gardner.

Should he call her again?

Pointless.

She was someone else who didn't want any fuss.

And she wasn't even from Yorkshire.

CLAMPED – Parking Fee Not Paid. Release Fee: £150.
Contact...

The notice flapped under the windscreen wiper.

Graham plucked it out and read it again.

£150.

Even two Mars bars were beyond his reach now.

A laugh escaped him as he screwed it up.

What else could he do... It was comical...

Somewhere beyond the car park, church bells chimed the hour. He'd missed his daughter's appointment. Another broken promise.

Graham plugged his phone into the battery with the stolen cable and waited. Eventually, the screen flickered to life.

Finally, a break...

Although it felt like too little, too late.

Leaning on his car, Graham felt a wave of nausea and unsteadiness. He should have stolen the flu capsules too!

The strawberry laces came to mind. Maybe sugar would help. Graham pulled out one of the packets, tore it open. Artificial strawberry smell. Chemical and wrong, but cheaper than real strawberries, and he'd never been able to afford a great deal of them for Lucy.

The synthetic sweetness coated his mouth as he bit into one and started walking. Sirens wailed somewhere nearby – he'd have to keep his head down now.

Outside, the busker had switched to something cheerier. The tourists and the Vikings applauded.

The city carried on, indifferent to his crisis.

Just like always.

Riddick brushed the containers of herbal tea aside and reached for his own box of Yorkshire Tea, which he'd labelled. The box stared back at him, empty.

Bastards...

In a way, he could understand colleagues dipping in for a freebie, but to take the very last one. That was a new level. The next box would have to be locked in his office drawer.

His phone beeped to remind him to take tacrolimus. What was the world coming to when he couldn't even wash down that shite with a cup of tea? After toying with the idea of nabbing some herbal tea, he decided he'd prefer overchlorinated luke-warm tap water.

From his jacket pocket came a small plastic container. He shook out two small white capsules, each containing enough immunosuppressive medication to keep his transplanted heart from being rejected by his own immune system. Deliberately poisoning himself to stay alive...

'Everything all right, sir?'

He jumped out of his skin.

'Bloody hell, it's Paul!' he said, turning to face Frost. 'And no amount of medication is going to keep me alive with shocks like that.'

She looked uncomfortable, and guilt washed over him as he swallowed his tablets with a glass of water. He returned the pill container to his pocket and sighed. 'Look, sorry for being rude.'

'Now or earlier?'

He narrowed his eyes. 'Both.'

'Well, I'm not surprised... everything you're up against.'

He raised an eyebrow. 'Eh?'

'I had to read your medical report.'

Had to? Christ. Of course she had. He'd forgotten about the mandatory health disclosure requirements. Three months into this deployment, and he still wasn't used to the idea that his medical condition was a matter of official record that everyone he worked with professionally was expected to read.

'Good on you for reading it,' Riddick said. 'I reckon most people here don't bother. Just tick the form to say they have.'

'Reckless.'

'Aye... but in fairness, I wouldn't have read it.'

'But it's important. No one should be going near you when they're sick.'

Riddick snorted. 'Like that's sustainable. Anyway, you'll be pleased to know that no one has coughed in my direction lately.'

She nodded at the glass. 'Wouldn't you be best on mineral?' She gestured at the sinks. 'Old pipes... you know—'

'I was unprepared. I wanted tea, but someone cleaned me out.'

'One moment...' She went back to her table, rustled in her bag and came back with a plastic container. 'Yorkshire tea, sir?' She held it out.

Riddick smiled and took the container.

'Nothing like the best tea in the world to well and truly break the ice. Still... it will only thaw properly when you pack in the "sir".'

She laughed.

Maybe she isn't so bad after all, he thought to himself.

10

Graham pressed himself against the limestone of the Minster wall, listening to the answering machine at York Hospital. 'We are currently experiencing higher than normal call volumes...'

Of course you are.

'You are number forty-three in the queue.'

Jesus.

Music. Vivaldi. *The Four Seasons.*

To calm you while your health deteriorates.

He kept the call alive but switched to another call to Samantha for the third time.

Voicemail again.

He left the same message. 'Did Lucy get there? Even if she was late by taxi they might still treat her. I'm stuck in the sodding queue. Call me back. Please.'

He switched back to Vivaldi.

A cough racked his body. His throat no longer felt sore. It was on fire.

Three crows watched him from the Minster wall. It made him think of his gran.

His gaze travelled down the ancient Gothic towers and over the streaming tourists below. A group of them clustered around a tour guide listening to a piece on the Norman architecture.

They all looked so sodding content.

Lives on schedule.

On the right course.

No chronically ill young children.

No frozen benefits.

No missed appointments and raging flu.

Just warm expensive coats and fully charged phones used to snap the sights.

'You are number forty-one in the queue.'

Alternating waves of heat and ice crashed through his body.

A school group passed by. Twenty or so kids in matching navy uniforms, about Lucy's age, all of them glowing with health.

Healthy kids. Packed lunches in their bags teeming with treats from M&S. At home, loving, happy parents who've never had to choose between heating and food.

A young lad stopped and stared at Graham, fascinated.

Due to the flu, he must have looked a state, like a homeless man.

It would explain the youngster's attention.

Graham straightened himself up, but the boy continued to stare.

Graham tried smiling.

The boy smiled back, before turning and running back to the crowd.

Graham loved kids. They didn't mind that he was desperate and sick. To them, desperation wasn't a deadly contagion to be avoided at all costs.

If only we listened to them, if only we paid more attention to each other, some of us wouldn't be in such a mess.

The Minster bells began to chime, deep bronze notes that seemed to vibrate through his chest. It was quarter past ten.

The sound reminded him of the church near their old house, where Lucy used to count the chimes and try to guess the time. She'd been good at it, better than him.

'Daddy, why do the bells sound sad?'

'They're not sad, honey. They're just... old. They've been ringing for hundreds of years.'

'How many times am I going to hear them ring before I die, Daddy?'

'You're not going to die, Lucy. I promise.'

He thought of her now, falling asleep with that ridiculous stuffed elephant, chewing on strawberry laces like it was the last sweet thing left in the world.

Deep down, he knew it was a promise he couldn't keep. But he'd never stop trying.

Graham pushed himself off the wall, swaying slightly as the world tilted.

He was now fortieth in the queue.

A man dressed as a berserker posed for photos with a group of students, his fake-fur cloak draped over modern hiking boots. Graham watched the charade with growing disgust.

Fake bastard.

Everything about this place.

All of you.

Your costumes, your smiles, your fucking games.

You think life is something you can dress up and play at? While real people are dying, while children miss hospital appointments because their fathers can't afford petrol?

The bitterness rose in his throat like bile. These people with their weekend entertainment, their historical fantasies. What would they know about real struggle? Real Vikings buried their children in frozen ground. Real Vikings knew the world was cruel and cold, knew that carrion followed armies because there would always be corpses to pick clean.

The phone went dead. He looked at it. Reception had dropped out.

The hospital was still twenty minutes away on foot, maybe twenty-five in his condition. And that was the motivation he needed. He was off again, pushing through the thickening Viking Festival crowds.

Graham looked up at the three crows again, watching him.

He froze and closed his eyes.

Suddenly he was lying on cobblestones, staring up. A murder of crows descended. Then came phantom pecks along his arms, his cheeks.

'The Morrigan chooses who lives and who dies. She comes as three sisters. Three crows.'

Graham opened his eyes and regarded the crows again.

Had they always been there, preparing him for something? This moment, perhaps? This fever? This desperation? The sick daughter who needed him even when his body was ready to fold?

The middle crow cocked its head.

I won't fold... Not today... not ever...

He pushed through the Viking crowd, not looking back at the crows. He knew they'd still be there when he returned. They always would be. Watching. Waiting. He stumbled forward, fever burning behind his eyes, Lucy's face swimming in his vision.

Time to fight for what mattered.

11

'Okay,' Riddick said, pulling out a chair for DS Frost, then one for himself. 'Now the report is done, and I've got a brew in me, let's try again.' They both sat. 'I'm DI Paul Riddick. Please call me Paul.'

She smiled. 'I will. I'm DS Laura Frost. I'm excited about being here, Paul.'

'It's good to hear.' He grinned. 'Okay, you know that I'm not a picture of health... but I would honestly prefer it if you didn't mention it. I appreciate that you are being kind, but I just can't stand discussing it... not because I'm rude... just... well... Full disclosure, I still feel like I'm operating my body remotely – everything slightly delayed, slightly disconnected. The immunosuppressants aren't content with merely dampening my immune response; they want to dampen all my responses too! I am going to come across as unsteady from time to time. So, please, no five-minute check-ins. Is that okay?'

'Hourly?' she chanced.

'Once a day.'

She nodded. 'Got it. However, if you ever need time away, I'm more than willing to help. Don't think—'

He held his hand up. 'I promise you'll be the first to know. But even though there's this layer of cotton wool between myself and the rest of the world, I do feel like I'm coping well. I try not to worry too much about whether someone's cough is going to kill me. And when I'm down, I practise gratitude. Or at least try to. A twenty-four-year-old motorcyclist from Leeds died so that I could live.' Even as he said it, he felt the steady rhythm in his chest – someone else's heart. A young man's heart. What would that heart be doing right now if its original owner hadn't died? Beating fast for a first date? Pumping him up for the final leg of a marathon? Instead, it was here, in Riddick's damaged chest, keeping a broken detective alive. And one that probably didn't deserve it. 'It's important I make the best of this situation and give back somehow.'

'Stoic and commendable.'

'Yes, there will be times when I'm distracted. The post-transplant regimen has been relentless. Twice-daily blood pressure checks. Weekly blood draws to monitor immunosuppressant levels. Every few months they stick a catheter into my neck and take samples from the heart muscle to check for cellular rejection. Today was one of those days.'

'Sounds exhausting.'

'Aye, but it's the price of admission. Now, before we work out how to untangle this investigative mess I'm partly responsible for... tell me about you.'

'There isn't much...'

'Nonsense... and I just spilled my guts. Why are you here?'

She sighed. 'Messy divorce. New start.'

'I see.'

A moment of silence expanded. She clearly wasn't ready to

elaborate, and he didn't have the patience to wait. He'd cross that bridge later. 'Right, tell me what you already know about the Hurren investigation,' Riddick said. 'I'll help you fill in gaps but there isn't much.'

Frost sat up straight as she started speaking. 'We have three months of surveillance reports, financial intelligence and witness statements. It started as petty retail crime, but there are signs it's escalating. No weapons as yet, but some violence against store managers and owners. Late afternoons, early evenings, when staff are tired and customers are distracted. They've been widening their geographical range over the past month – started around Exhibition Square, moved out towards Micklegate and Stonegate. You think they're testing response times, looking for soft targets. I saw that your informant was helping you build a picture of potential targeted areas with other individuals and gangs involved. I read about previous associates, Hurren's past convictions.'

'You come prepared then,' Riddick said. 'Jamie, my informant – or ex-informant now, Christ – thinks they're planning something bigger. A cash-in-transit robbery, possibly weapons. A professional crew brought in from outside York. Jamie's going to be a real loss.'

'Well, fresh eyes might spot something we've missed. I'll hop on the shared drive.'

Riddick smiled. 'Thanks for the tea bag.'

Frost nodded. 'Thanks for the welcome.'

'Is that sarcasm?'

'No... I've worked with far more abrupt people.'

His phone interrupted them. Standing and turning away, he answered. It was regarding a prescription he needed to pick up. When he turned back, Laura Frost was already at her computer, pulling up files.

Already, he recognised something in her – the focused efficiency of someone who needed the distraction, someone who understood that immersion in other people's problems was sometimes the only way to avoid confronting your own.

The signs were unmistakable because he'd been living with them for as long as he could remember.

He wondered if her problems had been caused by the 'messy divorce'.

Not that he had any experience of a messy divorce.

His experiences had been very different.

Less messy, but far more final.

12

Graham approached the renal unit, having spent most of his working life in hospitals. He could keenly sense the lives suspended between hope and statistics all around him. To him, it overwhelmed the smell of disinfectant like the most pungent of incense.

At reception, sweat poured from his brow despite the aggressive air conditioning. He caught sight of the door to Dr Wainwright's office and recalled their first meeting in that room. A desk, three chairs, a box of tissues placed carefully within reach. His daughter's small, cold hand gripping his with surprising strength.

'I'm afraid the blood tests confirm chronic kidney disease,' Dr Wainwright had said.

At that moment, he'd tightened his own grip on Lucy's hand. 'How?'

'The scarring pattern suggests post-streptococcal glomeru-lonephritis. Essentially, a throat infection she had – possibly that strep throat last year – triggered an immune response that attacked her kidneys.'

He had spent twenty years in the NHS working in IT. Over that time, he'd picked up enough medical terminology to recognise a death sentence wrapped in clinical language. How much nicer it would have been for ignorance in that moment?

'She'll need dialysis. Twice weekly to start. We'll monitor her closely, adjust as needed. She's young, which works in her favour for a transplant, but the waiting list...'

He knew what was coming at that point. He'd seen the statistics.

'Two to three years, typically,' Wainwright said. 'Longer for her blood type.'

Samantha, his ex-wife's mother, sat alongside them both, completely in the dark. 'So with treatment, she'll be okay?'

Samantha's hope was a wonderful thing for Lucy. Graham realised it would be invaluable during the dark times ahead.

Dr Wainwright, too, had offered her own form of hope, although it had sounded scripted and rehearsed. 'Many children with CKD live full lives.'

Wainwright left out the truth: a great many don't.

The waiting room brought him back to the present: plastic blue chairs, motivational posters about kidney health, a gurgling water cooler that had seen better days. He counted fifteen people waiting. All with their hope and statistics.

There were two people queuing in front of him. Behind the desk, a woman with kind eyes and tired shoulders. A familiar look – he'd worn it himself during his NHS years and seen it on many of his colleagues.

He felt the presence of someone behind him now.

Turning, he saw a man in his seventies with a ruddy complexion. He stood straight and looked pissed off. 'Ridiculous, isn't it?'

'What is?' Graham asked.

'My appointment has been delayed by forty-five minutes.' He puffed out his cheeks and shook his head. He looked like a man who was used to being heard, and woe betide anyone who didn't listen. 'Forty-five bloody minutes.'

Graham nodded and looked back. His throat felt like sandpaper. He certainly didn't want to talk, and he always felt one step away from a coughing fit.

'Don't get me wrong,' the man continued to the back of Graham's head. 'I understand they're busy. But you'd think after serving my country for forty years, there'd be some consideration.'

The lady behind the desk had just directed the two people in front of Graham to take a seat. He caught her nervous glance and wondered if it was because of him – he did look like crap, but then he caught the movement of her eyes and realised that it was the old man behind him who was intimidating her. This clearly wasn't the pissed-off veteran's first rodeo.

'How about that, eh?' the elderly man said loudly. 'Some more consideration for those who've paid into the system?'

Graham turned his head slightly. 'Lots of people here have paid into the system.' He then turned back and started coughing into his hand, tasting copper.

'Have they though?' the man asked.

Graham caught the stale smell of cigarettes. The elderly man had obviously moved closer to the back of his head.

'Mr Williamson,' the lady behind the counter said. 'Hopefully, someone will be along shortly, but please could you retake your seat.'

'For the third time?' he asked. 'You ask me to retake my seat?'

Graham swallowed.

'Yes, please,' the receptionist said.

'Since I've been here,' Williamson continued, 'I've seen people jumping the queue. One lass only waited five minutes.'

'I've explained this. Different appointments, different doctors and different needs.'

'So... nothing to do with where this lass comes from? I heard her talk. She was Polish,' Williamson said. 'The immigrants always get seen before me.'

Graham's skin crawled. Here it was, the ugliness.

'How do you even know she's an immigrant?' Graham asked. 'And how do you even know that her need isn't greater than yours?'

'There are things you learn to spot over time, son.'

Graham turned his head slightly, again. 'Listen. The delays... the waiting times... your discontent is not because of immigration.'

'Ha... What is it then?'

'Underfunding,' Graham said quietly. 'Systematic underfunding.'

Williamson snorted, and Graham felt a surge of irritation.

'Look around that waiting room, son.' He raised his voice. 'Just bloody look... Half the people here weren't even born in this country!' The bastard put a hand on his shoulder and eased him round to look into the waiting room.

It seemed to contract. A mother of Asian heritage pulled her sick child closer. A couple exchanged worried glances and spoke to each other in a European language. An elderly woman of African heritage lowered her newspaper, her face carefully neutral.

'Taking up resources that should go to people who've actually contributed,' Williamson added.

Graham felt his chest tighten, though whether from anger or his worsening condition, he couldn't tell.

Williamson pointed into the waiting room again at the intimidated patients. 'Health tourism, son. Plain and simple. These people rock up with sob stories and no documentation, and get treated before honest British citizens who've been waiting months.'

Graham glanced back at the receptionist who was now clearly phoning for assistance.

When he turned back and saw Williamson's pompous red face, and that finger, that pointing finger, moving around the waiting room, he fought off the urge to grab hold of it.

'Immigrants jumping the queue while the descendants of people who died fighting for freedom suffer and wait... in silence.'

'You need to stop,' Graham said. 'Now...' It suddenly felt as if the scene before him was underwater, warping and twisting with the ebb and flow...

Probably best if he does, Lou said. *Pretty sure he would, if he knew what you were really like.*

Not now, Graham thought. *Not now, Lou...*

'Stop with the truth?' Williamson laughed, a harsh sound that carried across the waiting room. 'That's what everyone wants though, isn't it? The NHS was perfectly fine before we had to treat every Tom, Dick and Ahmed washed up on our shores.'

Graham's hands clenched into fists. 'My daughter... my...'

'What about your daughter? Is she made to wait because of all the bloody tourists?'

'Convenient lies...' he said. 'The system is starved of resources.'

He recalled Lucy after her first few months of sickness, sitting in this waiting room, grey-faced and exhausted.

Williamson was too close... looking down at him... smoky breath... pompous, grotesque cheeks moving up and down...

'Let me past,' Graham said, trying to move around Williamson.

'Look at you, son.'

'Stop calling me son.'

'Look at how sick you look. Where's your priority treatment? A white, British male like you... what chance have you got today?'

'Your ideology is fucking ugly,' Graham managed.

'Ha. Just you wait till it's your kid on a slab, dying...' Williamson's voice dropped to a vicious whisper. 'Immigrants' kids get the beds while your daughter rots...'

He remembered Lucy on a hospital bed after one particular turn. Machines keeping her alive while politicians argued about funding and racists blamed immigrants for their own government's failures. He put his hands over his ears. 'Stop,' he whispered. 'Get out of my way.'

Here comes the Graham we all know and love, Lou said.

'Move...' Graham hissed.

'Not until you admit that I'm right,' Williamson said.

Graham shoved Williamson in the chest.

The elderly man slid down the wall with a theatrical moan.

'Help!' Williamson cried, his voice suddenly frail. 'He's attacking me! Security!'

Graham looked down at his shaking hands as he clenched and unclenched his fists. The desire to swing for Williamson, where he sat on the floor, was overwhelming.

He noticed several people in the waiting room were

standing now. Their eyes were no longer on the racist who'd been terrorising sick families, but on him. The man who couldn't keep control. The dangerous one.

They've seen you for what you are, Lou said.

They should be thanking me.

For pushing over an old man?

Williamson was pleading for help. The same man who'd been spewing poison moments ago was now just a frail pensioner attacked by a violent stranger.

One day, all that anger will sink you, Lou said.

Not now. He put his hands to his ears.

I warned you... How many times did I warn you?

At least I've always been there for her... Where were you? Australia? Running from her illness?

Anyway, get a move on. You'll be no good to our daughter from a jail cell.

He ran, pushed through the double doors, down corridors he knew by heart from years of IT support calls, his breathing laboured and his chest burning. He didn't stop until he was three blocks from the hospital, slumped against a brick wall with his phone in his trembling hands.

He phoned Samantha and was through to her voicemail again.

'I'm sorry... I'm sorry...'

He hung up, realising that his call would have been confusing to Samantha. There was no context.

But how many times do you keep saying you're sorry, Graham? How many times? Before someone gets hurt... or worse?

He slid down the wall.

He hadn't given them his name – that was something; although, it was probably only a matter of time before they identified him from video footage.

But the worst part of it all was that he was now unable to plead his daughter's case for missing that appointment. He'd just destroyed his one chance to advocate for Lucy, to explain why she'd missed it, to beg for another slot. They'd never listen to him now – wouldn't even let him through the doors.

13

After wrangling another cup of tea from his new colleague, Riddick spent some time browsing old Hurren surveillance files. Growing increasingly frustrated, he welcomed the interruption of a phone call. It was the desk sergeant, Jason Grimes, which could mean only one thing.

'There's been another?' Riddick asked.

'Theft and criminal damage in a store close to Exhibition Square. Minster Gifts,' Grimes said.

'Okay, I'll head over myself.' He ended the call and approached Frost, who was scrolling through CCTV time-stamps on her screen.

'Fancy a ride out?'

'Only if I drive. No offence.'

'None taken.'

'It's just you've had an operation today...'

'Hey.' He held up his palms. 'No need to justify. I hate driving – especially in town centres. You be my guest.'

'Okay, what's this trip all about then?'

* * *

Riddick was impressed with Frost's driving. She navigated the Viking chaos in the town centre as if she already knew the place, even though this was her first visit to York.

She also managed to point out a few decorative banners held aloft by plastic-horned tourists. 'This is just bizarre.'

It certainly was bizarre, especially when it was the backdrop to their police work.

En route, he felt a wave of unsteadiness. It was the familiar disconnect caused by the immunosuppressants. He closed his eyes and took a few steadying breaths.

Frost didn't ask. She'd clearly heard his plea earlier.

'Bloody festivals,' Frost said, braking behind a tour bus. 'Always feels like the city's putting on fancy dress while the real problems fester underneath.'

'Some would consider that a harsh assessment. York's a decent place, you know. And tourism helps the community.'

She snorted as they waited for a group of ersatz Vikings to cross the road. 'The Midlands taught me that tourist money and genuine community investment are two very different things.'

Something in her tone suggested some deeper experience. Riddick had spent so long carrying the unbearable weight of grief and cynicism that he'd learned to sense it in others. He knew better than to question her on it so early in their relationship, but human nature and curiosity got the better of him.

'What was it about a messy divorce that made you choose Yorkshire?'

Her glare was to be expected. 'An opportunity to advance my career.'

Total bullshit, of course. There were much better ways to

advance your career than becoming holed up in the Intelligence Analysis Unit.

They parked on double yellows near the square's edge. As they approached, Frost said, 'You know this is a waste of time, don't you?'

'What makes you say that?'

'Lone perp. Doesn't Hurren's lot always work in pairs?'

'Maybe one was taking annual leave?'

'Ha... but I sense you know that this is different anyway. A man who stole a phone cable?'

'And some strawberry laces,' Riddick added.

Frost laughed. 'So, you just fancied fresh air?'

'Well, I've spent most of this past year inside hospitals and incident rooms. Is it so wrong to grab any opportunity to get out and stuck in with both hands? And, after we confirm it's a waste of time, I'll buy you a coffee to make up for it.'

'I don't drink coffee.'

'Yorkshire tea then.' Just before they reached the door to Minster Gifts, he said, 'Also, something had me curious.'

'Ah... really? Curiosity killed the cat, you know.'

Riddick smiled inwardly, remembering Emma Gardner making similar observations in the past. 'How many lives have you got, Paul?' she'd asked him once, her eyes full of concern, while her voice was full of sarcasm. He missed that – her presence, her voice, the way she'd challenged him.

'What are you curious about?'

'The sick daughter,' Riddick said and went through the door. Because that changed everything. A parent fighting for their child operated from a deep desperation that could drive people to places they'd never imagined going. He understood that instinct only too well.

Clive Taylor was behind the counter reading a magazine.

Riddick showed his warrant card. 'DI Riddick and DS Frost. We were passing, thought we'd check everything was all right. We heard the place was a mess.' Riddick made a show of looking around. 'Looks in order.'

'Well, I tidied up. Sorry, why are you here? I didn't expect CID. Not that I'm complaining. Already gave a statement to uniform and thought that I'd be lucky to even hear back.'

'Just following up,' Riddick said. 'We like to stay on top of things around here. So, tell me again, exactly what happened?'

'I already made a report.'

'I know, I read it. But I'd like to hear it again.'

Clive glanced in Frost's direction, and then back at Riddick.

'He came in looking rough as anything. Coughing all over the place, running a fever by the look of him. Wanted a USB cable to hook up his phone to a battery... and some painkillers. When I told him about the fifteen-pound minimum on cards, he grabbed a couple of Mars bars and some strawberry laces. His card didn't work and then he went crazy. Knocked over a stand. Wrecked some of my merchandise. Assaulted me...'

Riddick pointed behind him at the stand behind the door. 'That one?'

'Yes.'

'But you were behind the counter...'

'Well, I was, but he was shoplifting.'

'We don't recommend pursuing shoplifters,' Frost said.

'Aye... but some of us have a living to make.'

'You have insurance?' Riddick asked.

'It won't cover the wire.'

'And the strawberry laces?' Riddick asked.

'Aye.' Clive narrowed his eyes, detecting the sarcasm. He hissed, 'That's right.'

Riddick caught a ghost of a smile on Frost's face as he

reviewed his notes. 'You described him as mid-forties, scruffy clothes, sweating like a pig.'

'Aye. And sick, like I said. Had that junkie look.'

'Junkie look?' Frost prompted.

'You know. Desperate, aggressive, ready to do anything for a fix.'

'And your CCTV doesn't work?' Riddick said.

'No... like I told the officer. Been bust for weeks.'

'It is really odd,' Frost said. 'Someone causing chaos over a phone charger and some sweets. Why didn't he take more? He forgot the Mars bars and the flu tablets?'

Clive nodded.

'Odd.' Riddick echoed Frost, nodding.

'As I said. Desperate. Angry. Had a chip on his shoulder about something.'

Glancing at his notes again, Riddick said, 'You didn't say much about what he said.'

'Because he spoke garbled rubbish.'

'Although you did tell the officer he said he had a sick daughter,' Riddick said.

'Yes... but he also said he used to work for the NHS. No chance. He said he was late for work... then he said he was late for an appointment for his daughter... or was it the other way round? You see, garbled.' Clive shrugged dismissively. 'The problem is the likes of him all have sob stories. It's why your lot will eventually let him off.'

Riddick looked at Frost. Frost was openly smiling. Riddick liked her.

Turning back to Clive, he said, 'Well, our lot would like to identify him. Did he say what the issue was with his daughter?'

Clive's expression suggested he thought this was pointless,

but he sighed and answered. 'Said she was ill. That he needed to get her to hospital or something, and his phone was dead.'

'That's why he wanted the cable,' Riddick said.

'Yes.'

'What if that was the real reason?' Riddick asked.

'It wasn't...'

'But what if it was... What if he genuinely needed to get his daughter to hospital?'

'It's bollocks.'

'But could you know that for absolute certainty?' Frost asked quietly.

Clive flinched and looked away. 'I run a business, not a charity.'

The temperature in the shop seemed to drop.

'So, he was sick, worried about his daughter, who had an urgent hospital appointment, and all he wanted was medicine and a phone charger,' Riddick said slowly. 'So why the strawberry laces?'

The shopkeeper's cheeks reddened. 'He said his daughter loved them.'

'The one that doesn't exist?' Riddick asked.

'I never said that.'

'Not those words, no,' Riddick said.

'Look, I've got rent to pay, stock to replace. Am I the one really in the wrong here?'

'Not saying that. How much you reckon it's cost you in damage?'

'A hundred or so.'

Riddick nodded and looked at Frost.

'Why? What you getting at?' Clive asked.

'Maybe you could have just helped.' Riddick shrugged. 'Sick

daughter needs hospital, he's ill and has to get her there. Paracetamol, a wire, strawberry laces... How much again?'

'Fifteen.'

'Not a massive deal if it was a lie... but if it was the truth? Gold dust, I guess.'

'I don't like this. That's not the point. I'm not the one in the wrong here.'

'No,' Riddick said. 'I guess not.' He turned to leave.

'Unless the point is basic human decency,' Frost said.

As much as it felt warranted, Riddick couldn't believe she said it. He turned back.

'What's your name again?' Clive looked at Frost, eyes narrowed dangerously.

'Grab a pen,' Riddick said. 'I'll give you my name and warrant number.'

'No, I want hers.' Clive pointed at Frost.

Riddick looked at Frost.

Frost shrugged. 'Grab a pen.'

Clive found one. 'Just because I'm a businessman, because I expect people to pay for things, suddenly I'm the villain!'

'Good shout,' Frost said calmly. 'And that will go down very well... unless...'

'Unless?'

'Well, unless you really were wrong about the real cause of that man's desperation,' Frost added.

Riddick nodded. 'Sounds like Russian roulette, that story. Going to come back and bite one of you.'

'It won't be me,' Clive said, narrowing his eyes.

Frost read out her warrant number and her full name. She rounded it off with: 'You know, Mr Taylor, people like to believe they still live in a community, even when it's not always true. Man with a sick daughter comes asking for help – if that turns out to be accurate, a hundred pounds damages will seem minuscule to the number of customers you might lose.'

Riddick noticed a muscle twitching near the Clive's temple. The shopkeeper looked away, suddenly finding a display of keychains intensely interesting.

Outside, walking back towards their car, Riddick said, 'He won't complain.'

'I know.'

He grinned. 'You're growing on me.'

Frost looked serious. 'I meant what I said.' She gestured back towards the shop. 'About community. About how we treat desperate people. It matters.'

'I know... and I agree with you. That was why I was curious in the first place. This wasn't your average robbery.'

'Still, it could be something, could be nothing, but it's nothing to do with Hurren,' Frost said. 'Which means what?'

Riddick sighed. 'Means we need to get back to the gloomy incident room—' Just then his phone buzzed with another medication reminder. Mycophenolate. More pills to stop his body from rejecting the heart keeping him alive. He silenced the alarm – he'd take them back at the station.

Back in the car, Frost sighed.

'Nice to fight the good fight though?' Riddick asked.

'Hmm. Wouldn't be the first time someone chooses not to help someone desperate,' Frost said. 'And it won't be the last.'

'It's sad, though, and at least you got him to realise that. And look, it's cost him £100 and a blow to his pride.'

She smiled, but after she started the engine, the smile fell away. 'The desperate father, you think he's still out there?'

Riddick nodded. 'Desperation has a nasty habit of lingering.'

As they pulled away from the square, threading back

through the Viking Festival crowds, Riddick found himself thinking about desperation and the choices people made when the world stopped listening. He knew that territory intimately – knew what it felt like when grief became so heavy that every morning began with the realisation that your worst nightmare hadn't been a dream. When desperation started to whisper its insane solutions, which seemed perfect from the inside, but anything but to those on the outside.

Solutions like the ghosts he'd lived with – the conversations with the dead. Not to mention the whisky and self-loathing.

Somewhere in York right now, was a father with a sick daughter following the same dark path?

14

Near St Sampson's Square, Graham pressed through the crowd. Paranoid about the police now, he kept his eyes down on the cobblestones, which shifted back and forth in peculiar ways under the force of his aggressive fever. At one point, he detected movement above and saw a crow swooping low to the medieval rooftops.

When it was gone, he wondered if it'd been a fevered hallucination.

What wasn't a hallucination were the plastic horns and polyester fur coats all around him. Forty thousand visitors, apparently. A weekend of dress-up while the NHS crumbled.

He could barely remember what it was like to have disposable income. Even when he was earning, things had been tough. The prospect of getting his car unclamped seemed impossible now, as did feeding himself for the next few weeks with sanctions on his universal credit.

Jesus, he wished he'd taken those flu tablets from Clive! His thoughts were scattered, and now more than ever, he really needed to think straight.

A tour guide's amplified voice drifted across the square: 'The Vikings first arrived in York in AD 866, establishing Jorvik as a major trading centre.'

Some festival stalls were selling 'authentic' Viking jewellery at twenty quid a pop!

Twenty quid! He could feed himself for a couple of days on that.

This made him think of the food banks. It was highly likely that he would have to visit one. Looking ahead down Parliament Street, he recognised the anonymous doorway of a food bank, squeezed between Costa Coffee and more festival tat. No bunting there, funnily enough. Some locals moved in and out of the food bank, heads down, looking at the cobblestones like Graham had been doing – albeit for completely different reasons.

When he drew closer, he saw two women in NHS scrubs entering.

Heart sinking, he remembered clapping the nurses during Covid. Every night.

He wondered if they had been sick of it.

The simple fact was: clapping didn't pay the bills.

The two nurses parted to allow a young woman out of the food bank. She was manoeuvring a pushchair with one hand, while in the other she held a bulky plastic bag. The child inside the pushchair couldn't be more than two, bundled up against the cold in a coat that had seen better days. Unlike the many others who kept their faces downward from shame, she held her shoulders back and pushed her child proudly. She was doing everything she could, and she knew it. He felt some affinity for her.

I was like you, doing everything right, he thought.

Eventually, he considered with sadness, she would realise that it didn't matter. That she would still lose. Like he had done.

Like his daughter, Lucy.

A tin of beans spilled from the top of the mother's bag. She stopped pushing to retrieve it before it rolled to the kerb. As she bent to try and grab it, the voice of someone close to them cut through the festival racket.

'Tony... fuck me, look at that!' The accent was southern. Posh, too, despite the foul language.

Graham sized up the three young men in their Viking costumes, designer trainers incongruous next to their cheaply made historical gear. Early twenties, perhaps. Cans of beer in their hands, flaunting laws because they could. The police wouldn't be warning them on a busy day like today.

'Fit, isn't she? An absolute treat,' one of the others, potentially Tony, responded.

He sounded even posher. Home counties, probably; privileged, and drowning in money.

Graham clenched his jaw.

Not again, Lou said. He heard her snort in the back of his mind. *You can't go anywhere these days...*

And if it was you, Graham thought, *you wouldn't want someone to step in?*

Of course not... I wouldn't need a knight in shining armour. Besides, you have your own concerns... your own problems... Leave her to hers.

He shook his head. *But that's just it, isn't it? Leaving everyone to their own problems. Where has that gotten us?*

Having heard the young men, the young mother decided to abandon the tin that had rolled off the kerb and come to rest by a grate. She wanted to return to her child. One of the three, the tallest who hadn't yet spoken, blocked her path.

'Hey. You okay?' This one was slurring. He radiated drunken confidence. He winked. 'Want me to give you a hand?'

'I'm okay,' she said, navigating around him.

The drunken one reached out and took her arm. She looked down at his hand and then up at his face. 'Let go...'

He released her arm and held up the palms of his hands. 'Just trying to help...' He smiled and then said under his breath, 'No need to be a bitch.' Their laughter was ugly, arrogant.

She started to push her child again, but her dignity had been shaken from her. The pushchair wheel caught on an uneven cobblestone, making her stumble. She kept her feet though, meanwhile the three had regrouped and were moving in her direction.

Graham went to the kerb and retrieved the tin of beans.

As he turned, Graham heard one of them say, 'I could be your kid's daddy for a couple of hours.'

Graham clenched the tin tightly in his hand, while his other hand balled into a fist.

Doing everything right...

Yet...

How long, he thought, *how long until she also had that bone-deep exhaustion on her face?* Until she had the look of someone who'd heard it all before and was too tired to fight for her child any more?

In ten years' time, this could be Lucy; struggling, vulnerable, nobody helping.

'Leave her alone.' The words scraped out of his raw throat.

The three turned to look at him, smirks plastered on their drunk faces. Even pissed, they all looked steadier than he felt. His world was hot feverish chaos.

'Who asked you?' the tallest one who'd grabbed her arm said.

'She's got a child,' Graham managed, his tongue feeling thick.

'I know... we're offering to help.' All three laughed their presumptuous laughs again.

Graham closed his eyes and took a deep breath. His lungs felt inflamed, but at least he didn't cough. The breath did little to calm him though.

Opening his eyes, he asked, 'Where... where do you even come from? Speaking to people like that?'

The dark-haired one laughed. 'Surrey. Ever been? Lovely this time of year.' More laughter.

'Weekend warriors with Daddy's credit card, treating York like a personal playground,' Graham said.

Two of them continued laughing, while the tallest one stopped, his face frozen in anger – he clearly had some sort of chip on his shoulder about it. 'What the fuck does that mean?'

Enough was enough. Graham stumbled forward, meaning to position himself between them and the woman. The movement was clumsy, uncontrolled. The tall, angry one barely had to push him – just a palm to the chest – and Graham staggered backward into a tourist who quickly moved away, eyes down.

You can barely stand, Lou said. *This is madness.*

I didn't ask you...

The young men were moving towards the woman again, emboldened by the tallest one's show of bravado. The poor child in the pushchair had started crying.

The kid was picking up on his mother's fear.

And then something snapped in Graham, and not for the first time today. However, this time, it felt more familiar. A primitive rage. One that had been kept hidden, repressed even, allowed now some freedom to respond. Looking at the tin in his hand, he felt its solid weight. Real. Right now, it was the only real thing in a world gone truly mad.

The taller one who'd pushed him was saying something more to the mother, but Graham was past the point of hearing the words. There was a roaring inside his head now that drowned everything. In a way, it felt good, and it allowed him to move faster than his fevered body should have allowed.

He struck the tall one's head with the tin.

There was a wet crunch, before the Viking hat clattered across cobblestones as the lad dropped.

The roaring in Graham's head started to subside, replaced by gasps from other pedestrians and tourists around them.

The young mother stood with her hand on her mouth, wide-eyed. Graham looked down at the fallen man, blood already pooling, shocking red against ancient stone.

'Milo! Jesus Christ!' The one who'd started all of this off with his comment knelt beside his friend, hands hovering uselessly over his prone body. 'What have you done?' He looked up at Graham. 'What the fuck is wrong with you?'

Everything is wrong with him, Lou said.

'She was minding her own business,' Graham heard himself say, though his voice sounded like it was coming from someone else. He looked around the concerned gathering crowd. 'Looking after her child.' He stared hard at the one that may or may not have been called Tony, and then inched towards him.

Tony backed away, hands raised. 'Okay, mate. Okay. You win. You've made your point.'

'Have I?'

'Yes, I promise. We're done.'

But Graham didn't feel done. The fever, the desperation, the months of watching Lucy fade while the world offered nothing but bureaucracy and blame – it had all poured out through the tin in his hand so elegantly, so perfectly...

Are you not worried? Lou said. *About becoming everything you hate? Everything Lucy would hate?*

The thought would usually stop him dead in his tracks.

But not today. No, today was different. Today, Graham saw Lucy's face in his fevered vision – pale, tired, disappointed that Daddy always failed her.

Graham swayed, suddenly aware of the crowd gathering, the phones being raised to record, the sirens that would surely come.

Tony was fumbling for his phone.

What did you think would happen? That lad with the split head will have private healthcare. He'll be fine. They'll also be able to afford the best lawyers. What's your plan, Graham?

'Give me your wallet,' he said to Tony.

Tony was clearly in no mood to argue and the wallet was thrust into his hands. It was thick with cash that could buy medicine, pay fines, maybe even get Lucy a private consultation. Money these boys probably spent on a single round of drinks.

A thief now? Lou said.

No, just taking what's fair.

He took a twenty and a ten. Then, he handed the wallet and the rest of the cash back.

Walking over to the young mother, whose face was white with shock, he looked down at the child, who'd stopped crying now.

'What's her name?'

She didn't respond; she just stared at him with wide eyes.

What did you expect, gratitude? Lou said.

'Her name, please?'

She's terrified.

'Mary.'

'It's a nice name.' He slipped a twenty into the top of her plastic bag. 'I have a daughter too.'

The young mother nodded nervously.

'Her name's Lucy. And she's not too well.' He nodded. 'I know how it can get. I understand.'

He smiled and went to walk away, suddenly remembering something. Turning back, he offered her the dented tin of beans.

She looked at it without moving.

He proffered it again.

She took it. 'Oh, and also...' He pulled a packet of strawberry laces from his pocket. He put it into the woman's plastic bag. 'Lucy loves them... I reckon Mary will, too.'

He turned and walked away. Nervous people parted to allow him past. Slipping the ten pounds into his pocket, he decided on his next move. Medicine. Water. Maybe, some food. Without those three things, he could come to a crashing halt. And now, the police really would be on his back. And he wasn't ready to stop.

He caught sight of the crow again.

Not yet.

15

The tour bus in front of them hadn't moved in five minutes.

Frost drummed her fingers on the steering wheel.

Costumed Vikings wove between the gridlocked traffic like they owned the medieval streets. Which, Riddick supposed, they did for one week every February.

He switched on the news, recognised the voice of the man being interviewed about the housing crisis, and turned it back off.

'Who was that?'

'Marcus Crist, MP for York Outer. Not my cup of tea.'

'Which party is he with?'

Riddick shrugged. 'He's a politician, that's enough for me. His name is mud down the station. Apparently, he voted in favour of a ton of cuts last year after promising never to.'

'Sounds so, so familiar.'

'Yes. What is interesting is he runs a free community group for people of faith to come together and talk.'

'Eh? Any faith?'

Another shrug. 'Dunno. Sure won't be mine. Not unless

they're accepting people who've had religious experiences on operating tables. I've seen the light three times – turned out it was just the surgical lamp.'

She laughed. 'If it's just one religion... is that even allowed?'

'Guess it's just freedom of speech.'

'But he's an MP.'

'Seems to me that no one has freedom of speech like a bloody MP.'

Frost turned her attention back to the traffic and sighed. 'God, this bloody traffic. Why did I let you talk me into this?'

'Hardly talked you into it... and it's not like you weren't passionately invested back there. Almost had to drag you off the wit—'

Riddick flinched when Frost broke from the traffic to take a sudden right turn.

'Bloody hell!'

She navigated onto a side street, only to find it blocked by a heritage tour group photographing some bloody plaque about Viking massacres.

'Shittingpissinghell,' she said.

Riddick laughed. 'Comprehensive swearing there!'

Her eyes narrowed. 'I can be more creative than that.'

'Don't doubt it.'

A particularly enthusiastic re-enactor wielding a foam axe walked in front of their vehicle. 'In fact, right here is some inspiration... so cover your ears if easily offended.'

Riddick listened, and had to agree, her latest creation was particularly offensive.

Fortunately, the car windows were closed, and the Viking didn't have to hear it.

Frost made some ground before having to stop again.

'Christ,' she said. 'How do you lot cope with this amount of chaos every year? We've barely made it two streets from Exhibition Square.' She reached the end of the road, hit the indicators and turned. 'You have to be taking the absolute piss,' Frost said.

There was a festival barrier.

'I think you'll find they are,' Riddick said with a grin.

'Bloody medieval city,' she said.

'I know!' Riddick snorted. 'Who wants it? Let's do away with the eight-hundred-year-old architecture.'

She laughed. A three-point-turn later, she found another side street to drive down. This one was quieter, so she increased the speed.

'Easy does it, Laura, this isn't *Smoky and the Bandit*. This is Yorkshire. *Last of the Summer Wine* territory.'

'Bloody hell. In that case, I'll speed up and get us out of here.'

She didn't make good on that promise. Then, after a minute of quiet, calm driving, she said, 'You knew that robbery wasn't about Hurren.'

'I told you... I was just curious.'

'It was the sick daughter angle that had you interested.'

Riddick regarded her from the corner of his eye. This was unexpected. 'What made you say that?'

'I just saw the way it was affecting you when he started talking about the man's desperation.'

Riddick felt exposed, caught off-guard. He'd thought he'd been hiding it better, thought he'd mastered the mask after all these years. But apparently his face had betrayed him, shown her exactly what he'd been feeling. 'And how was that?'

'Well, you went quieter.'

'Only because you wouldn't let me get a word in edgeways at that point!'

'It wasn't that. Remember, I've read your files. I had to...'

'Oh, I see... so you really get me now.'

'No, but I know about what you've lost.'

His attention drifted to two kids, maybe seven and nine, coming past the car, wearing helmets—

'Sir?'

'Paul,' he corrected automatically. 'I thought we had that sorted now?'

Detecting his dismissive tone, she nodded. 'Look, I get it.'

'Get what? A desperate man wanting to help his sick daughter? Wouldn't anyone feel a response? You had one too if you haven't forgotten!'

'Clive didn't have one.' She shrugged.

'Maybe that's the difference between decent people and sociopaths.'

His chest felt tight and he winced.

'You okay?' Frost asked, stopping a metre or so from another coach.

He nodded. 'Yes. Just reeling from the fact that I called myself a decent person. A fair few people would object—'

Movement outside caught his eye. A man stumbling more than jogging. He wasn't dressed for any kind of exercise and was sweating heavily in his shirt and trousers despite the February cold. His hair was plastered to his forehead. He came close enough to slam his palm on their bonnet, using it to pivot around their stopped car. The man then pressed his hand against the rear passenger window to push himself onwards, leaving a smeared print behind.

'I guess if you're in a rush this is some kind of obstacle course,' Frost said.

'Yes,' Riddick said. 'Did you look at him, though? He's either on the back end of a serious drinking session, or he really isn't that well.'

'You want to check it out?' she asked.

'Well, we'd have to do it by foot, you'll not get the car around in this...' He looked in the wing mirror, but the man had gone.

The thought of chasing after someone following his experience earlier made his stomach turn.

'You want me to go?' Frost asked. 'You can take the wheel?'

Riddick thought about it for a moment and then shook his head. 'With this crowd, be like a needle in a haystack. Like I said, probably just someone partaking of the Viking mead... long overdue a lie down.'

'Okay...'

A commotion up ahead caught Riddick's attention. He opened the window and the sound of raised voices in the distance came into the car.

They exchanged a glance. It didn't sound cheerful and festive.

The car was at a standstill, so he stepped from the vehicle. There was definitely a thicker crowd swarming up ahead. And the raised voices were definitely sharp and panicked.

He leaned into the window. 'I'm going to check it out.'

Frost nodded. 'I'll probably still be stuck here.'

'No, I can see the traffic peeling off right ahead. If I'm not back by the time you get there, pull over, mount the kerb if necessary, put your hazards on.'

Riddick didn't go at a fast pace. He wanted to do everything he could to keep his adrenaline and heart in check. But despite the assistance of a cooling breeze and deep breaths, he couldn't shake the sense that desperation was loose somewhere.

And that, in turn, caused something to start wriggling free in Riddick's gut.

Dread.

16

Graham half-jogged, half-stumbled along the narrow width of Museum Street, dragging one hand along the rough brick wall and the glass storefronts for support as tourists moved to allow him past.

No one said anything. After all, they weren't moving for him, they were moving for themselves. No one fancied catching whatever he had.

Graham caught his deterioration in every window. His shirt was soaked. His hair hung in lank strands across his forehead. To these visitors, he must look as if he was patient zero in a new plague.

He was looking for the familiar green cross of a chemist, but so far, he'd been overwhelmed by useless modern pretentiousness – expensive chocolate displays, artisanal cheese shops, galleries selling watercolours of York Minster at prices that would feed everyone visiting that food bank for a month.

Then, something caught his attention. Not a chemist, but rather a charity shop.

Gift of Life.

Out of breath and sweating, he reached out and touched the window.

This charity shop was a beacon of hope in a gold-flecked canal of privilege. He knew it well. The window display featured mannequins in running gear – 'Run for Life! Support Organ Donation!' – surrounded by pamphlets about joining the register. A poster showed a smiling girl, not much older than Lucy, with the caption: 'Emily got her second chance. You could give someone theirs.'

He placed his other hand against the window and closed his eyes. He could hear people muttering behind him, some deciding to move further away, while the occasional person suggested asking if he was all right, before a companion would quickly change his mind.

Emily got her second chance, he thought. Her gift of life.

Graham recalled being in Dr Wainwright's office after Lucy had endured months of treatment.

'I'm so sorry. Lucy's kidney function has deteriorated significantly.' The doctor's voice had been gentle but direct. 'We're looking at stage four chronic kidney disease.'

Some would say knowledge is a blessing. But the knowledge given to Graham by his time in the NHS was anything but. He knew exactly what his daughter was in for.

'She's having dialysis,' Samantha had said. 'And I thought it was going well?'

'Dialysis is a treatment, not a cure. Given the rate of deterioration and the scarring patterns we're seeing...' Wainwright paused, choosing her words carefully. 'Lucy needs a transplant more urgently than we thought. Months really.'

'You said it would be years,' Samantha said.

'We will try to expedite.'

Expedite.

Graham snorted. Both doctor and grandmother looked at him.

'Are you okay, Mr Blanks?' Wainwright asked.

'Yes... sorry... just shocked to hear that my daughter's life is now a lottery.'

'Graham, I know both you and Samantha have been tested for compatibility, but I see her mother still hasn't been tested?'

'It isn't an option,' Graham said, looking at his ex-wife's mother. 'My ex-wife doesn't love Lucy enough for that.'

'I'm sure that—'

'She doesn't.' Graham cut her off sharply. 'It's not worth discussing.'

'But even if we explain the situation to her?' Wainwright asked.

Samantha weighed in. 'My daughter doesn't do much for others. Not even her own...' She broke off, tears in her eyes. 'Where did I go so wrong?'

But Graham hadn't wanted to listen to that then. Lou's self-ishness, and her mother's dismay, were old news. Expedite was very recent news.

'What will happen if we can't get one in time?' Graham had asked. He knew the answer, of course, but it was better that Samantha heard it from a professional. Then she, too, could be ready for the challenges.

'We will start to see infections becoming increasingly dangerous. More organs may become compromised. We'll need to increase monitoring to weekly visits.'

Back in the present, the door to Gift of Life chimed.

An older man came out but struggled with a step.

Graham went forward to offer him help.

'Cheers, son. Sorry to hold you up,' the man said. 'Slowly or no way is my motto. My other is: Keep at it, because when I no longer am, then I no longer can.' He smiled.

Graham smiled too. He appreciated the fight in the old man's tone, even though both those mottos sounded particularly sad. He waited until the old man had passed, then coughed into his arm.

He thought of Lucy.

He had to be there for her. No matter what. No matter the cost.

'Keep at it, because when I no longer am, then I no longer can,' he said under his breath and went into the shop.

17

'Police,' Riddick called out, badge raised. 'Move aside.'

Sirens wailed in the distance.

When Riddick broke through the rubberneckers, he saw a young man slumped against the wall beside Costa, and his breath caught in his throat. Blood covered the lad's face and hair, as well as most of his Viking costume.

He was conscious, although judging by the occasional loll of his head, barely.

Another young man, dressed as a Viking, was kneeling to the side of him, holding something against the back of his head. A third lad paced close by, while talking into his mobile. Two staff members from Costa lingered, trying to help.

Riddick stepped around a pool of blood on the cobblestones as he approached the side of Costa.

Off to his left, commotion caught his attention. Two community support officers, who must have arrived before him, were trying to establish a perimeter. The crowd weren't playing ball. Everyone had their bloody phones out.

Irritated, he went over but knew that this would already be going out live on someone's device, so he kept his irritation in check. Riddick held up his badge. 'Detective Inspector Paul Riddick. If you can read this badge, you're too close to a crime scene.'

'But we can't see what's happening from back there,' someone said from the crowd.

'That's rather the point.' Riddick gestured for them to move back. 'This isn't entertainment.'

He held back on adding: Move back or I'll have you moved. He would become a massive hit on YouTube if he did that.

Sometimes he missed the good old days, pre-technology.

The crowd widened, and one of the community officers – a woman with a relieved look on her face – came over. 'Thanks for that.'

'No worries. Completely surprised the rank still has an impact. I expected something to get thrown at me. Anyway, what happened?' He had to raise his voice over the intensifying sound of the sirens.

'Assault with a tin of beans is the best I could get,' she said. She indicated the lad pacing on the phone. 'That lad, Tony, claims a madman just walked up and attacked them with the tin. Hard enough to kill him, he reckons.'

Riddick raised an eyebrow as he surveyed the cobbles again. 'Well, there's a lot of blood.'

'Then, Tony reckons the madman took his wallet.'

'Right,' Riddick said, nodding.

He wandered over to the injured man. He knelt in front of him and his friend. The sirens were really near now, so Riddick had to raise his voice. 'That's the sound of help.' The lad's eyes were all over the place – he was going to have one hell of a concussion; hopefully, nothing worse. He addressed the lad's friend directly. 'What's your name?'

'Col Webster.'

'Well, Col, you think that this was more than just a mugging?'

Col shrugged. 'Well, he took Tony's wallet, so...'

'But he's given your friend quite a whack.'

'Isn't that what muggers do?'

'Sometimes,' Riddick said, not adding: But most try to avoid making the step up to murderer. This was not a careful mugger by any stretch.

The third lad hung up his phone and came over. 'This is totally unacceptable. When we find out who he is, we're going to sue him for everything he has.'

Riddick stood and looked at Tony. 'This isn't the States, Tony... Besides, doesn't sound like he has much if he's robbing tourists. He took your wallet... What was in it?'

Tony looked away. Something going on here, Riddick thought. Young lads were really shit at keeping things from the police. 'He did take your wallet, didn't he?'

'Not exactly.'

'What do you mean – not exactly?'

His face went red. 'He asked for my wallet... took thirty pounds out and gave the wallet back.'

More thievery then – was it the same man as earlier?

Strawberry laces...

Giving a wallet back was a rare thing to do.

'Fortunate he gave it you back... Saves you cancelling all your cards. Rarely hear of muggers handing it back though... especially ones who can't even control how hard they swing. Could I see your wallet?'

Tony took it out. 'Nothing to see, really.'

'I can see there's still money in it.'

Tony gave a reluctant nod.

'Why didn't he take it all?'

Tony shrugged. 'How would I know? The man was mad!'

'Maybe he wanted to leave you enough to get a taxi home?'

'Was that a joke?'

Best not, Riddick thought. 'Do you know where he went?'

Riddick looked at where Tony pointed. It was the direction in which the man had come past him and Frost. It suddenly looked highly likely it was him.

Christ, maybe he should have sent Laura after him!

'What did he look like?'

'Like shit, coughing... very sweaty... sick...'

It was their shoplifter then.

'A junkie, maybe?' Tony suggested.

Clive, the store owner, had said the same thing.

Riddick scanned the crowd. 'Anyone else see what happened?'

Tony sighed. 'I don't know.'

The ambulance was here; the noise of the sirens had stopped and two paramedics were coming through the crowd.

'Come on... let them through.'

Riddick recognised Frost's voice. She came up to Riddick, while the paramedics rushed over to the injured lad. At that moment a woman with a pushchair emerged from the crowd.

She stepped a few metres ahead of the crowd. The community officer that Riddick had been speaking to was darting over to request she move back.

'Just a moment,' Riddick said, coming forward. 'I think she wants to talk to me.'

And look what she has in her hand. A tin of beans.

'Ma'am,' Riddick said. 'Are you okay? What's your name?'

'Amanda Ruston.'

'Did you see what happened?' He didn't address the beans in her hand just yet.

She pointed over at the lad being looked over by the paramedics. Col was still with him, but Tony had come closer to Riddick, clearly curious as to what was going on. 'They were harassing me,' the woman said. 'Making vile comments.'

'Bollocks,' Tony said.

Riddick turned. 'You've had your chance to speak.' He turned back. 'Go—'

Tony interrupted again. 'Hardly—'

Riddick swung. 'You were too busy worrying about suing someone who took thirty pounds from your wallet and left you the lion's share. Last warning.'

'The man who took the money from him stuck up for me,' Amanda continued.

Riddick turned back and saw she was offering the tin.

'I dropped it, you see. They started to make filthy suggestions and—'

'Bullshit!' Tony said.

Riddick glared at the boy and then looked at Frost. 'Would you like to do the honours, Detective Sergeant?'

Frost walked towards Tony, who went pale and held up his hands. 'Okay... okay...'

The woman with the child continued. 'The man asked them to stop. He didn't look well, and he did get angry, too angry, but he was trying to help.'

'Yeah, I saw,' someone called from the crowd. 'Decent of him, if you ask me.'

Riddick held a hand up. 'Let me speak to one person at a time.'

'Decent?' Tony hissed. 'My mate was assaulted.'

'Tony,' Frost warned. 'You've been asked a number of times now.'

'Your friend pushed him first,' the woman said. She was pointing at Tony, now.

'That's lies.'

'He did!'

'It's true,' someone else called from the crowd.

The woman nodded, relieved to have people in her corner. 'Then, he picked up the beans—'

'And went batshit!' Tony said, raising his voice.

Riddick took the can of beans, noting the significant dent. Batshit was one word for it. The force behind that blow could have been fatal. He looked back at the paramedic trying to keep the lad awake. Could still turn out to be fatal.

'Can you describe him?' Riddick asked.

'Forties maybe? Looked ill, really ill. Sweating and shaking. After, he gave me this twenty-pound note.' She held it out.

'That's not hers,' Tony protested.

'Nor yours any more,' Riddick said with some satisfaction. 'It's evidence.' He looked back at Amanda. 'Do you know why he did that? Did he say anything?'

'He asked me my daughter's name and then told me he had a daughter too.' The mother shifted nervously.

'I see,' Riddick said. 'And what's your daughter's name?'

'Mary.'

'It's a nice name.'

'That's exactly what he said.'

Maybe we have a lot in common, Riddick couldn't help but

think. After all, he'd also been called batshit on numerous occasions.

'He also said he knew how it could get,' she continued. 'Implying it was hard. That's why he gave me that money. Maybe he saw me coming out the food bank?'

Bloody hell, Riddick thought; from desperate father to Robin Hood?

'He said she was sick.'

The final confirmation, if they even needed one, that it was the same man. Sick daughter. Needing money. He only kept ten pounds for himself. What does he think he'll need ten for?

Food? Drink? Another weapon?

'He really didn't look well,' the woman added.

'No shit,' Tony muttered.

Riddick ignored him.

'He gave Mary a packet of strawberry laces, but she wouldn't have it.'

Riddick acknowledged this with a slight nod. He knew he needed to find this man.

'Said his own daughter, Lucy, loved strawberry laces.'

Something cold settled in Riddick's chest.

Lucy.

'Come again?' he said.

'Strawberry laces.'

'No, the name?'

'Lucy.'

A familiar disconnection washed over him – that medicated distance from the world that usually protected him from sharp emotional edges. 'Thank you.' He turned away. 'Laura, if you need anything, I'll be over there.'

He took a few steps, then leaned against a wall.

He closed his eyes and took several measured breaths, the

way his grief counsellor had taught him. In through the nose, hold for four, out through the mouth. The technique that was supposed to help when the past ambushed the present.

It wasn't working. Not fast enough. Lucy's name echoed in his head, pulling him back to school mornings and bedtime stories.

And a life that felt increasingly like it had never been his.

18

Graham passed by the donated clothing, which was sorted by colour. It was a rainbow of discarded items.

Bittersweet, he thought.

Behind the counter, an elderly woman was sorting jewellery. She wore a Gift of Life volunteer badge on her cardigan. He had the urge to reach out and touch it but kept his trembling fingers in check.

Her eyes, magnified behind thick glasses, widened as she looked up.

'Oh my dear,' she said, running her fingers through a tangle of necklaces. 'Are you quite all right?'

'Yes... Rather, no... Do you have any paracetamol? Painkillers?'

She didn't answer immediately. Graham presumed that she was stunned. After all, why would a sick man request medication in a charity shop?

In the end, however, her response was calm and efficient; she'd undoubtedly seen all manner of people walking through these doors.

'There's a Boots five or so shops down. Would you like me to point it out?'

'No... that's okay...' How had he not spotted Boots' familiar logo? His senses were a mess. 'Gift of Life,' he said.

'That's us,' she said and smiled.

His trembling fingers touched the sign on the counter. Donations welcome. He pulled the crumpled ten-pound note from his pocket and placed it on the counter.

'I want to donate, but I need change.'

'Ah... the sign refers to donations we can sell. Maybe you'd like to purchase something?'

'Yes... I would.' The words tumbled out before he could stop them. 'My daughter is on a waiting list. For a kidney. I know what you try to do here.'

The woman put down the jewellery and lifted her glasses onto her forehead. 'Oh, the poor thing.'

'Yes, she's been waiting over six months.'

'I will pray that it happens soon for her – what's her name?'

'Lucy.'

'Lucy. How lovely. I cannot imagine how hard it must be.' She reached out and touched his trembling hand. 'I can see you love her very much.'

'More than anything.'

'And she needs that in her life. A good person... a good father... in her life.'

He flinched.

'Are you okay?'

Graham shook his head. 'I'm no good.'

'I don't believe it.'

His gaze fixed on her. 'We had a match, you know. Months back it could all have been over. She could be well... getting better.' His voice cracked.

The woman touched her chest. She opened her mouth to speak but then closed it again. Discomfort crossed her features.

'The NHS had my old phone number. I can't afford internet, and my phone was out of credit. By the time I saw the email, they'd given it to someone else. There is only a short window. I missed it. I hadn't updated the contact details.'

Her hand reached for his again, but this time, left it there.

'I'm sure I had done...' Graham shook his head. 'I filled out all their forms... I updated that number...' Eyes closed, he saw the email notification twelve hours too late. 'I'm sure I did... I am...'

'I'm sure you did. Mistakes happen. How awful this happened to you.'

'Such a short window. Twenty-four hours. Someone else's child got Lucy's kidney because of that number.' Opening his eyes, he stared at the donation posters on the wall. 'But I remember standing at the reception desk, writing it clearly.'

'Well, there you go then. It may have gotten lost somewhere between that desk and their system.'

'Yes, I know. At least, I think so... but what if I'm wrong?' He pulled his hand from underneath hers and touched the side of his head. 'What if I made it up in here... to take away my guilt... except, well, except, I still have guilt.'

'I'm sure you didn't.'

'Everything seems so hazy these days.'

'But I'm sure you wouldn't mistake a thing like that.'

'I'm not so sure of much any more.' Graham took a couple of steps back. The ten-pound note was still on the counter.

As he picked up the note and turned away, his eyes swept the shop, landing on a collection of toys near the back.

Maybe he could treat his daughter to something by way of donation.

After all, he'd given most of the strawberry laces away by now.

The wooden kitchen set drew him over. Miniature wooden pots, pans, oven and microwave. She'd had one just like this! He saw her, six years old, wearing an apron that pooled around her feet. Smiling, he closed his eyes as he remembered the moment.

'What would you like today, Daddy?'

'What do you have on special offer?'

'This wooden spoon is very special. It makes the best porridge in all of England.'

'All of England? That is special. How much?'

'One hundred pounds!'

'One hundred pounds, really!'

'Okay... for you... free... because I love you.'

'Best shopkeeper ever!'

When he opened his eyes, tears ran down his face. Turning from the toys, he noticed real kitchen utensils not too far away. Frying pans, colanders, tin openers.

Knives.

Graham moved over, his hand settling on a three-piece knife set in one of those impenetrable plastic containers.

Unused.

He picked them up and turned them around, reading the information: Non-slip soft grip handles. Protective covers. Dishwasher safe.

Seven pounds.

He reached out to put them back when he saw those sneering, rich boys from the south, terrorising that young mother. And that bigot at the hospital – intensifying the pain and vulnerability felt by those sick people in the waiting room.

Clive, the shop owner, who couldn't give one fuck about

someone's desperation – not like this kindly woman working, potentially volunteering, at Gift of Life.

Graham went over to the woman with the knives. 'For my wife. She loves cooking. We've been meaning to get a set like this for a while.'

Her gaze dropped to the knives, then lifted again. Looking at the state of him, she should really be concerned. But maybe she saw him like so many others didn't these days? A tired, sick man, who lived only for his daughter.

A good father.

What possible concern could you have for a man like that?

He placed the ten pounds down again. She gave him a five-pound note back.

Graham shook his head. 'They're seven.'

The woman shook her head. 'You need some for Boots, remember?'

'Paracetamol isn't expensive.'

'Maybe get a treat for your daughter, too?'

'No.' He shook his head. 'It's better here – she would understand that more.'

The kindly woman smiled, slipped the knives into a plastic bag and then gave him three pounds change.

'Thank you.' He turned to leave.

'Wait,' she said.

Graham looked back. 'I shouldn't, but...' She reached into her handbag behind the counter and pulled out some flu remedy capsules. 'I had a dreadful cold last month. You look like you need these now, not after waiting in a queue in Boots.'

'I can't.'

'You can, and you will.' Leaning over, she put them in his hands. 'I'll only be throwing them away anyway.'

Graham accepted them gratefully. 'Okay... thanks.'

'Just promise me you'll head home and get some rest.'

He nodded.

Outside, he swallowed two capsules. Then put the packet into his pocket.

As he headed further down the street, he looked at the plastic bag in his hands and thought about his purchase.

Why had he bought them?

He didn't quite know, but he did feel different somehow.

Like he had more control, perhaps.

Let them push him about now, just let them try.

It was time for the world to take a leaf out of that woman's book. And stop pretending to care about desperate fathers and sick daughters.

19

'What's wrong, Paul?' Laura asked.

'Nothing... just thinking.' But even as he said it, he knew she wouldn't buy it.

Lucy.

Not an uncommon name, but still...

Strawberry laces hadn't been his daughter's thing, but fizzy bottles... now she absolutely loved them.

'What are you thinking about?'

Riddick pushed himself away from the wall he was leaning against. 'Escalation.'

'I agree. Whoever our sick, desperate father is, he's spiralling. He was provoked, but did you see that lad, and that tin of beans? He's lucky he isn't facing a murder charge.'

'I'm also convinced we saw him... before.'

'The man who ran past our car?' Laura said. 'Seems plausible.'

'More than plausible. It was definitely him.'

'How can you know for certain?'

'I just know.' Riddick shook his head. 'I should have gotten out of the car.'

Laura shrugged. 'Not sure your cardiologist would have approved of that.'

Riddick glared at her.

'Sorry.'

Realising he was being over the top, Riddick took a deep breath and sighed. 'No, you're right. Anyway, I was rattled when he told me his sick daughter was called Lucy.'

'Okay...' Laura was clearly stopping herself from asking why – despite the fact her expression was practically screaming it.

'My daughter was called Lucy.'

Frost's inquisitive expression softened. She paused, clearly recalling something. 'Yes, I remember now...'

Riddick rolled his eyes. 'It was in my file, wasn't it?'

She nodded, her face reddening. 'Sorry.'

'Why are you sorry? Riddick's tragedy is out there in print for mass consumption – hardly your fault!' The anger was there, yes – hot and immediate. But underneath it was something more complicated. Shame, maybe. Or exposure. His most private pain had been turned into bullet points in a personnel file.

Loss of wife and two children in a terrorist incident.

As if that sentence could possibly contain the reality of what he'd lived through!

Still, anger was much easier to show than vulnerability.

'I understand. Hearing your daughter's name like that... with a father beside himself and struggling.'

The simple, direct sympathy hit harder than elaborate condolences ever had. Looking at her, he noticed something different. He'd sensed it before, and he sensed it again. They shared something.

Riddick was just about to quiz her over this and maybe sarcastically suggest that he'd like to read her file when he noticed the injured Viking being loaded into an ambulance.

He'd trained himself not to dwell on thoughts of those sirens heading towards the wreckage of his car, and his family – too late to do anything to help them.

Laura was right though – this whole event had certainly stirred his settled mind.

After the ambulance had left, tourists started to flow again.

They watched as very few people noticed the blood on the cobblestones, and Riddick reflected on how obliviousness quickly replaced panic and violence.

Riddick waited until they were back in the car Frost had mounted on the pavement before continuing the conversation.

'My eldest, Lucy, loved fizzy cola bottles... I know... it's a long way from strawberry laces.'

'Close enough,' Frost said.

He nodded. 'The youngest, Molly, liked chocolate.' He took a deep breath. 'Although, neither were opposed to the other's treats! They knew how to share. I hear about siblings, but my two, they were joined at the hip... Sorry...'

'For what?' Frost asked. 'They are your children. Talk about them.'

'And become a walking sob story?'

'No, be like everyone else. It's healthy to talk about your loved ones whether they're still here or not.'

'You sound like you're talking from experience.'

She looked away. Realising it was unkind to be that blunt if she wasn't yet willing to talk about whatever was weighing on her, he continued talking about his daughters. It had been so long since he'd had someone to talk to about them. Really talk, that is. Not just the clinical discussions with therapists or the awkward silences with colleagues who didn't know what to say. Gardner had understood. She'd listened without that uncomfortable pity in her eyes, had asked real questions, had made him feel like talking about Molly and Lucy wasn't just wallowing in grief but honouring who they'd been. God, he missed that. Missed her. The way she'd known exactly when to push and when to just sit with him in silence.

'Yep,' he continued. 'Mol and Luce shared everything – right down to that same little scar on their chins from when they both tried to slide down the banister on the same day. Luce went first, Mol right behind her. Couldn't bear to be separated, even for something as stupid as that.'

Frost laughed. 'Sounds like me and my sister, Bridgett.'

'Well, I'm glad you and Bridgett, and my daughters, had a lot of fun. I remember, after that little stunt, we were worried about them day and bloody night.'

'Parents worry anyway.'

'Now, isn't that the truth. Crazy to think that, well...' His voice dropped. 'That it was nothing they did in the end... it was something I did!' A lump formed in his throat, and he turned away. 'You know already, don't you? What happened? About Ronnie Haller?'

There was no need to look at her; he knew she did. 'That saves us some time, then.'

And the need to recount that horrendous tale.

'Nothing I read suggested it was your fault.'

Riddick snorted. 'Very kind of them.'

'Boss... Paul, sorry, you put a bad man away. A very bad man. Doing your job. A dangerous man off the streets – you will have saved many lives.'

'Just a shame I didn't save the ones that mattered most to me.'

'No, but you wouldn't have left him out there, would you?'

Riddick shrugged.

'I don't think you would have done.'

'No, but maybe I wouldn't have expressed such pleasure in putting him away. I got Haller's back up. I gloated and—'

'You genuinely think that was the reason he did that?'

Another shrug escaped him.

'Do you? Honestly?'

'Probably not.'

'Of course not. He wasn't cornered. He was beaten. What he did then was savage and completely unpredictable. It takes a certain person to do that, and you couldn't have known.'

Riddick nodded. If she'd have been saying this to him several years back, he'd have laughed in her face and sought out the nearest public house. But this wasn't years ago, and he'd had a rather sobering near-death experience.

He knew she was right.

'I hear Haller died in jail,' Frost said.

Riddick looked away. The memory of Gardner's face surfaced – when she'd discovered that it was Riddick who'd arranged that murder.

A look of disappointment on her face.

He certainly didn't want Frost sensing his guilt now. She was proving very effective at sensing things.

A sarcastic comment dismissed it. 'Couldn't have happened to a nicer bloke.' Then Riddick took a deep breath and rubbed his face again. 'How long is that bloody file anyway? I could summarise it in a page. Your version sounds like *War and Peace*.'

She laughed.

'I guess it's just full of warnings and strategies to engage with me. Probably a good call. I'll give you a tagline for the cover: Know your broken colleague, understand his limitations.'

More laughter from Frost. 'I wouldn't say you were broken, and there is very little mention of limitations. In fact, you are regarded as highly effective.'

His glare met her eyes. 'Look, don't blow smoke up my arse. Keep your wits about you. Things don't always end well when knocking around with me. Grief has a strange way of, I don't know, creeping up on you...' Again and again, he thought. Like now for example.

He caught a look of agreement in her eyes, and his senses tingled again.

How have you been damaged, Laura?

A moment of silence settled between them, filled with the distant sounds of the festival crowds.

'So, what's our next move?' she asked, her voice carefully neutral. 'This crazed man isn't really our thing, is it? Armed robbery, commercial burglaries – that's what we're supposed to be investigating. Besides, they'll have a fair chunk of the force on the lookout for him now.'

'Staking out every supermarket and tinned goods aisle in York.'

'Ha. So shouldn't we head back and get on with our case?'

They were Intelligence Analysis. Danny Hurren and his crew were planning something big, and every hour they spent chasing a desperate father was another hour the real criminals had to prepare.

'Probably,' he said and sighed.

'Except?'

He didn't respond.

'You don't want to head back, do you?'

It wasn't really a question. There was something almost hopeful in her tone, as if she needed him to say it out loud.

'Guess not.' A family walked past – mother, father, daughter about Lucy's age. The girl was skipping between her parents, healthy and carefree. 'A tinned-bean-wielding maniac on the loose in York – it should be all hands to the pump.'

She nodded. 'But...'

Here it comes, he thought – a concern based on that file. She'd probably read a section entitled 'watch out for these warning signs'.

'It's not because his daughter has the same name,' he said.

She nodded again. 'Okay...' Then she looked at him. 'And it isn't because you suddenly think you understand him, is it?'

'Of course not! I don't know him from Adam!'

However, she'd read him like a book. It was everything to do with a desperate father's concern for the health of his little girl.

'Didn't think so,' Frost said, and he caught the ghost of a smile. 'So, what now?'

'We put in a request for other incidents in the area. Is it just the shop and the drunken Vikings, or has something else happened? We need hospitals contacted for appointments today involving a Lucy – young girl. We keep pressing for CCTV around all these areas – catch a glimpse of him – although we won't be the only ones doing that. So, I suggest we park better, get out on foot – head the way we saw him go. He said he needed painkillers, right? Maybe he's sick. Let's see if there's been any stops at a chemist.'

Riddick's heart was suddenly beating faster than it should be. And this wasn't just down to the transplanted organ's unpredictable rhythms. This was something else. Adrenaline. The thrill of the chase mixing with something deeper: the recognition that this case mattered. That finding this desperate father before something worse happened felt more important than surveillance reports and robbery predictions.

He reached for a beta blocker, but knew the pill couldn't slow what he was really feeling.

20

The kind lady had done Graham a service.

The flu remedy had brought the fever down. His shirt still clung to his skin, and the world still swam at the edges, but he no longer felt at death's door.

On a weathered stone bench near York Minster, he read the packaging of his new knife set: Non-slip soft grip handles. Protective covers. Dishwasher safe.

Short, concise statements from the salespeople. An attempt to bring simplicity to a cluttered world but ironically stitching you up with more clutter for the home.

The packet was easier to open than he'd first anticipated. The corner had warped, allowing him to get a fingerhold and pull the two pieces apart.

The largest blade emerged from its protective cover. Eight inches of surgical sharpness caught the weak February sun.

Tourists surrounded him, so he was careful not to spend too long examining. After replacing the protective cover, he dropped all three blades back into his bag, still sheathed. He slipped the label in with the knives, but the empty plastic container stayed on the bench.

Time to try Samantha again. 'It's me again,' he said, watching tourists flow past. Best to leave out the hospital altercation with the bigot. 'I still don't know if Lucy made it to the hospital.' Which was the truth. Although he'd not seen Lucy or Samantha there, they could have managed to get a taxi. They might have been in a room being seen by doctors. 'If you could just let me know... put my mind at rest. If we have missed it, then we need to press them—'

The words died in his throat when a family of three walked past – father in an expensive wool coat, mother carrying a designer handbag. The girl looked about Lucy's age, rosy-cheeked and vibrant with health.

'The world is not a place for everyone, Samantha.'

The little girl giggled as she shared a joke with her parents.

'Some bask and glow... while others...'

His hand found the bag while keeping the phone pressed to his ear.

I wonder if this glowing girl got a new kidney.

'Not everyone has to sit and wait their turn.'

His fingers touched one of the knife handles.

'We hang over the edge, don't we, Samantha? Me, you... Lucy.' The grip felt solid in his palm. 'Maybe it's time for answers.'

The four-inch paring knife came free.

He closed his eyes and hung up.

When his eyes opened, the glowing girl had vanished into the crowd. In her place, three crows perched on the Minster's limestone wall, their heads cocked at identical angles, watching him. The same three. Always the same three. His grandmother's voice echoed from decades past: 'When the Morrigan sisters gather, someone's thread is about to be cut.'

The middle crow cawed once – a harsh sound that cut through the tourist chatter.

Not yet, Graham thought. But soon.

The crows took flight as one, circling overhead before settling on a medieval rooftop across the square. Still watching. Always watching.

Graham rose from the bench and stood among the insulated, the paring knife in its protective cover now nestled in his trouser pocket. At the bin, the other two knives clattered against empty coffee cups and food wrappers. He only needed one.

Do they see us?

The uninsulated?

I mean – do they really see us?

The insulated don't queue.

The insulated don't suffer.

And only the insulated have answers.

But the funny thing about the insulated and the uninsulated?

His fingers found the knife handle through the fabric of his pocket.

We all bleed the same way.

21

Riddick soon started struggling on the uneven cobblestones.

By the time York Minster's twin towers came into view, his chest was tightening. You have to be kidding. Not again.

Frost was no mug. 'Here.' She pointed at a stone bench. 'Let's rest for a moment.'

He pushed along an empty plastic container and sat down. 'I'm sorry.'

'Why?' Frost said, sitting alongside him. 'Because I need a breather? It's bloody rammed round here.'

'Ha,' he said. 'I'm too long in the tooth to be arsed about saving face. You can spare my feelings. Just tell me – do I look like shit?'

'I didn't know how you looked before today, so I'm limited on comparison material. You could be looking the best you've ever looked for all I know.'

'Well, I can assure you that's not the case. However, I think I've looked like shit for a very long time... prior to today... so most people wouldn't notice the difference.'

'Well, you must look better without the substance abuse?'

'Yes – well, I knocked drinking on the head a while back.'

'I'm talking about the heroin.' She didn't look at him, just left it hanging there for him to decide whether to address it or not.

'Jesus wept. Is there anything you don't know?' he asked.

'*War and Peace*, remember?'

'Look, there was a reason for what happened...'

'Not arguing. I know.' She looked at him, her eyes glassy. 'What you did? Those kids you saved? It's a shame not everyone has it in them to make such sacrifices.'

Riddick almost added that he'd been near suicidal around that time, making the sacrifice all the easier, but he knew she'd just shoot that one down. It was an argument Emma Gardner had shot down countless times before.

'Anyway...' He nodded upwards at the Minster. 'Turn your eyes from me onto something worth looking at.'

The Gothic architecture rose above them in breathtaking vertical lines, eight centuries of limestone reaching towards grey February skies. He liked to consider the sheer audacity of medieval craftsmen who'd built something so magnificent it still dwarfed everything around it.

'It's impressive,' Frost said.

'First time seeing it properly?'

'Yes. The Midlands doesn't compare.'

Riddick felt the weight in his chest easing again. Closing his eyes for a moment, he let the sounds of the festival wash over him – distant Viking horns, tourist chatter in multiple languages, the steady flow of feet on ancient stones.

When he opened them, Frost was turning over the thin plastic container he'd brushed aside in her hands.

'What's that?' Riddick asked.

'Just some rubbish. Looks like it might have had some tools in it,' Frost replied.

'You always pick up rubbish?'

'Yes, and I put it in the bin when I can.'

Before Riddick could respond, his phone buzzed.

Taking it from his pocket, he read the subject line on a new email:

CCTV Footage – St Sampson's Square Incident

'Here we go,' he said, opening the attachment.

They huddled over his phone screen as the grainy black-and-white footage began to play. The timestamp showed 11.35 a.m. The camera angle captured most of St Sampson's Square, though the festival crowds obscured much of the detail.

'There.' Frost pointed to three figures in Viking costumes near the edge of the frame. 'Our charming alphas.'

The video quality was poor, but their body language was unmistakable – the aggressive posturing, the drunken movements.

The woman with her pushchair came into the shot. It was obvious that the idiots were giving her a hard time. 'A couple of beers and they're like gorillas in a jungle claiming their prize,' Frost said.

'I think you're being rather harsh on the gorillas,' Riddick said.

'Look at the way these dickheads are moving,' Frost said. 'Did you see the taller one grab her arm?'

'Milo,' Riddick said. 'His impending injury couldn't have happened to a nicer bloke.'

'Unbelievable. The casual confidence of predators who've never faced real consequences,' Frost said. 'And look at the great

British public.' Pedestrians went past, heads down, unwilling to get involved. 'No one thought to say anything.'

'Here's the knight in shining armour,' Riddick said.

'You were right – it was the man who came past us in the car before!'

'Looking just as messed up. He should be resting up, not playing vigilante.'

'He does look like he's trying to reason with them and get past to—'

Then came Milo's push.

'I wouldn't be doing that, fella,' Riddick said.

'It does look worse than it was... what with him being weak on his legs.'

'Still a push.'

The man struck with sudden, devastating efficiency. Milo dropped immediately, blood soon visible even on the grainy footage.

'Our man didn't seem too weak on his legs then.'

'Never seen someone just come alive like that. He looked half-dead a moment back,' Frost said.

'Aye,' Riddick breathed. 'Like a boxer down for a count of nine, who gets up and delivers a knockout blow immediately. He's obviously not on the same drugs I'm on.'

'Adrenaline I guess.'

'Really?' Riddick said. 'Can you buy it in bulk?'

They watched the father demand Tony's wallet and take out thirty pounds. Then, they watched him approach the woman with the pushchair.

It seemed to play out in exactly the same way that the young woman had suggested.

'Not exactly your typical violent criminal,' Frost said.

'A regular Batman. Put that on the news and half the general public will be cheering for him.'

'You included?' Frost said, eyebrow raised.

'Nah, he was too gentle with Milo. I'd have used a sack of potatoes... Heavier.'

She laughed, then regarded him, probably hoping he was, in fact, joking.

'And I'd have given that Tony one for good measure.'

The footage ended with the man walking away, leaving behind a scene of confusion and blood. No sound meant they couldn't hear what had been said, but the visual story was clear enough: a sick, desperate man defending a vulnerable young woman from privileged bullies.

'That'll make the news,' Frost said.

'Probably,' Riddick said.

He read the attached email and sighed.

'Go on.'

'Public enemy number one is not in the system,' Riddick said. 'At least his image is about to find its way to a lot of officers in this vicinity.'

His phone buzzed again and he read another email.

'So, there have been seven reported crimes in the city centre this morning. We have: a Wispa chocolate bar lifted from the Co-op... that's been ruled out by CCTV – elderly woman. Criminal damage – graffiti on Bootham Bar. Hmm. Our man doesn't strike me as the gang-tag type. The phone wire stolen from Clive, so another strike. A drunk tourist urinating on medieval wall. Bloody hell, it's only just gone midday. Okay, so he was wearing a Viking helmet – not our man. A taxi driver punched by fare-dodger – different description entirely. Criminal damage – wing mirror kicked off parked car, witness described suspect as a teenager.

And assault at York Hospital, renal unit reception – male suspect, forties, fled scene.' He looked at the timings. 'It could work if he headed to St Sampson's Square straight after the hospital. Renal unit? The sick daughter. He mentioned the hospital to Clive...'

He texted back his contact:

> Get me everything on that hospital assault this morning. Suspect description, witness statements, CCTV if they have it. Cross-reference with our Exhibition Square and St Sampson's Square incidents – is it the same man?

'I'm okay now,' Riddick said, standing and pocketing his phone. 'Let's continue until we hear back about the hospital.'

'Okay.' Frost went over to the bin and threw away the plastic container.

22

Graham stopped dead in his tracks when he saw the brass plaque.

Quinn Vale Private Medical Centre – Excellence in Independent Healthcare

He reached out to touch the honey-coloured stone of the Georgian property.

'Excellence in Independent Healthcare,' he said under his breath. The sales team were at it again. Concise simplicity in a cluttered world.

He touched the paring knife in his pocket. Non-slip soft grip handles. Protective covers. Dishwasher safe.

He went inside, down a short corridor and into an empty reception area. It was so different from any medical centre he'd ever been to! No antiseptic tang here. No plastic chairs or industrial carpets. Instead, there was a marble coffee table laden with copies of *Country Life* and *The Lady*. Persian rugs. Cream leather furniture. Not a single person waiting.

But wasn't that obvious? Why would the insulated queue?

'Can I help you?'

Behind a mahogany reception desk that looked like it belonged in a bank rather than a medical practice, a young woman looked up from her computer screen. Perhaps twenty-five, blonde hair swept back in a neat bun.

'I don't know,' Graham said, fingers finding the knife handle in his pocket.

'Do you have an appointment?'

He approached the reception desk and read the nameplate. 'Sarah Crossfield, Patient Services Coordinator.'

'I'm sorry – what name should I look under?'

An uncomfortable expression settled over her face as she took him in properly.

'It's so calm in here,' Graham said. 'So quiet... so unlike outside... unlike the morning I've just had.'

'Sir, I need your name to check our system.'

'Why? My name doesn't matter. At least not to you. Not to anyone in your world. I don't have an appointment.' He smiled and noticed a nervous twitch in her cheek. Her eyes were cataloguing his appearance now – the feverish sheen, the sweat-stained clothing.

'Are you feeling all right? Should I call someone for you?'

'Do I look that unwell?'

Sarah rolled her chair back slightly, edging closer to a door behind her. 'You seem... Yes, you don't look well.'

'Then I suppose I need to see a doctor.'

She swivelled towards a side desk and reached for the phone.

'What are you doing?'

'I can call an ambulance. They'll be here quickly... be better equipped—'

'But this is a medical practice, isn't it?'

She regarded him with confusion, not grasping his point. Did she think he was simply thick?

'Well, is it?' he pressed.

'Yes, but—'

'So I can see a doctor here?'

'It doesn't work that way. This is a private facility. Dr Phillips only sees patients by appointment.'

'Ah.' Graham surveyed the empty waiting room. 'And you're remarkably busy, I see.'

She looked down. The hand gripping the phone trembled visibly. Guilt flickered through him. This young woman hadn't done anything wrong. She was just following rules, doing her job. He'd stood up for that mother against those thugs because intimidating innocent people was wrong. And now here he was, doing the same thing to Sarah. The fever made it hard to think clearly, but some part of him still recognised the hypocrisy. Still, what choice did he have? Lucy needed him. 'Is Dr Phillips with a patient now?'

'No, but—'

'So I'd like to see him.'

Sarah chewed her lip, clearly calculating her options. 'Look, if this is urgent, A&E would be free. No waiting for insurance verification or—'

'But why burden them when there's a doctor here? Available?'

'I could book you an appointment for next week, but there's paperwork, insurance verification—'

'What if we skip the paperwork?'

'Do you have private medical insurance?'

'National Insurance, yes. Don't we all?'

'No, I mean private cover. Bupa, AXA, something like that?'

'Is that different from the NHS?'

Of course he knew the difference. Twenty years in the NHS had taught him exactly how the system worked – how private patients got seen immediately while others waited in pain. He was being difficult on purpose, forcing her to articulate the inequality, to say out loud what everyone pretended not to see. Make her uncomfortable with the reality of it. Maybe then she'd understand why he was here, why he couldn't just accept 'proper channels' any more.

'A consultation starts at two hundred pounds, before any tests or treatment.'

Graham sighed and looked down, fingers tightening on the concealed knife. 'Let me understand this. You have a doctor here. I'm clearly unwell. He's free.'

'I'm sorry,' she said, unable to maintain eye contact.

'Would it help if I mentioned I'm on Universal Credit?'

Her brow furrowed with genuine confusion and discomfort. Why did privilege always squirm when confronted with actual need?

'I'll just call that ambulance—'

Graham's cough erupted, harsh and prolonged. When he finally caught his breath, he rasped, 'I'm ill, yes. But not ambulance ill.'

'I could ring for a taxi to York Hospital?'

'How thoughtful, except I have no money for a taxi.' He pulled three pounds from his pocket, placing the coins on the marble counter. 'Perhaps you could cover the difference?'

'I... The hospital's only a twenty-minute walk. I can give you directions.'

Graham pretended to consider this. 'Actually, I'm exhausted. Let's return to my original request. The available doctor.'

Sarah shifted uncomfortably, trapped between corporate policy and human decency.

He began pacing the reception area. 'My GP's next appointment? Eight weeks out. For chronic insomnia. Imagine how I'll be sleeping by then.' He picked up a copy of *Country Life*, flipping through pages of manor houses and hunt meetings. 'Exhausted.' The magazine slapped shut. 'But someone with the right insurance could walk in here and see someone immediately?'

Silence.

He stared at her. 'Sarah?'

'Sorry?'

'Could they?'

'If they have cover, yes.'

'If they're insulated.'

'I don't follow—'

'Wealthy. Protected. While the rest of us wave government vouchers at closed doors.' The words came out sharper than he intended, loaded with a bitterness that surprised even him. She probably didn't make much more than minimum wage herself. But knowing that didn't stop the hot, corrosive anger building in his chest.

It felt like such a waste of time. After all, Lucy needed him, and instead he was here taking his fury out on this young woman suffering the misfortune of being the face of a system that didn't give a shit about people like him.

But every time he tried to pull back, he just thought of every closed door he'd ever encountered.

Every policy.

Every 'we can't help you'.

Sarah's professional mask slipped momentarily – pity or

distaste, he couldn't tell. 'This is a private facility. I don't make the rules.'

'Of course not.'

He tried to dispel his building fury by turning his attention to an ornate vase by the window. Expensive looking, though what did he know about such things? He gestured at it. 'Ming dynasty?'

No response.

'Sarah? Is it Ming?'

'I wouldn't know.'

'Course not.'

The vase held plastic flowers – perfect plastic petals that would never wilt, never need water, never die. He touched one cold bloom. 'All the answers,' he murmured. 'All this time watching Lucy deteriorate, begging for help...' He turned back to Sarah. 'The answers were here all along, weren't they?'

'Sir, I need you to leave now, or I'll have to contact security—'

'My daughter's kidneys are failing.' The words came out flat, matter-of-fact. 'She's eight years old, and she's dying because we can't afford to jump the queue.'

Sarah's eyes widened.

'Eight. Years. Old.'

'I'm so sorry.'

'Genuinely?'

A small nod.

'Then put down the phone. If you actually care, put it down.'

After a moment's hesitation, she replaced the handset.

Graham returned to the flowers, running his finger along synthetic stems. 'Excellence in Independent Healthcare. That's your promise, on the plaque.' He glanced back. 'Tell me, what's excellent about turning away sick people?'

'I'm truly sorry about your daughter—'

'Can my daughter access your excellence?'

'That's not my decision—'

'No, it never is. Unless...' He gripped the vase. 'Unless we make it our decision.'

'I don't understand.'

'Then let me clarify. Call the doctor. Now.'

'He'll be furious if I interrupt—'

'Plastic bloody system.' Graham tilted the vase. It teetered on its pedestal, suspended for a heartbeat, then shattered across the Persian rug. He studied the ceramic shards and scattered plastic flowers. No water pooled on the carpet.

'Not even water for fake flowers.' He approached the desk again. 'Though they don't need it, do they? They're only plastic. Like we are to you – plastic people with plastic problems. Is my daughter plastic? Am I? Don't we deserve your excellence?'

Sarah had already lifted the phone, fingers moving over the keypad.

Graham drew the knife from his pocket, thumbed off the protective cap, and held it where she could see it clearly.

The emergency operator's voice leaked from the handset.

'Put it down,' he said quietly. 'Put it down and nobody gets hurt.'

She replaced the receiver, tears now flowing freely.

'Good. Now tell Dr Phillips he has an emergency consultation.'

Rising halfway from her chair, she whispered, 'Okay,' her entire body trembling.

He raised the blade, hating himself for it. Every cell in his body screamed that this was wrong. He was threatening a young woman who'd done nothing but her job. But Lucy's face swam before him, pale and desperate. What other choice did he have left?

'No. Stay seated. Use the desk phone.'

'Please, I—'

The knife point hovered near her face, his hand trembling slightly. He saw the fear in her eyes and felt sick. 'Make the call, Sarah.' His voice cracked. 'Please. I don't want to hurt you. I just need him to see me. That's all. Just make the call.'

23

It was approaching one o'clock, and Riddick had to stop and rest twice more on Museum Street.

During the second stop beside a flower boutique, his phone buzzed with the hospital CCTV footage. The video that loaded was grainy but clear enough – the timestamp showed 10.43 a.m., the renal unit at York Hospital.

Frost moved closer to see the screen. There was no sound, but they watched the altercation unfold between the dishevelled desperate father and the elderly man.

'Batman's about to lose his hero status,' Frost said.

'Maybe not.' Riddick scrolled through the accompanying report. 'Says here he was confronting a bigot. Racist comments about immigrants draining NHS resources.'

'Christ. That'll split opinion.'

'Completely. The elderly man – Williamson, seventy-three, ex-military apparently – been attending renal appointments for six months.' He continued reading. 'Started ranting about queue-jumping, health tourism. Claiming foreign families were getting priority over "proper British citizens".'

'That old chestnut.'

'Mm. Our desperate dad's going to be Marmite now. There'll be plenty cheering him on, and just as many baying for blood.' Riddick squinted at the screen. 'According to witnesses, he tried talking first. Asked Williamson to stop, said underfunding was the real issue, not immigration. But the old boy kept at it, targeting other patients, making everyone uncomfortable.'

'Then what?'

'Then Williamson apparently said something about our man's sick daughter – something like she was suffering because immigrants were getting preferential treatment.'

'Ah. Red rag to a bull.'

'Exactly. Another adrenaline surge, and—'

'Lucky there were no tins of beans handy this time.'

'Very lucky. Williamson's frailer than our Surrey boy.' Riddick frowned at the next line. 'Here's something odd though – there were no appointments scheduled for any Lucy.'

Frost's eyebrows shot up. 'What? But he said he needed to get his daughter to the hospital. I mean, he wasn't lying – he actually went there.'

'I know. Makes no sense.'

'Wrong department maybe?'

'Could be. Or...' He rubbed his temple, thinking. 'Look at the state of him. Running that kind of fever, he could be confused, delusional even. When you're that ill, that desperate, reality can start sliding.'

She gave him a long look. 'Speaking from experience?'

'Unfortunately.' He fired off a text to his contact. 'I'll get them to check every department for any Lucy with an appointment today—' He stopped. 'You know what's bothering me?'

'What?'

'If there's no Lucy in the system at all.'

'Then either he's completely lost it—'

'Or something else is going on.' They stood in silence for a moment, processing the implications.

'We should probably pick up the pace,' Frost said eventually. 'His pattern's escalating. Shop owner, elderly patient, young man with a tin...'

'Each one worse than the last.' Despite everything, Riddick felt a grudging respect for the man's determination. 'You'd think whatever's making him this ill would slow him down.'

'Instead, he's speeding up.'

'Which means—'

'Someone's going to die if we don't find him.' Frost paused. 'Probably him.'

'And he's someone's father.'

They moved on, Riddick's legs already protesting. The immunosuppressants made everything feel like wading through treacle, but something was nagging at him. They were on one of York's priciest streets, surrounded by boutique shops, private galleries, professional services that regular people couldn't afford...

By the third rest stop, he was leaning against a Georgian building's honey-coloured stone, breathing hard. He felt the cold of a brass plaque against the back of his neck. It was soothing.

'Where would you go?' he asked suddenly. 'If you were desperate, sick, angry at the system?'

'Well, I imagine first, he'd like to return to his daughter.'

'That doesn't help us now. Somewhere else?'

'Somewhere to help him with his health? His daughter's health.'

'Okay, good point... hence the hospital. But he's burned his bridges there because of Williamson, so now what? The next hospital along?'

'Maybe, or a doctor's surgery?'

Riddick nodded. 'Well, that wouldn't narrow it down. Needle in a bloody haystack, but at least it's a start.'

24

Graham paced back and forth, broken vase crunching under his brogues, paring knife in hand. The two occupants on the sofa kept their eyes down, their faces etched with anxiety. Neither Sarah nor Dr Phillips seemed willing to look up, clearly too nervous to meet his gaze.

'What's your first name?' Graham asked.

Dr Phillips – a man in his late fifties, immaculately dressed in a tailored suit far nicer than anything Graham had ever worn – lifted his eyes, touched his chest, and said, 'Me?'

'Well, I've already met Sarah.' Graham tried smiling at her, but she didn't look up, and a tear ran down her face. 'In a fashion. So yes, Doc, your name?'

Look at them both, Lou whispered. *Terrified of you. Is that what you want?*

'Ron,' the doctor said.

'Well, Ron, I like your suit.'

'Thank you.'

'Non-slip soft grip handles. Protective covers. Dishwasher safe.'

Ron creased his brow. 'Sorry?'

Graham smiled. 'You look professional. Fit for purpose.'

The doctor nodded, his brow still creased. 'So, how can I help you?' Ron ventured.

Graham continued to pace, bobbing his head as he thought. Heat prickled his scalp. Was the fever building again? 'I've already explained that.' Graham pointed at the door behind the reception desk with the knife. 'When you came through that door, I told you to sit over here with Sarah.' He turned and pointed the knife at the sofa. 'I apologised for your vase... and then I told you I wanted you to listen to what I have to say.'

'Yes, I recall.'

'And if you do that, all will be good.'

'Great... so, I'm ready, then.'

'For what?'

'To listen?'

Graham stopped, laughed and pointed at him with the blade. 'Ah... of course...'

Silence stretched between them as Graham studied the two terrified individuals. He forced away any feelings of sympathy; after all, when had any of these people ever shown him sympathy, really? And he'd been living in a state of perpetual fear for as long as he could remember.

'There is a problem though, Ron. Quite a large one.'

'I see.'

'Are you actually listening?'

'Yes, of course.' Ron nodded frantically.

Graham moved nearer. 'No, I mean really listening.'

'Yes—'

The blade thrust outward, closer to the doctor's throat.

Ron shook and pressed himself deeper into the sofa. 'Please God.'

Graham backed away smiling. 'I mean, I'm threatening to cut your throat... of course you're going to listen.' He snorted. 'I don't think I've ever been able to hold someone's attention so... so... rigidly! The problem is, now I have it, well... I'm not sure how to begin really!'

Sarah continued to sob quietly in the corner of the sofa.

'Maybe you could help me. I mean, you look like a man accustomed to deference and respect.'

Ron's smile was transparently fake as he shook his head, trying to keep some composure. 'I don't know about that.'

'Come on now! A man like you!'

'Not sure my wife shows me much deference or respect.' He paused. 'Or my children for that matter.' The emphasis on 'children' was deliberate, calculated.

Clever boy, Graham thought. *Trying to instil some sympathy in me.*

'I imagine your children are all grown up now,' Graham said.

Ron nodded and lowered his eyes.

'Guess it's sad when they don't need you any more?'

'Well, I don't know about that. They still manage to hang off our coattails—'

'Quit the smarm.' Graham's eyes narrowed. 'Always smarm with you people. Salespeople, the lot of you.'

'I'm a doctor,' Ron said defensively. 'I'm not a salesman.'

'Oh, really?' Graham gestured around the waiting room. 'I may not have had the education you've had, but come on... look at this place. It's designed to separate rich people from their money.'

'We provide legitimate medical services—'

'I'm not disputing—' A violent coughing fit seized him and Graham stumbled back, one arm covering his mouth while the other hand kept the knife extended. *Don't you dare, Ron*, he thought. *Don't think you can make a move while my body attacks me. I'm not as weak as you think.*

When the coughing subsided, Graham wiped his mouth and took several deep breaths. The doctor hadn't moved – a wise choice.

'I can see that you're sick,' the doctor said carefully. 'I can help with that.'

'Can you? Really?' Graham pointed the blade at Sarah. 'Your Patient Services Coordinator seemed to suggest otherwise.'

The doctor looked at Sarah, then back at Graham.

'Well, maybe she wasn't aware that I always make an exception for those in desperate need of help.'

Graham shook his head. 'She seemed to have no idea of your charitable side.'

'Well, we're always so busy.'

'Until someone has some power, I guess,' Graham said. 'Usually in the form of money. However...' He sliced the air with the blade. 'Power comes in many forms. But no, I don't think you can help me. I think we're past that. All you have to do is listen. That is all I can expect.'

'Let me at least try. What's wrong with you?'

Graham found this hilarious. 'Wrong with me? With me?' He touched his chest. 'Try this... I'm bleeding inside.'

'Internal bleeding?' Ron's professional instincts kicked in despite his fear. 'Have you been diagnosed? Are you on blood thinners? Any history of ulcers, varices? Have you been vomiting blood?'

Graham shook his head. 'Worse than all that. I feel like I've had my insides ripped out.'

'I... I don't understand.'

'You really don't get the metaphorical, do you? Everything is so black and white, so linear with you people. Are you not able to work on an emotional level?'

'Well, yes, of course... we do have doctors for that.'

'I know. Tried them. They thought the answer for me lay with chemicals.'

'I see. And do you take them?'

'Not any more. They blunted everything. It was nice to be clear for a time, but then, of course, the clouds return. Some days it's hard to see the wood from the trees.'

'I have a colleague—'

'I bet you do. How much will he charge me for his services?'

Ron straightened, his professional dignity reasserting itself. 'You are being...' He broke off before potentially offending his captor. 'We've dedicated our careers to helping people—'

'People with money.'

Anger flashed across Ron's face.

Careful, Doctor, Graham thought.

'I worked in the NHS for fifteen years!'

'Twenty years for me. In IT services.'

Ron's eyes widened. 'Really? In what capacity?'

'In the poorly paid, overworked capacity. But I took pride in what I did.'

'Me too.'

'Was that before you realised you could make more money treating rich people's tennis elbows than poor children's cancer?'

'You make everything sound simple.'

'Isn't that how you all like it?' Graham moved closer. 'Simplified and less cluttered. Some for them. More for us.'

'You're not making any sense.'

In one swift movement, Graham had the blade an inch from Ron's eye. 'You know exactly what I'm talking about.

Whatever else you say is a lie. I told you to listen, not to lie to me.'

Ron squeezed his eyes shut. 'Please...'

'Another lie and I'll puncture your eye, do you understand?'

'Yes.'

'Okay, listen, and when you speak, you tell the truth.' Graham glanced at Sarah, who was now pressing herself into the corner of the sofa as if trying to disappear into the leather.

Switching the professional-quality knife between hands, Graham knelt in front of them both. His face was level with Ron's now, the doctor's eyes still closed.

'Look at me, Ron.'

'Please...'

'Open your eyes and look at me!'

Ron's eyes snapped open.

Graham waited until the terrified doctor was maintaining eye contact. 'Good. Imagine I'm an agitated patient, which, in a way, I guess I am. Don't take your eyes from me. Try to soothe me. Now listen – you provide excellent care.' Graham's voice took on a mocking tone. 'That's what your sign says outside. Excellence in Independent Healthcare. Is that the truth?'

Ron opened his mouth to speak.

'Remember, no more lies,' Graham cut in.

Ron closed his mouth.

'Answer from your heart. Don't be a salesman.'

The doctor's face contorted with the effort of finding the right words. He reminded Graham of Bilbo from *Lord of the Rings* trying to solve one of Gollum's riddles.

Eventually, Ron said, 'Many have commented on the fact that we do.'

'Clever. But what do you think?'

Ron took a deep breath. 'We try our best.'

'You try your best?'

The doctor nodded, squinting as if Graham was about to strike.

'I believe you.'

Clear relief washed over Ron's face.

'Next question. This "trying your best" – it's only available for the insulated?'

'Sorry?'

'Those with means. Money. Not a pleasant question, I know, but I must insist on the truth.'

'Even if the truth makes you angry?'

'I'm already angry, in case you hadn't noticed.'

Graham watched Ron's face. The doctor was calculating, trying to find the safest path through the conversation. Twenty years in the NHS had taught Graham to read people like this. The ones who measured their words like medication doses, afraid of liability, of lawsuits, of saying the wrong thing to the wrong person.

'Look, I told you I used to work for the NHS—'

'That wasn't my question.'

Ron closed his eyes and opened his mouth slightly as if to speak. Was this the universal gesture of someone about to admit an uncomfortable truth?

'I don't have all day, Ron.'

'Yes, it costs money.'

'Okay, how much for a consultation?'

'It's £199.89,' Ron said quietly.

'Not cheap then.' Standing up, Graham resumed his pacing. The ceramic vase crunched underfoot. 'I'm sorry about your vase.'

'It's all right,' Ron said.

'Still, it must be annoying. The broken vase.'

'It's fine, really.'

Graham stopped. 'It's not though, is it? If you came into my home and broke something, I wouldn't be happy about that either.' The absurdity of apologising for a vase while holding them hostage with a knife wasn't lost on him. But manners, no matter the circumstances, cost nothing. One thing they can never say about him, no matter how far he went, was that he didn't care about civility.

'No?' Graham prompted.

'It was okay, I guess.'

'Sarah?'

'Umm... yes.'

'Sorry, both of you, about the vase.'

'Okay,' Ron said, while Sarah nodded, tears still streaming down her face.

Graham stopped again, prodding the plastic flowers with his foot. 'You know what, I've had an idea. Want to hear it?'

Ron's nod was enthusiastic and clearly false.

'Really? You're interested in what I have to say?'

'Yes...'

'Stop nodding, Ron.'

The nodding ceased immediately.

He felt a tiny rush of power. For the first time in months, someone was listening to him. Really listening. Not dismissing him, not telling him to fill out forms, not checking their watch while he talked.

Even in his fevered state, he couldn't delude himself into thinking that Ron was paying attention for any other reason than the fact he was terrified. So why savour it?

Because of the insight? Because of finally discovering what control felt like?

Was this what it meant to be taken seriously?

He'd never wanted to be this person, but now that he had it, was it better that he did?

'Okay, my idea is this: maybe you should add something to your "Excellence in Independent Healthcare" sign. How about: "Only for those who can afford it"?'

Ron stared at him.

Graham turned to Sarah. 'Do you like that idea?'

Sarah nodded mutely.

'Ron?'

'We can look into it.'

'Fantastic... unless... was that a lie, Ron?'

The doctor lowered his head.

Of course he's lying, Lou said. *They all lie when they're scared.*

'Ha, just messing, Doctor. I get that you're scared. I'd promise anything if someone was waving this about.' Graham gestured with the knife. 'I did kind of trick you with that one. I think the chances of you adding that to your sign are virtually zero, wouldn't you say?'

Ron nodded with a resigned sigh.

'Virtually or just plain zero?'

Silence.

'I definitely want the truth this time.'

'Zero,' Ron said. 'Okay, we've listened. I've been truthful. Please, what else do you want?'

Graham touched his chest. 'To finish. Is that too much to ask? I've got more to say.'

A flash of frustration crossed Ron's face, making Graham smile. 'Tell you what, I'll press on. I want to talk more about the monetisation of healthcare.'

Ron looked confused. 'Haven't we done that?'

'It's a massive subject.' Graham shrugged. 'Let's start with your views, Ron.'

The doctor glanced at Sarah, sighed, then looked up fearfully. 'Healthcare has costs – equipment, staff, maintenance. Running a medical facility is expensive.'

'I worked in the NHS, remember? I understand the economics.' Graham moved closer. 'My concern is more with the ethical.'

Ron shook his head. 'We've done nothing wrong. At least let Sarah go.'

'If I do that, I won't get a chance to finish! Now come on, Ron, talk to me about the ethics of what you do.' Graham gestured around the pristine waiting room. 'About all of this.'

'I think this is enough.'

'I will decide when it's enough!' Graham's voice rose sharply.

Ron flinched and nodded.

Graham touched the doctor's cheek with the point of the blade, considering a nick, maybe a quick slice, just a little persuasive flavour. 'Shall I help? The NHS tries to treat everyone, regardless of ability to pay. You treat people based on the size of their bank account.'

Still no response.

The blade pressed harder, the skin creasing around its tip.

'Ron – I'm trying to help.'

'We work within a different model, yes, but we still follow medical ethics—'

Graham pulled the blade away. 'Providing that excellent care, yes? Or at least "trying to", as you said.'

The doctor nodded. Sarah pressed a tissue to her nose, her breathing shallow.

'So shall we talk about those who don't have money?' Graham wiped sweat from his forehead with his free hand. He noticed that the hand holding the knife was really trembling now. 'Well... shall we?'

'Look, everyone knows the arguments for and against. I do. You do. We could go back and forth. It won't solve anything. This doesn't have an outcome.'

'Doesn't it?' Graham narrowed his eyes.

The doctor shook his head.

'What if I was to cut you open?'

Tears welled in Ron's eyes. 'It won't change anything, so please don't.'

'Probably not. But I want to make a point.'

'I know, but nobody will give you the time of day if you make a point in this manner.'

Graham darted forward, the knife trembling in his grip. 'Time of day? Nobody has ever given me the time of day! You think if I let you walk out of here, I suddenly get the time of day?'

'No.'

'At least you're still being honest.' The admission should have made him angrier, but instead he felt oddly grateful for it. Truth, finally. How rare that had become.

Graham resumed his pacing. 'But maybe it will make me feel... I don't know... better.'

'It won't. It can't. You'll regret it.'

'Will I? You sure? Do you know me, Ron? Maybe as I spike you, I can think of all those people waiting eighteen months for a specialist appointment while those with bank balances are seen the very first day.'

'The NHS and private sector serve different functions. They exist, and will continue to exist, whether you hurt me or not—'

The blade swished past the doctor's face. 'Different functions? What functions? You're both treating the same conditions, the same ailments, using the same specialists, the same equipment. The only difference is how much money people have – how quickly life can be restored to normal. In other words, some have more hope than others. You think I'm mad, don't you?'

Ron looked like he was going to be sick.

Good. Let him feel nauseous. Let him feel a fraction of what I feel every waking moment.

'No.'

'You're lying.'

'Angry, yes. Not insane.'

'Still lying.' Each breath suddenly felt as if it had to fight its way in. 'Look, maybe I am insane, but I know this for a fact: I have a daughter. She's eight.' His voice broke.

'Think of her.'

'I am thinking of her, fuckwit. Her kidneys are failing.' Graham lowered his head. 'She needs a transplant.'

'I'm so sorry.'

'Are you? Really?' Graham snorted. 'Or is it just because of this?' He raised the knife. 'Non-slip soft grip handles. Protective covers. Dishwasher safe.'

'I don't understand.'

'Sarah was the same. She sounded sad too, but I don't think she cares. Not really.'

'I do,' Sarah said, her voice barely a whisper. 'I really do.'

'Prove it then.'

Sarah's mouth opened as if to suggest something, but then closed again. Her face dropped.

'Exactly.' Graham turned back to Ron. 'Do you know how long the NHS waiting list is for paediatric kidney transplants?'

Ron looked genuinely sad but said nothing.

'Two to three years. Minimum. If she's lucky. Will she survive that long?' Graham's voice rose again. 'Now if I had money, if I could pay your fees, then I would get excellent healthcare. How long would it take then?'

The doctor's eyes suddenly widened, as if a lightbulb had gone off. Something that might just save his life. 'It's the same! You're wrong! Private healthcare doesn't typically handle organ transplants!'

Graham knew this already. 'But you could fast-track the assessment, couldn't you? Private consultation, private tests, private referrals. Jump the queue at every step.'

Ron shook his head, still looking somewhat elated. 'That's not how it works. Really. I'm telling the truth. There are no advantages when it comes to transplants.'

'Come on, Ron. Let's look at the facts. Is everyone waiting their turn?'

'As far as I'm aware.'

Graham's hand shot forward, slapping Ron across the face with enough force to knock him sideways.

The crack echoed through the waiting room. Graham looked at his stinging palm.

More violence, Lou said. *It really is becoming your default.*

Ron collapsed against the sofa, clutching his cheek, sobbing.

'You're all in on it together. You're part of it all. Both of you. Tell me, when did you last treat someone on benefits? When did you last see a patient who couldn't afford your consultation fee?'

Through his sobs, Ron said, 'I can't give you the answer you want.'

'The truth is what I want. How many fucking times?'

'The model,' Ron said desperately. 'The model doesn't cater for people on benefits. But that doesn't mean—'

'The model.' Graham's pacing intensified, ceramic shards

grinding under his feet. 'The model. The fucking model. Right.' He stopped and steadied himself against the reception desk. 'And what happened to "do no harm", Doctor? Isn't that part of your oath?'

'Of course it is, but—'

'But it doesn't apply if people can't pay?'

'That's not what I said.'

'It's what you meant, though.' Graham's agitation was building visibly. 'You took an oath to do no harm, to help people, to heal the sick. But only if they can afford it.' Graham spun to face him. 'My daughter is dying while people with money get immediate care. I understand that the system I worked for, the system I believed in, has been carved up and sold to the highest bidder.'

Dr Phillips tried a different approach. 'Your daughter's situation sounds desperate. Have you spoken to the hospital social workers? There are sometimes emergency provisions—'

'Emergency provisions?' Graham's voice dripped with incredulity. 'You mean the scraps? The charity cases? The oh-so-generous system throwing us a bone when it feels like it?'

'That's not what I meant—'

'What would you do?' Graham interrupted. 'If it was your child? If your daughter was dying and you had the choice between NHS waiting lists and private care?'

'I would... I would do whatever I could to help her.'

'Whatever you could afford, you mean.'

Silence stretched between them.

'Answer me!' Graham stepped closer. 'If your child was dying, would you wait two years for NHS treatment, or would you pay for private care?'

Dr Phillips's professional mask slipped. 'I would want the best care possible.'

'The best care money can buy.'

'Yes.'

'But my daughter doesn't deserve that because I'm poor.' Spit flew from Graham's lips as he shouted. 'You're saying that some children deserve to live and others deserve to die, based on their parents' bank accounts!'

'Please, calm down—'

'Calm down?' Graham's laugh bordered on hysterical. 'My daughter is dying, and you want me to calm down? You sit in your private clinic with your expensive vases and Persian rugs, treating rich people's headaches while children die waiting for NHS care!'

Graham looked down at the knife in his hand, then back at his terrified hostages, both trembling on the sofa. He pointed at his chest. 'Twenty years of helping people get their appointments, get their treatment. I was one of the good ones.'

And then he heard Lou laughing somewhere deep inside him.

Not again, he thought.

One of the good ones? You've never been anything but an angry, bitter little man skulking in the shadows.

'Skulking?' Graham said aloud. 'You call this skulking?'

Look at you. Our daughter would be horrified.

'How dare you, you sanctimonious bitch. Where are you? In Australia with your fucking toy boy?'

Okay, have it your own way, Graham – maybe you are a nice guy. Whatever you want to believe.

'Not any more. Nice guys finish last while their daughters die.'

The terrified pair stared at him, clearly stunned by the conversation he was having with his absent ex-wife.

'How about emergency care, Ron?'

'Sorry?'

'Emergency care. As a doctor, you'd treat someone in an emergency, wouldn't you? Someone dying in front of you.'

'Of course. I'm not a monster.'

'I don't believe you.' Graham turned his hand over and pressed the blade against his wrist. 'What if I slit my wrist here? Would you treat me then? Would you stop the bleeding, or would you ask for my insurance details first?'

'This is ridiculous—'

Graham glanced at Sarah. 'Or would you just go back to calling that ambulance – pass me along?'

The blade pressed harder against his skin. A laugh escaped him. Part performance, part genuine curiosity about whether he'd do it.

Would it hurt?

Would it be quick?

But most importantly, would Lucy forgive him?

Blood began to bead around the blade's edge.

Just a little deeper now, Lou's voice whispered seductively. *Spare us all. Spare your daughter. Spare yourself.*

God, his ex-wife had always known how to get under his skin. All the fever, the pain, the injustice, the agony of his helplessness in the face of Lucy's suffering – it could all be over with the flick of a wrist.

No more fighting a system that didn't care. No more watching Lucy fade away. No more being the father who couldn't save his child.

'Stop!' Ron lunged forward from the sofa. 'Don't do that!'

Graham felt the doctor's hands grabbing for the knife, trying to prevent the blade from cutting deeper. The doctor was stronger than he looked, or maybe Graham was just weaker than ever.

He's trying to save you, Lou's voice observed.

What a bloody time to start trying to do some good, Graham thought.

Ron gripped Graham's wrist with both hands, the one holding the blade. But sweat and blood made everything slippery, and Graham could feel the doctor's grip failing.

Let him save you, Lou insisted.

No, Graham thought. *It's just another lie. Another way to pretend to care. Another performance to protect their interests.*

Graham threw his weight forward, the knife still trapped between them.

They crashed to the floor together, Ron underneath, Graham on top. The ceramic shards from the vase scattered beneath them as they struggled. Sarah screamed from the sofa.

The knife?

Where was the knife?

It was pinned between them. No one was in full control.

So this is who you are now? Lou's voice was almost sad. *This is what you've finally become?*

No, Graham thought as he wrestled for control of the blade. *This is what they made me.*

25

When Riddick heard a woman's scream coming from inside the Georgian building he was leaning against, he pounced forward, turned and read the brass plaque.

Quinn Vale Private Medical Centre
Excellence in Independent Healthcare
Dr R. Phillips MD FRCP – Dr M. Sterling MD

'The needle found us,' Riddick said, throwing open the door and charging in. He sensed Frost just behind him.

'Paul, careful—' Frost called.

He held up his hand and waved her on after him down the corridor; if his physical limitations couldn't stop him, then Frost sure as hell wouldn't be able to.

He burst into the waiting room and took in the scene quickly.

A young woman – blonde, mid-twenties – knelt beside a much older man who was clutching his side. Blood seeped between the man's fingers. The remains of a smashed vase were strewn beneath them both. She was on her mobile phone – calling for an ambulance, by the sound of it.

Riddick surveyed the scene for the assailant. The woman looked up at him, tears streaming down her face.

'Police!' Riddick said. 'Where—'

He broke off because she was already pointing towards a door behind the reception desk.

Not wanting to risk Frost, Riddick moved around the desk and pushed through the door despite his body's protests.

'Paul, wait!'

The corridor beyond reception stretched deeper into the building – cream walls, expensive artwork, the hushed luxury of private healthcare. Three doors on the left, two on the right, all standing open except the one at the far end.

His chest tightened as he moved down the corridor, each step sending shooting pains through the catheter site from this morning's biopsy. His breathing was laboured, but he forced himself forward, checking each room methodically.

First room: consultation office, mahogany desk, medical certificates on the walls. Empty.

Second room: examination room, leather chairs, diagnostic equipment that looked straight from a private hospital's wish list. The room was clear.

Sirens wailed in the distance, growing louder.

Third room: another consultation office, computer still logged in, papers scattered across the desk as if someone had left in a hurry. No one here.

The corridor felt endless.

Fourth room: treatment room, medical supplies in glass cabinets, a window – closed, locked from the inside.

The sirens were much closer now.

Fifth room: the door at the end stood slightly ajar. He

approached cautiously. Through the gap, he could see an office in disarray – chair overturned, papers scattered, and there—

The window was wide open.

Cold February air rushed in. Riddick moved to the window and looked out into a narrow alleyway that ran between Museum Street and the parallel road behind.

Perhaps fifty yards away, where the alley opened onto a side street, a figure was stumbling along. Even at this distance, Riddick recognised the unsteady gait from the CCTV footage. The man caught himself against a wall, then disappeared around the corner.

His transplanted heart hammered against his ribs, each beat reverberating through his skull. For a moment – just a moment – Riddick considered pursuit. Then a sharp pain lanced through his chest. Reality check.

'Damn it.' He'd never catch him. He leaned against the wall, counting breaths until the pain subsided.

As he returned to the waiting room, he called it in.

'Control, DI Riddick. Suspect has fled on foot from Quinn Vale Medical Centre, Museum Street. IC1 male, forties, dark clothing, heading towards Stonegate via the alley system. Subject appears to be in medical distress – unsteady gait, possible high fever. He's armed with a knife and dangerous.'

'Received, DI Riddick. Units responding to Stonegate area.'

'Be advised – suspect has mentioned a sick daughter named Lucy requiring medical treatment. May attempt to access other medical facilities. Approach with caution.'

'Understood. Confirmed ambulance has been called by Sarah Crossfield. Ambulance ETA two minutes for your location.'

'Thanks.'

Blue lights were already painting the Georgian facades

outside. Soon the building would be swarming with uniforms, paramedics, scene-of-crime officers – all the machinery of justice responding to violence.

A desperate father was out there somewhere, armed and dangerous, his love for his daughter twisted into something darker.

A father like Riddick had once been.

He knew with absolute certainty what that meant.

If this man's daughter was in trouble, then this was far from over.

26

Graham was drowning.

Or, at least, it suddenly felt that way.

He managed to get to the end of the alleyway and around the corner before having to lean against the wall. The coughing came violent and wet now. Doubling over, he braced one hand against the medieval stonework, the other pressed to his mouth.

Copper flooded his tongue. Graham spat.

A thick glob of greenish phlegm streaked with red landed on the cobblestones.

Is that my blood?

He looked at the hand that he'd put to his mouth.

Ron's blood.

Graham spat again and again, trying to clear his mouth. It didn't work. His stomach heaved once... twice... Nothing came out.

Eyes closed, he took deep breaths. Eventually, the sensation of drowning, and the disgust he felt, began to subside. When he opened his eyes, he stared down at the cobblestones – his bloody phlegm was just another stain among many.

Stains from centuries of human suffering.

He saw some Viking tourists waving festival scarves.

Ah... to be one of them.

The insulated.

Their biggest worry – finding a decent pub with an available table for lunch.

A hand touched his shoulder.

Graham spun, wild-eyed, expecting police.

He almost thrust in defence, but realised he'd dropped the knife in the alleyway after fleeing Quinn Vale.

A weathered face with kind eyes confronted him. Graham estimated the man was in his sixties – he reminded him of the pleasant woman who'd given him the painkillers in Gift of Life.

'You all right, mate?' the man asked, genuine concern in his voice. 'You look proper poorly.'

Graham opened his mouth to respond. Not certain what to say. Maybe thank him for getting so close to help a man in need, when everyone else gave him a wide berth. But then the man's kind eyes widened as they settled on his shirt. Following the gaze, Graham looked down at himself for the first time since fleeing the clinic.

Blood. Dark stains across his chest – he recalled the tangle on the floor with Ron after stabbing him.

The man took a step backward.

'It's not mine,' Graham said quickly. 'I mean – it's not what you think!'

But it is what he thinks. It is exactly what he thinks. Lou's voice, sharp and unforgiving, returned, cutting through his skull like a blade.

The stranger was backing away, palms out. 'I'll leave you be.'

And there it is. You've become what I always said you would become. A violent man. A dangerous man.

'Shut up!' Graham snarled, pressing his hands to his temples as if he could physically push the voice out of his head.

The helpful stranger backed away further, hands raised defensively. He stumbled.

'I wasn't talking to you,' Graham said desperately. 'I was... it is my ex-wife... she's—'

If he didn't think you were barking mad before, he does now!

'It's my daughter, you see. She's dying. No one will help!'

No one can help, Graham. For pity's sake, accept it!

'That's not true!'

The stranger turned and jogged off into a stream of Vikings.

Probably looking for the nearest copper. Although, is there any need? Haven't you heard all the sirens?

He had, of course. But he'd been too busy coughing up gunk and tasting Ron's blood to consider them.

But now the reality of what he'd done suddenly dawned on him.

You shouldn't have stuck a knife in him.

'It was an accident.'

He was trying to help you. Stop you cutting your wrists.

'He came at me too fast.'

Is that what you'll tell them?

'If I have to.'

Ha... an accident. Like you're the victim. Even though you robbed Clive? And you thumped that old racist. Let's not forget the lad you clobbered with the tin.

'He wasn't a kid!'

Tell me, who are the real victims here, Graham? Give yourself up. Don't waste everyone's time. Soon they'll have descriptions, CCTV footage, a manhunt...

Graham pushed himself off the wall and stumbled deeper

into Stonegate, crossing his arms, trying desperately to cover his blood-stained shirt.

A narrower alley opened to his left – darker, the kind of forgotten space that existed in the gaps between York's tourist attractions. The cobblestones here were uneven, worn smooth by centuries of feet, slick with moss and February damp. Halfway down, he spotted a pile of old coats and cardboard arranged in a doorway. Someone's makeshift bed, temporarily abandoned.

The homeless knew these hidden places, the spaces where you could disappear from the world for a few hours.

Graham crawled into the pile of discarded fabric – old coats, mouldy blankets, carrier bags full of possessions that reeked of damp and desperation. The stench was overwhelming, but they offered concealment.

He pulled a stained sleeping bag over his head and pressed himself against the cold stone, making himself as small as possible.

He tried to picture Lucy, with her sweet face and trusting eyes, believing her daddy was one of the good ones. Lucy, who still thought the world was fair and that people helped each other when things got bad.

Lucy will be ashamed of you.

'Stop it.'

Terrified of what you've become. Just like that man in the alley.

'Please...'

Just like Sarah Crossfield... just like Dr Ron Phillips. Watch them all cross the street. Watch them run from you...

Graham pulled the sleeping bag tighter around his head, trying to block out the voice and the sirens that were getting closer.

27

The paramedics had cut away Dr Ron Phillips's blood-soaked shirt.

Riddick winced when he drew closer and saw the ragged gash on the left side of his gut. The sight brought back memories of his own knife wound – surviving the blood loss had been one thing, but surviving the infection that had destroyed his heart had been an entirely different ball game.

Good luck, Doctor, he thought.

'Okay, Doctor,' one of the paramedics said, adjusting an IV line. 'You're doing great. Just keep breathing for me.'

Ron groaned softly.

Turning back to Frost and Sarah Crossfield, Riddick observed the young woman wrapped in a blanket behind the desk, staring vacantly into the distance.

She'd just finished giving a full account to Frost of what had happened.

They now knew that Lucy was eight years old and needed a kidney transplant – information that would help them identify the desperate man sooner rather than later.

Riddick touched the scar on his own chest through his shirt. Transplant.

So many coincidences... too many... and they just kept coming.

Frost was now on the phone arguing for armed response. It turned out there'd been a shooting in Acomb, and a potential terror threat at the football stadium. Armed response was hard to come by. Her voice was raised. 'We've got a mentally unstable suspect with a knife in the city centre. A Viking festival and forty thousand tourists.' A pause. 'Then pull them from traffic duty. Pull them from wherever. Just get me backup within twenty minutes or I'm calling the chief constable myself.'

The steel in her voice impressed him.

He looked down at his notes.

Broke the vase... plastic flowers... kept talking about 'insulated' and 'uninsulated' people. Subject seemed genuinely distressed about daughter's need for kidney transplant. Subject claimed those with money are protected from real suffering. Expressed belief that private healthcare creates two-tier system. Twenty years' NHS service mentioned repeatedly. Strong class-based resentment. Subject stated 'Excellence in Independent Healthcare – only for those who can afford it.' Witness stated subject appeared to be hallucinating, talking to someone named who wasn't present.

Forensics were starting to arrive. A younger officer was cordoning off the scene.

Soon the place would be marked with numbered placards – the shattered vase, blood spatters on the Persian rug.

His notes continued: subject threatened to cut his own wrist during confrontation. Dr Phillips intervened to prevent self-harm, resulting in struggle on floor. Knife wound may have been accidental during attempt to disarm subject.

Accident or not, Riddick reasoned, the escalation continued.

And if Ron Phillips survived the operating table, there was still a very good chance the next victim might not be so lucky.

'Right then,' the lead paramedic said. 'Ready to move, Dr Phillips? Vitals are stable. Let's get you to theatre.'

Another soft moan escaped the doctor's lips.

They hoisted him on a count of three. As the stretcher passed, Riddick noticed the doctor's eyes were unfocused, glazed with shock. The lead paramedic caught his look and mouthed, 'Lost a lot.'

The memory of his own blood loss made Riddick's stomach turn – that helpless feeling of life draining away, drop by drop.

Dr Phillips's eyes suddenly sharpened, focusing on Riddick's face. His lips moved weakly.

'Sir, please,' the paramedic said gently. 'Save your strength.'

'Officer...' The word was barely a whisper.

Riddick leaned in closer.

'Sorry...' Phillips's voice was thread-thin.

'What for?'

With surprising strength for someone so close to shock, Phillips gripped Riddick's forearm. 'His daughter... Find her... Please help her...'

'We will,' Riddick assured him.

As they wheeled the stretcher towards the door, Riddick stood frozen. Unbelievable. The desperate father had somehow made his victim feel guilty about a system neither of them could change.

Frost appeared at his shoulder. 'Armed response is over an hour out. Best I could do with a shooting in Acomb and some threat at the stadium. Not ideal.'

'An hour?' He shook his head. 'In an hour either he or some other poor soul could be dead.'

28

Twenty-five minutes of breathing in piss and sweat was all Graham could manage.

His muscles had cramped from staying still and as he pushed himself up from the makeshift bed, pins and needles shot through his left leg.

The shirt beneath told its own story – he looked like he'd spent the morning in an abattoir.

A hooded sweatshirt lay crumpled near his feet. Graham picked it up and sniffed it. Not as bad as the bed and smelling slightly off was much better than walking through York advertising his crimes.

The sleeves hung past his hands when he pulled the hoodie on. Rolling them back, he checked the pocket. A child's toy – a small plastic dinosaur, worn smooth from handling. Someone's treasure, kept close for comfort.

He placed it carefully on the makeshift bed where it would be the first thing any returning occupant would see, then steadied himself against the alley wall. The limestone felt rough under his palm.

The coughing remained persistent, but the flu remedy still had his fever under control. For now. His hand found the packet in his pocket – still there.

Graham pulled up the hood and started walking.

The alley was narrow, barely wide enough for two people to pass. These ancient passages had seen eight centuries of desperate souls passing through. The walls had been worn smooth by countless hands seeking support, seeking escape, seeking something they'd never find.

Soon he was among the crowds again.

A couple in expensive coats marched towards him. He stood his ground, but at the last second she steered her partner around him with the practised efficiency of people who'd learned to navigate urban poverty without acknowledgement. Another homeless person to be avoided, edited out of their curated experience of historic York.

Two police officers ran past, heavy boots echoing off cobblestones, stab vests obvious beneath their high-vis jackets. The couple who'd swerved around him had inadvertently blocked the officers' line of sight.

They probably wouldn't have spotted him anyway, but it was nice not to have left it to fate.

Deeper into the maze of passages he moved, staying off the main tourist routes. The drugs were working, but every now and again, exhaustion – emotional and physical – brought him to a standstill. The walls seemed to breathe around him, expanding and contracting like the throat of some ancient beast.

You think you're the only desperate father to have ever walked these stones? Lou asked.

He groaned. After twenty minutes of respite, she'd returned.

Emerging onto Goodramgate, he found himself face to face

with his reflection in a shop window. The man staring back was unrecognisable – hollow-eyed, hooded...

With that blood on your hands. Literally, as well as figuratively, eh?

Daddy? He could hear Lucy's voice, confused and frightened.

Don't, he thought. *Don't do this to me.*

Do what? Lou said. *The man who made Lucy laugh with his silly jokes is gone. The father who'd been someone worth knowing – that man is gone. Is that my fault?*

He turned away from the ghost in the glass and his breath caught.

Two police officers stood at the far end of the street, positioned like sentries. One spoke into his radio while the other studied every passing middle-aged man with clinical attention. Graham watched them stop someone and request his details.

His shoulders caved inward, mimicking the protective hunch he'd seen outside the Jobcentre – that particular angle of defeat that made people look away rather than look closer. Shuffling forward, he let his feet drag.

One of the officers glanced his way as he approached. Graham held out his hand – the one not stained with Dr Phillips's blood – palm up in the universal gesture of need. His voice came out in the flat monotone of someone who'd said these words a thousand times:

'Spare change for a cuppa?'

The officer's expression shifted from professional interest to instinctive dismissal. 'Move along.'

Not unkind, just automatic. His partner didn't even look up from checking the other man's ID.

Graham shuffled past, maintaining the broken posture until

he rounded the corner. Only then did he allow himself to breathe properly.

From somewhere nearby, a PA system crackled: 'The Jorvik Viking Centre will be closing early today due to a security incident. We apologise for any inconvenience.'

Did you ever imagine yourself as a security incident?

His phone buzzed. As always, he fumbled desperately for it – could be an organ match, could be news about Lucy.

It wasn't.

Neither was it Samantha.

No, this wasn't a pleasant call.

Not at all.

As he listened to the voicemail, church bells chimed the hour. The sound carried over the medieval rooftops, marking time's passage with bronze-tongued indifference.

But he was unable to feel that same indifference. Instead, his blood started to boil all over again.

Something watched from above – he could sense it. His eyes searched the skies for a crow.

Nothing.

Maybe these crows watched from the shadows.

He listened to the voicemail again.

He gritted his teeth and changed direction.

29

Riddick answered a call from an unknown number. 'DI Riddick—'

'Paul.' The voice was measured, professional, with a West Country accent bleeding through.

'Mike.'

DCI Michael Yorke, Emma Gardner's old mentor from Salisbury. The man she believed had shaped her into the formidable detective she'd become.

'Are you alone?' Yorke asked.

When Gardner had returned to Wiltshire following Riddick's recovery, she'd deliberately cut him out of her life while she became obsessed with finding out why two of her colleagues had died. She'd claimed it was because she didn't want to drag him into danger while he was recovering. He imagined that was part of the truth, but not all of it. She'd needed headspace. A new relationship wouldn't have afforded much of that.

There had been no getting through to her, so he'd been

forced to try and get updates from Yorke – who'd assured Riddick that he was keeping a close eye on her.

Yorke had been well-meaning to begin with, but contact had dried up these recent months. After being hounded by Riddick for over half a year, his well of compassion had clearly run dry. He'd stopped returning calls.

'I need to take this,' Riddick told Frost.

They'd only just got back in the car, so they were stationary. 'I'll wait outside.' She mouthed and exited the vehicle.

'It's been a while,' Riddick said. 'In fact, we must be in double figures of unreturned calls.'

'If I returned every one of your calls, I'd have to take early retirement.'

Riddick snorted. 'Maybe if you kept me updated, I wouldn't need to pester.'

'There's been very little to update you on...' He broke off.

Riddick's blood ran cold. 'What's happened?'

He recalled phoning Gardner earlier today and getting the message to only contact Yorke.

There was a long silence, followed by a sigh. 'I was hoping you might have heard from her?'

Riddick leaned forward in his seat, fighting the familiar tightness in his chest. 'No... Is she okay?'

'I don't know.' Yorke sounded rattled. The man was renowned for being unshakeable. Not a good sign.

'Will you get to the bloody point?'

'Right. Listen, Paul, I don't want you going off half-cocked. Losing it now won't help matters.'

'I can be very efficient when half-cocked.'

Yorke sighed again. 'She's gotten too close to something, and I don't know where she is.'

Riddick's free hand clenched into a fist. 'Bollocks!' He squeezed his eyes shut. 'You were supposed to be watching her.'

'I was... I am...'

'Clearly not closely enough.'

'I had her checking in every day!'

'Is that it? Where Neville Fairweather and his associates are concerned, not to mention her psychotic brother, you think that's enough?'

'So, what would you have done? Twenty-four-hour surveillance?'

'If that's what it took.'

'And how do you think that would've gone down? You do know Emma, don't you?' Yorke's frustration bled through. 'Look, this is all beside the point – I just need to find her.'

'Is it Fairweather?'

Neville Fairweather: wealthy businessman, government connections, shadowy past. The man had inserted himself into Gardner's life, claiming to have her best interests at heart while clearly pursuing his own agenda.

'Not certain yet.'

'Her brother, then?'

Jack – Emma's sociopathic brother who'd nearly killed her when they were children, recently released from prison through Fairweather's machinations.

'I'm sorry – it's too early.'

'Bloody hell! You're heading up SEROCU, aren't you?'

The Southeast Regional Organised Crime Unit dealt with the kind of people who made ordinary criminals look like choir boys.

'What's that supposed to mean?' Yorke asked.

'Aren't you supposed to have your finger on the pulse?'

'Listen, Paul—'

'You've been helping her, feeding her information—'

'Within boundaries, yes—'

'Not tight enough boundaries, clearly.'

'She's always gone above and beyond. You know Emma.'

He did. And Yorke was exactly right. She wouldn't be letting anything go, no matter how dangerous.

Riddick hit the dash. 'You must have some idea what's happened based on what you've shared with her?'

'Only theories right now.'

'How long has she been missing?'

'Twenty hours. She checks in every morning at eight, without fail. She missed this morning. First time ever.'

Riddick's hand trembled as he checked his watch. 'I reckon I could be there in four hours if I leave now.'

'To do what exactly?'

'Find her.'

'Come on. I've got the entire resources of SEROCU at my disposal. If we can't locate her, what makes you think—'

'No offence, but she's missing on your watch.' Riddick heard Yorke's sharp intake of breath.

'I know all about your health issues. Your recovery.'

'Apparently everyone does.' Riddick glanced at Frost, who was leaning against the wall, absorbed in her phone. 'It's well documented, I hear.'

'Not from documents. Emma talks about you constantly.'

The words hit him like a bucket of ice water. He closed his eyes, remembering the moment he'd woken after nearly dying from the infection in his transplanted heart. She'd been there, holding his hand.

He'd told her then that he wanted to be with her. And she'd wanted the same – he'd seen it in her eyes. But that was before. Before their colleagues died. Before everything went to shit.

'Truth is,' Yorke said, 'she asked me to look out for you, same as you asked me to watch her. You're both as stubborn as each other.'

Riddick found himself without words.

'Why do you think I kept you informed, against my better judgement? She wanted you kept at a safe distance, and she still does.'

Riddick exhaled slowly. 'There must be something else. Where she might be?'

'Promise me you won't come charging down here. Not until I've got a handle on this.'

Riddick knew the promise meant nothing, and Yorke knew it too. 'Fine.'

'Okay... she was meeting a contact about Fairweather's financial network. Someone claimed to have intel on shell companies, offshore accounts – the machinery keeping his operation running. Meeting was set for Fleet Services on the M3. We had surveillance in place, ready to move if needed. But she never showed. Her car never left her flat.'

'But she did?'

'She's not there now.'

'Kids?'

'With their father this week.'

'Public transport? Taxi?'

'All checked. Nothing.'

'So someone collected her.'

'We're canvassing neighbours, pulling CCTV. Could be innocent – a friend picked her up, plans changed.'

'A boyfriend?' The question tasted bitter.

'Not that I'm aware of. She was still single. But even so, it doesn't explain the missed check-in.'

'No, it doesn't. If the wrong people have her, what then?'

The question hung between them, heavy with all the things neither of them wanted to say. Riddick's transplanted heart beat faster, that familiar flutter of arrhythmia threatening. He'd survived losing his family. He didn't know if he had enough left in the tank to survive losing Gardner.

Yorke paused. 'We can't spook them. These aren't street thugs, Paul. They're connected, careful. If we go in heavy, it'll make things worse.'

'Give me something else. What had she found recently? What got her close enough to grab their attention?'

Another pause.

'You've got my word. What else do you want, a blood oath?'

'Remember the podcaster? Tanya Reid?'

'The one who died in the house fire. She was about to expose Aegis Dynamics, where Fairweather has major holdings.'

'Her death wasn't an accident. Emma found evidence.'

'Christ. And you think—'

'They won't hurt her. They're not stupid enough to escalate that far.'

'Your confidence is overwhelming.'

'They know about SEROCU, about me, about the shitstorm that would follow. If they have her, it's for leverage. That's why you charging in won't help. If they want something, they'll contact me. If not, she'll surface with a warning delivered.'

'This is already beyond warnings.'

'I know. But trust me on this. Please.'

'You'd better be right.'

'If I'm not, I couldn't live with it either. I need to go. I'll update you every couple of hours.'

'Every hour.'

'Or you'll be on the next train?'

'Flight, actually. Already looking.'

'Your promise lasted all of thirty seconds.'

'Where Emma's concerned, I don't make promises I can't keep.'

'I know. She feels the same about you. Remember that she wanted you away from this. She knows what you've been through. She wants you safe.'

Or she chose Fairweather's world over whatever we might have had, Riddick thought, though he knew that wasn't the whole truth.

'I've started my watch. I expect your call before three.'

The line went dead. His hands shook – immunosuppressants, cold, pure adrenaline. Hard to tell any more.

'Bloody hell, Emma,' he muttered, rubbing his forehead. 'What have you gotten yourself into?'

And here he was, useless. Over two hundred miles away. Sick, broken, barely able to chase a suspect down one street without his borrowed heart protesting.

No use to anyone. A hindrance rather than a help.

Outside, a solitary crow landed on the wall where Frost had been standing. It fixed him with one black eye, head cocked as if in judgement. Waiting. Watching. Then, with a harsh caw, it launched itself southward.

In the direction of Wiltshire, perhaps?

Towards Emma?

Riddick watched until it disappeared into the grey February sky, thinking of her hand in his as he'd faced some of his darkest moments.

He wouldn't be alive if not for her. Emma.

It was beyond question.

The car door opened. Frost leaned in, her eyes bright with urgency. 'We know who he is.'

30

Hunkered down in an alley behind Coney Street, Graham pressed play to listen to the voicemail for a fifth time. His chest rattled with each breath, and the fever that had been briefly suppressed was creeping back, making his vision swim at the edges.

You can't help yourself, Lou said. *You just can't let it go.*

And she was right. He couldn't. He felt trapped and helpless, the anger inside him boiling like never before.

But he'd heard something, too. Something on the third and fourth listen that could be relevant.

'Dennis Hartley, again, from York Jobcentre Plus...' The timestamp said 12.47 p.m. Nearly two hours ago.

Smug, smug fucker, he thought, remembering those bloody awful striped shirts that pulled too tight across Hartley's stomach.

'...reference number YRK-3847-GDB.'

Do you remember that first time, Dennis? You wouldn't look me in the eye. You wouldn't look away from that screen to acknowledge I was even human.

'Following your failure to attend your Work Search Review at nine o'clock this morning, this constitutes your third consecutive missed appointment.' There was no compassion in the professionally neutral tone – he'd perfected the art of sounding helpful while destroying lives.

My daughter, Lucy! I had to get her to the hospital. Tell me, Dennis, if your kid was as sick as mine, what would you do?

'As previously warned, this triggers an automatic higher-level sanction under regulation 27 of the Universal Credit Regulations 2013.'

Oh, how you love it. Those words. Higher-level sanction. Does wielding that power make you feel important?

'Your Universal Credit standard allowance will be reduced by thirteen pounds ten pence per day for ninety-one days, effective immediately.'

Graham's fevered brain did the maths again, though he knew the answer: £1,192.10. More than three months' full payment.

Twenty years he worked for the NHS. Twenty years making sure people got their appointments, their treatment. Without people like him, the whole system would have collapsed. And now they wanted to take away what little he had left.

A violent coughing fit seized him. He doubled over, spitting phlegm onto the cobbles. In the distance, police sirens wailed – they were still hunting him. He pulled the stolen hoodie tighter.

'This means your payment due on February twenty-eighth will be reduced from £334.91 to £144.91.'

The bastard was enjoying this – calculating it from different angles like twisting a knife.

'You have the right to request a Mandatory Reconsideration of this decision. You must apply within one calendar month.

The form can be downloaded from your Universal Credit journal or collected from your local Jobcentre.'

Mandatory Reconsideration: four to six weeks if you're lucky. Then tribunal: another six months minimum. Lucy didn't have six months.

'Please note that benefit payments will remain reduced during any appeal process.'

Of course they will.

I'll either be dead or in prison by then, Dennis. Is that what you're hoping for? But who'll help my daughter then? Samantha's pension won't stretch that far.

He heard office chatter in the background, someone laughing, mundane workplace banter while they destroyed his life.

'If you're experiencing financial hardship...' Hartley continued.

You think?

'...you may be eligible for a hardship payment. This is a recoverable advance that must be repaid from future Universal Credit payments at a rate of up to 40 per cent. You can apply through your online journal or by telephoning—'

A loan. The cruellest joke yet. Borrowing from his future self to survive today, at 40 per cent interest from benefits already cut to nothing.

Then, he heard again what he'd picked up on the third and fourth listen! Clearer now. A female voice in the background: 'Henry VII at three, Dennis. Say goodbye to Steve.'

Henry VII, a pub on Micklegate.

Three – it must be an early finish for them.

Micklegate was close enough to walk from the government buildings, far enough from tourists. Ironically, they'd held Graham's own leaving do there three years ago, everyone buying him pints and pretending to be sorry about the redundancies while secretly relieved it wasn't them.

He checked his watch through blurred vision. Twenty-five to three. The Henry VII was maybe seven minutes' walk, straight down from Coney Street to Micklegate.

'If you have any questions about this decision, you can contact us through your online journal or call 0800—'

He stopped the message, though Hartley's voice continued echoing in his skull like sandpaper on exposed nerves.

Graham stumbled out of the alley onto Coney Street. Tourists everywhere, clutching Viking Festival programmes and overpriced coffees. A busker was murdering 'Wonderwall' near the Jorvik Centre entrance. Normal people living normal lives while his world burned down around him. A police officer stood at the corner – Graham shuffled past, head down, invisible in his homeless disguise.

Your Universal Credit standard allowance will be reduced by thirteen pounds ten pence per day for ninety-one days.

Ninety-one days. Spring would come. Summer maybe.

And Lucy? Would Lucy still be alive?

The crows watched from the medieval rooftops, three of them in a row. Waiting.

But don't you worry yourself, Dennis. Have your pint. Laugh with your colleagues about the desperate people you've sanctioned today. Swap stories about the excuses you've heard. It's not you left outside in the cold with the crows, is it?

Graham's hand found the empty space in his pocket where the knife should have been.

He needed another way.

Don't worry, Dennis. I won't be late to this appointment.

31

Back in the car, Frost managed to get them free of the crowds and drive them to Tang Hall with purpose.

The medical centre had delivered the clearest camera footage yet, and facial recognition software had identified Graham Blanks. He had no previous record, and most information had come from a hit on his passport, so information was still rather limited. But they knew he was forty-three and they had his home address. He was claiming Universal Credit and was currently living alone with one dependent. Lucy Blanks.

Yorke's update on Gardner, and his insistence that he stayed put, still had Riddick rattled, but fortunately, he now had something to distract him. He was currently updating armed response.

Tang Hall was one of York's less picturesque neighbourhoods, and a world away from the area that Graham had spent the morning rampaging around.

After the call to response, Riddick turned to Frost. 'They're still twenty minutes out from the centre. I've requested they divert some units to his home to meet us, but that'll take a touch longer. You think he could head home?' he asked.

'Possible, I suppose.'

Riddick nodded. 'Still, if he's in his car, he'll be spotted.' There was now an APB out on his vehicle. 'Maybe a taxi? Be a tricky one for him if he's low on funds.'

'We'll be at his house in fifteen minutes,' Frost replied. 'Ten minutes before response. We should probably wait them out in case Blanks is back.'

'Safer, yes.'

Riddick received some more information. Blanks had worked in IT support for the NHS until three years ago when he was made redundant in a restructure. He'd mentioned this fact to Clive and at the medical centre, but it was good to clarify. Another call indicated that Graham's registered vehicle was clamped at the NCP car park near Exhibition Square. Looking at the time, Riddick reasoned that it must have happened while he was in the shop. 'So, that's how he ended up on foot.'

They were still waiting on information from the NHS on Lucy Blanks.

'Five minutes,' Frost said, then hesitated. 'So, what was that call about before?'

The late afternoon sun caught the precise edges of her blonde ponytail, highlighting the tension in her shoulders. She clearly hadn't wanted to ask but it had been eating at her – it would have eaten at him too. He owed her some explanation. 'Someone I know may or may not be in trouble.'

Frost nodded. 'Okay... How so?'

Riddick sighed. 'It's a long story. I'm not being rude, but we just don't have time for it now.'

'You're not going to disappear at the drop of a hat, are you?'

'Wasn't planning to,' he said, thinking, *I was talked out of that.* Or rather warned out of it. 'We're having too much fun, aren't we?'

She guffawed. 'Is that what you call it?'

Compared to the last three months working behind a desk and speaking to a single, scatty informant – very much so, yes, he thought. 'In a fashion... I was just starting to get used to you.'

She laughed. 'That easy to figure out, eh? Wish you were!'

'Well, I'm quite easy to figure out, I suspect. It's just the getting used to me that's proved the stumbling block. Most people don't succeed there.'

She winked. 'Maybe we're more similar than you think?'

'Elaborate. I don't have a file on you.'

'You're not the only one who's had problems with top brass.'

'Well, I'm assuming it's not substance abuse. How about maverick, off-the-rails behaviour?'

She shrugged. 'Probably not.'

'Okay, so what were the problems?'

'Swearing at management.'

'Tame.'

'Hmm... I threw coffee over the chief constable.'

'Okay, now we're getting somewhere. Hot?'

'Not hot enough.'

'Shame, you should make them all count.'

She laughed again.

'Why did you do that?'

She grinned. 'Long story. Don't mean to be rude.'

Riddick laughed. 'I see what you did there.'

His phone beeped with an update that the doctor remained stable.

'He's a lucky boy if he makes it. Blanks could have easily

killed either Ron or Milo.' He regarded her out of the corner of his eye again. 'Okay... hot coffee over a chief constable... that's literally all I know about you. Yet my bones have been practically picked clean.'

She shrugged.

'What happened with the marriage?' he asked.

'Bit personal.'

'So is that bloody file you studied! Go on...'

Pain flickered across her face. A pain he recognised intimately.

'Kids?' he said.

The satnav announced a left turn.

She took a breath. 'One. A daughter. Sophie.'

She took the corner with mechanical precision. The houses were getting smaller now, post-war council builds with pebble-dashed walls and UPVC windows. Some had attempted cheerfulness – garden gnomes, hanging baskets – but February had leached most of the colour away.

'And?'

Silence stretched between them and her shoulders tensed again. He recognised these responses.

'I'm so sorry, Laura.'

She glanced at him, then refocused on the road. 'That obvious?'

'Probably not to most. Again, I'm sorry.'

She nodded. 'Thank you. I guess your sympathy carries weight. Most of the time people don't get it.' She broke off.

'Yes. Isn't that the truth? You could use this opportunity then?'

Frost slowed the car as they entered a cul-de-sac. Number 47 was at the end, a tired-looking semi with an overgrown hedge.

She pulled up three houses short of their target, engine still running. 'When Sophie was twelve, she was diagnosed with leukaemia...' Frost's voice remained steady, professional. No tears, just that steely determination she'd shown all day.

'Christ. Horrible illness. I'm sorry.'

'No, Paul.' She turned to face him properly. 'She beat the leukaemia. Took her three years, but she beat it.'

'I... Really, so what—'

'It was a nineteen-year-old drunk driver that killed her.'

Riddick felt his blood run cold.

'Imagine... beating cancer, only for some bastard to come along and do that.'

Riddick took a deep breath, giving her space to either continue or stop.

'August twenty-ninth, four years ago. Sophie had been at her friend's house. They were celebrating their GCSE results. I was supposed to pick her up, but I got caught up at work.' Her knuckles whitened on the steering wheel. 'She decided to walk. It was only a mile, broad daylight, busy road.'

She paused, gathering herself. 'She was on the pavement when it happened. Driver tried to overtake at the wrong moment, clipped an oncoming car, mounted the kerb. Three times over the limit. Middle of the afternoon, absolutely steaming. Nineteen years old.' Her voice hardened. 'Nathan Pierce.'

'Jesus.'

'He was out after only three years. Good behaviour, showed remorse, attended all the programmes. Turns out his dad used to beat him. He had a good solicitor who reeled out every excuse.' She stared straight ahead. 'You ready for the kicker?'

He gulped. He really wasn't.

'Started an app development company two months after

release. They just got bought out by some Silicon Valley firm. Eight figures.'

'Jesus Christ.'

'I know. Great start to his new life. Meanwhile, mine had been obliterated.'

'I'm so sorry.'

'Marriage couldn't survive it. We blamed each other, blamed ourselves. I should have picked her up. He should have insisted she wait. Round and round, eating each other alive with guilt and rage. He wanted to move on, said we needed to accept what happened and heal.' A cold look crept into her eyes. 'Sometimes I wonder what it would feel like to hold a knife to Nathan's throat.'

Riddick averted his gaze. He thought of Lucy and Molly, of the bomb that had taken them, of Ronnie Haller dying in a prison cell because Riddick had made sure of it. Different grief, same rage. Maybe they were more alike than he'd realised.

She killed the engine. 'Her ambition was to be a doctor. Paediatric oncology, specifically. Said she wanted to help children like those she'd met during treatment.'

Riddick reached over and squeezed her shoulder. 'I'm sorry, and thank you for telling me.'

Her eyes glistened. 'Tell me... Is there anything, anything at all, that can fill the space?'

For Riddick, it had been alcohol and self-destruction. Then arranging a murder. 'I wish I knew.'

Some tears finally broke free. She wiped them away and looked down the street. Number 47 looked empty – no lights on, no car in the drive.

'So, what's the plan?'

He knew what he wanted to do. But it wasn't always about

what he wanted. The last couple of years had taught him that much.

He opted for the right response, rather than the natural one. 'I say we wait.'

She studied him for a moment, then shook her head. 'Nah.'

She exited the car and leaned down to look at him through the window. 'You coming, Paul? Maybe this is what we both fill the space with.'

32

'Are you okay?'

Graham's eyes shot open.

A middle-aged woman was leaning over him, proffering a bottle of water.

Thoughts swirled in his head: *What's happening? Where am I?*

He'd been on his way somewhere important.

Why?

His throat was swollen and dry. He took the water. 'Thank you.'

The kind woman said something about how horrendous it was that people in this day and age could still be allowed to suffer without a home. She offered him a ten-pound note. He clutched it with his clammy hand as she walked away.

Reference number YRK-3847-GDB.

Everything came flooding back. Dennis Hartley... Henry VII... Micklegate...

Shit, he must have been out for almost ten minutes.

He stood, reached into his pocket for the flu capsules,

popped two out and swallowed one dry. The water followed, stinging his swollen throat. The world swayed slightly, but he couldn't stop now. Carrying on might kill him... but stopping meant a rendezvous with the police anyway – which was probably even less appealing.

Collecting himself, he bought a caffeine-laced energy drink from a newsagent with the ten pounds, pocketing the change.

When he reached Micklegate, the ancient bar towered above him – a massive stone gatehouse straddling the road. Three storeys of limestone and red sandstone rose up, punctuated by narrow arrow slits that gazed down. The central archway yawned dark beneath, still forcing modern traffic to squeeze through its medieval throat one vehicle at a time.

Graham tilted his head back, vertigo swimming through his fever, suddenly seeing the spikes that were once thrust between the merlons.

Heads. Row upon row of them, mouths agape in silent screams. There were Jacobites, skulls glimmering in the sunlight, warning all who entered that this was what happened to traitors.

And Richard Duke of York's head, rotted, crowned with paper in mockery. He saw the three crows again – the same trinity that had haunted him since childhood, since his grandmother whispered of the Morrigan's sisters. They'd watched him at the Minster, perched near St Sampson's Square, and now here they were again, picking at the duke's noble features, rendering them clean.

Closing his eyes, he took a deep breath and felt the first hit of the caffeine and flu remedy. When he opened them again, the empty spikes were gone, replaced by health-and-safety-approved railings.

Graham stumbled through the archway onto a street lined

with gastropubs and wine bars, disguising a street built on bones and suffering. People used to gather here, swilling ale, watching the executions.

The stone heads carved into the gateway's walls watched with blind eyes, their features worn smooth by centuries but still witnessing. Craft beer menus couldn't hide the truth. The veneer was transparent to those eyes. York had always been hungry for spectacle and suffering.

The Henry VII pub stood halfway down Micklegate, its mock-Tudor frontage a Victorian attempt at medieval authenticity. Black beams crossed white plaster, bottle-glass windows distorting the warm light within. Unlike the gastropubs that had colonised most of the street, the Henry VII remained stubbornly traditional – a government workers' haunt where civil servants could drink away the decisions they'd made that day.

He crossed to the opposite side of the street, finding shadows in the doorway of a closed shop. His legs trembled. The medication was helping his fever, so this had to be adrenaline – anticipation of what he was about to do.

What's the plan, Graham? Lou asked him.

Only then did he realise he didn't have one.

Hartley's eyes never left that computer screen when I met him. He reduced my Universal Credit despite knowing about my daughter.

Lou began to mimic Hartley: *I understand your situation is difficult, Mr Blanks... but the rules apply equally to everyone.*

On the other side, a group of office workers approached Henry VII.

Graham shrank deeper into the shadows.

He saw Dennis Hartley was among them – striped shirt stretched across his stomach, just as Graham remembered.

He knows about Lucy, Graham thought. *He knows she could*

die. How could he know something like that and still do what he did?

It's his job, Lou said.

It's wrong.

When they turned towards the pub entrance, Graham started to cross over.

Are you just going to march up to him in a pub? Lou asked.

Why not?

Then what?

I want him to acknowledge what he is – what he's done.

Same as Dr Phillips? You wanted him to acknowledge, except, it didn't end like that, did it?

That wasn't my fault.

Lou's laughter burned inside his skull.

As he neared the pub, and the crowd of office workers, every breath wheezed in his chest. He forced back the coughing, not wanting to alert Hartley just yet.

The workers went into the pub, apart from Hartley.

He stood there, checking his phone, thumb swiping with practised ease. Probably sanctioning someone else right now.

Your Universal Credit standard allowance will be reduced by thirteen pounds ten pence per day for ninety-one days, effective immediately.

Graham drew closer.

Why aren't you going in?

A metre behind the bastard now. A plume of vapor rose around the short, squat man.

The scent hit him – strawberry.

Hartley had phoned to reduce his Universal Credit, then come to a pub where two pints cost more than a day's sanctioned benefits and was now vaping strawberries.

Graham coughed and Hartley turned. They stared at each other.

Now what, Graham? Lou asked. *You have what you want. You and him within spitting distance.*

I'll ask him: How do I help my daughter with no money? How do I get her to appointments with no petrol? How do I keep her warm when I can't pay the heating?

So, what are you waiting for?

'Can I help you, mate? Jesus Christ—' Hartley covered his nose. Not willing to mask his discomfort. Compassionate as always.

Graham opened his mouth to ask those questions but all that came out was: 'Reference number YRK-3847-GDB.'

'Eh?'

'Reference number YRK-3847-GDB.'

Recognition dawned on Hartley's face. 'Graham? Graham Blanks?'

Graham nodded.

'Bloody hell, you look... Are you all right? You smell like—' He stopped himself. 'What are you doing here?'

Laughter erupted as someone opened the pub door. Graham caught a glimpse of the warm interior – brass fixtures gleaming, fire crackling in the hearth. The door swung shut. A young couple brushed past them, giving them a wide berth.

Dennis was looking him up and down. There was no fear, just mild annoyance mixed with disgust. The look you'd give a persistent fly.

Hartley continued to vape, using it as a barrier between them.

'How did you know I'd be here?' He didn't look concerned.

'Your colleague. Behind you on the phone. Said about Steve's leaving do.'

Hartley snorted. 'Christ. Ha! Unprofessional.' He put a finger to his lips. 'Don't you be saying anything.'

'I want to—'

Hartley silenced him with his hand. 'I can't discuss your case outside office hours. You know that.'

'I don't want to discuss it.'

'Then what? You've followed me here to what – intimidate me?'

'Are you intimidated?'

'Ha... no! You think you're the first? I've had people wait outside my house, mate. Outside my kids' school.'

'Maybe you should be intimidated this time.' Shit, he wished, so desperately, he still had the knife. He'd felt so powerful before with Ron back at the centre.

'Why?'

'My daughter is sick.'

'You've mentioned her. Multiple times.' Hartley took another drag of strawberry vapor.

'So why sanction me?'

'The rules don't change because—'

'It's cruel.'

'The system is the system. Three missed appointments trigger an automatic—'

'Cold. Can you not reconsider?'

There goes your dignity, Lou said.

His ex-wife was right. 'You're making me beg.'

'I'm not making you do anything. Look.' Hartley sighed. 'I've got to go. Put in the Mandatory Reconsideration. Include all the evidence regarding your daughter. The review team might—'

'Four to six weeks.'

'I'm trying to help.'

'Are you?'

He shrugged.

'Four to six weeks,' Graham repeated.

'That's not my problem.' The words came out sharp, then Hartley seemed to catch himself for once. He rolled his eyes. 'Look, it's not something I can control even if I wanted to. It's all automated now anyway. Computer says no, and all that.'

That's when Graham saw it. The truth naked on Hartley's bland face.

You see it, don't you? Lou insisted.

The thought was repulsive.

He's going to enjoy telling this story inside, Lou continued. *In fact, he's already composing it as he looks at you with pity and disgust. 'You'll never guess who ambushed me outside... that nutter from this morning's sanctions. Looked like death warmed up.'*

'Stop it,' Graham said.

'Stop what?' Hartley asked.

They'll laugh. Buy him drinks. Pat him on the shoulder. Say things like 'Poor Dennis, dealing with the dregs.'

This feels different to the doctor.

Because it is. Here, there is no point in words. They won't change him. And threats won't do anything, either.

'I can see that now,' Graham said.

'You're losing it, mate,' Hartley said.

Words won't change him, Lou continued. *Threats won't matter. Dennis Hartley will go back inside, finish his evening, go home to his heated house, sleep soundly. Tomorrow he'll reduce someone else's payment. The day after, someone else's. A production line of despair, and he was just a well-fed, content cog who vaped strawberries.*

Graham's fists clenched.

The pub door opened again. Two men stumbled out, already drunk at three in the afternoon. They barged past, one of them shoulder-checking Graham.

'Watch it, you smelly bastard,' one slurred.

Graham took steps away from Hartley.

Coward, Lou said. *No knife, and you lose your balls.*

He lifted his fists.

Hartley raised an eyebrow. 'You got the energy to swing?'

Pathetic, Lou said.

'Fuck off,' Graham said.

'No, you fuck off,' Hartley said.

Graham unclenched his fists, and made it ten yards down Micklegate.

Well that was ridiculous—

'Just shut up!'

A couple gave him a strange look as they passed.

He paused and noticed a middle-aged woman close by. Wool coat, sensible shoes. She was standing by a silver Vauxhall Astra, fumbling in her purse by a parking meter. The car door was ajar, the interior light on.

He drew closer.

The engine was still running.

His eyes flicked between the idling car and the woman digging for coins.

The world beats you down and you can't fight back, Lou said.

'You want to see fight?' Graham said and went to the driver's side of the Astra.

The woman turned at the sound of his question; her mouth opened in shock. He climbed into the vehicle, closed the door, locked it. It was an automatic, so he slipped it into drive.

The woman banged on the window.

He dropped the handbrake and accelerated. The car was picking up speed faster than his own, which would still be clamped back near the souvenir shop.

He felt the caffeine, the medicine and the surging car

rushing through him. The adrenaline made him feel alive again, as he'd done earlier with that misogynistic Viking... with Clive... and Dr Phillips.

The woman screamed.

He saw Hartley. He'd come further away from the entrance to Henry VII to see what the commotion was.

Graham mounted the pavement. Hartley's eyes widened.

You scared now?

Hartley started to back away, but it was too late now. Graham had picked up speed. The cold bastard was too slow – too many years behind desks ruining lives, too many good meals at the expense of those suffering.

Soft and slow.

'Enough,' Graham said as the Astra's front corner caught Hartley at hip height. The impact folded him over the bonnet with a wet crack. His head bounced off the windscreen, leaving a spider web of cracks and blood.

He slowed, and Hartley remained limp on the bonnet.

Screams erupted on Micklegate.

Hartley was somehow lifting his bloodied head.

Graham slammed the car into reverse and surged back.

Hartley slipped from the bonnet.

He shifted the car into drive again, while watching the bastard trying to crawl away.

'I said enough.'

He accelerated again.

The wet crunch was definitive. The front of the car lifted, came down and then clipped some railings. He stopped.

Dennis would be under the car.

Graham pushed it into reverse again. The front lifted again and thudded back down.

He moved to first gear, swung around the bloody mess on Micklegate and accelerated away.

The screaming and shouting was intense.

Graham shook his head. Once upon a time, people had drunk ale while watching executions.

Now, when the street ran with blood and justice was swift and brutal, they couldn't stomach it.

It'd be there inside all of them.

Buried.

Hopefully, this would help them remember.

Graham drove without direction, taking random turns until the sirens were far behind him.

33

With a dying patch of grass, wheelie bins askew, and curtains drawn tight against the world, Graham Blanks's bungalow wasn't out of place in the February gloom.

Riddick checked his phone. No signal. A dead zone.

Figures...

The front door was solid UPVC, the kind installed by councils in the early 2000s. Security bolts visible.

They knocked, but as expected, there was no response.

'Round the back?' Frost suggested.

'Wait.' He tried the handle. It turned and they exchanged glances.

Unlocked doors weren't unheard of. People popped to neighbours, forgot to lock up. Or left through the back door and forgot to secure the front, but it was still unusual.

'Trap?' Frost whispered.

'In a rush? He's sick... might have just forgotten or...'

'Past caring?'

'You're developing an uncanny knack for finishing my

thoughts,' he said. 'Be careful though… someone might still be inside.'

The door creaked open, releasing a wave of damp air. The stench of rotting food hit them immediately.

'Hello?' Riddick called into the gloom.

He waited. Nothing.

'Police!'

Still nothing.

They entered onto torn carpet. A wheelchair sat abandoned in the hallway, an NHS property tag still attached.

Riddick ran a finger over the handles and showed Frost the dust on his fingertips.

'Months,' he said quietly.

The kitchen was through the first door – dishes piled high, mould creeping across abandoned plates. A child's drawing clung to the fridge with a magnet: *Me and Daddy xx* written in crayon.

The paper had yellowed at the edges, curling away from the fridge door.

On the table, a pile of scrunched tissues surrounded two boxes of flu remedy capsules.

Frost's eyes found his, her concern evident. 'Those tissues look fresh. He's been here recently.'

'I won't touch anything,' he assured her, already regretting handling the wheelchair. 'But if his daughter really is sick and awaiting a transplant, these conditions…'

'Would kill her,' Frost finished.

The living room was worse. Empty takeaway containers covered every surface – sofa, coffee table, windowsills. The smell of rotting food mixed with something medicinal.

In the corner, a dialysis machine lurked beneath a white

sheet like furniture in an abandoned house. Boxes of supplies stacked beside it: tubing sets, needles, saline bags.

Frost examined the labels. 'These expired six months ago.'

'The wheelchair, now this.' He studied the untouched equipment. 'Either Lucy hasn't needed treatment in months, or...'

'She's getting it elsewhere?'

'Or not at all.'

The room at the end of the hall stopped them both.

Pink walls. Stuffed animals arranged with mathematical precision on the bed. Books lined up by height. Bed made with hospital corners. A complete contrast to the chaos they'd walked through.

Despite his promise not to touch anything, Riddick ran his finger across the bedside table and held it up. Clean.

'Even smells different in here,' Frost said softly. 'Like he's been using air freshener, cleaning products.'

'He lives in squalor but maintains this room like a shrine.'

'If she was still living here, she'd have to walk through that biohazard to leave the house. No parent who cared enough to keep this room spotless would allow that.'

'So where is she?'

'That's the question, isn't it?' He pulled out his phone again. 'The NHS should have responded by now, but there's no signal.'

Frost checked hers. 'Dead too.'

'Tang Hall's always been a black spot – too far from the towers, too low priority for upgrades.'

They lingered in Lucy's room, perhaps because it was the only space that didn't assault their senses. Photos covered one wall: Lucy through the years. A healthy toddler becoming a tired-looking child. Then gaps in the timeline. The most recent photos showed brief moments of colour returning to her cheeks

– Lucy beside a Christmas tree, Lucy holding a 'Happy New Year' sign.

'When do you think these were taken?' Frost asked.

'The Christmas one... look at the decorations in the background. That style of tinsel hasn't been in shops for years.'

'One more room,' she said, nodding towards the door opposite. 'His bedroom, presumably.'

The door was locked.

'Interesting priorities,' Riddick said, finding the key on top of the doorframe. 'Can't secure his front door but locks his bedroom?'

He turned the key and pushed the door open. The smell hit them first – stale sweat and something else, something chemical.

'Jesus Christ,' he breathed.

'What is it?' Frost asked, stepping beside him.

They both stared at what Graham Blanks had locked away.

34

After reaching Tang Hall, Graham abandoned the Astra in a quiet residential street he knew well.

He looked at the dented, blood-stained bonnet and considered wiping down the door handle, wheel and gear shift with a tissue he plucked from his pocket.

Are you serious? Lou said.

He heard the thrum of a helicopter overhead.

I think we're past that point, don't you?

He left the keys in the ignition and walked away.

Graham ducked through the gap between number 42 and 44. He'd used the shortcut a thousand times before. The caffeine and tablets had taken the edge off his fever, and at least his vision had cleared enough to keep him upright, rather than bouncing off the walls.

So, what now Graham? Going to kill everyone who's ever wronged you? If I remember right from our marriage, that's a lot of people. Everyone pissed you off.

'No, I just need to get Stripes.' His breath came in wet rasps.

You're being ridiculous.

'I'll get Stripes from home for Lucy, she'll know who I really am then. She'll remember that she needs me...'

She needs a father who isn't a murderer.

The back gardens blurred; Mrs Patel's washing line, the Johnsons' broken trampoline. Normal things from his normal life, before everything went wrong.

The helicopter circled close by.

They'll be at the house soon, if not already.

'I know.'

Then what the hell are you doing?

'I told you.' The words came out desperate, fevered. 'Stripes.'

A stuffed toy?

'Whatever it takes.'

He emerged onto his own street, keeping his head down until he reached his bungalow.

When he reached his doorstep, the first thing he noticed was that his door was ajar. The second thing he noticed were the low voices from inside.

You've really gone and done it now.

He sighed.

So aren't you going to run?

He shook his head and went inside. 'Stripes.'

35

Newspaper cuttings covered every inch of every wall.

Overlapping; layered; recent ones pasted over old. The headlines screamed from every direction:

NHS Waiting Lists Hit Record High – Cancer Patients Dying Waiting for Treatment

Universal Credit Sanctions Drive Families to Food Banks

Private Healthcare Profits Soar While NHS Struggles

Sections were highlighted in different colours. Red pen annotations crawled across margins. Post-it Notes flagged certain images like evidence markers.

Housing Crisis: 2,000 Homeless While Luxury Flats Remain Empty

Mental Health Services Cut by 30% Despite Rising Suicide
Rates

'Christ,' Frost breathed.

'The government's wall of shame,' Riddick murmured.

'This is... obsessional.'

Gardner's investigation wall flashed through his mind –
Yorke had described it months back. Emma had covered her
spare room with connections between her brother, Fairweather
and whoever else she could link to the whole conspiracy. But
that had been the careful curation of investigation.

This was different. This was rage distilled into newsprint.

Child Poverty Rises to Highest Level in Decade

Council Spends £2M on Tourism While Closing Libraries

Pharmaceutical Companies Post Record Profits Amid Medicine Shortages

Not investigation – truth-gathering. Or at least, Graham
Blanks's version of truth.

Benefits Assessment Deaths: 200 People Die Within Weeks
of Being Declared 'Fit for Work'

Yorkshire NHS Trust Faces £1M Deficit While CEO Gets
£300K Bonus

'This is years of accumulated rage,' he said.

One cutting had been circled so many times the pen had
torn through the paper. A small article about benefit sanctions.

About a system designed to save money by letting people fall through the cracks.

Frost moved closer to the torn article. 'This man didn't just snap.'

'No. But why the escalation? Why now?' His hand went instinctively to his pocket, checking his phone. Still no signal – Tang Hall's dead zone. 'Something's changed with his daughter. Maybe she was the only thing keeping him from going over the edge.'

'So what's different today?'

'Good question,' a voice rasped from the doorway.

Ice flooded Riddick's veins. The face from the CCTV footage peered at them. Hair plastered to his skull with sweat. Skin the colour of old concrete, slick with fever. The man should have collapsed hours ago. But his eyes burned with terrible clarity.

Frost edged forward, palms raised. 'Mr Blanks, you need medical attention—'

'Don't I bloody know it.' Graham slammed the door closed.

'Shit!' Riddick lunged for the handle, but it was too late. The lock clicked home with finality.

He pounded on the oak. 'Graham! I'm Detective Inspector Riddick. We're not here to hurt you. We want to help.'

Through the door, a muffled reply. 'You've seen my wall then.'

'Yes.'

'Read it properly, Detective Inspector. So many crimes.'

The man was wheezing now, each word an effort. Riddick pressed closer to the door. 'I don't disagree, Graham. Some of what's on that wall – it's wrong. The system's broken.'

'Crimes... against humanity.'

'Some of them, absolutely.'

'And yet.' A wet cough. 'Here you are. For me.'

'You know why, Graham.'

'Do I? Read the wall again.'

'You stabbed Ron Phillips. He's in intensive care.'

A pause. 'He's alive?'

'Yes.' For now. 'There's still time to stop this. Whatever you're planning.'

'Planning?' Another cough, deeper. 'I'm not planning anything any more. It's done.'

Riddick's chest tightened – not his heart, but dread. 'What's done?'

'I just... I won't be pushed around any more. None of us should. The uninsulated.'

'The uninsulated?'

'People with nothing.' The voice was fading, moving away. 'Against people with everything.'

'Graham, listen to me. Armed response units are already surrounding this house. You must have heard the sirens getting closer. This only ends one way unless you open this door.'

'Maybe that's... that's how it should end.'

'And your daughter, Lucy? Have you thought about her? Have you thought about how it will end for her?'

'That is in hand. She will know how I feel about her.'

'Where is she? We've been in her room.'

'Have you now? Very clever of you. Do you not know she doesn't live here any more?'

They hadn't received a notification to the effect, but what they'd seen made it look clear.

'Where is she?'

'Do your job properly, Detective Inspector, it isn't too hard.'

I could if I had some bloody reception, Riddick thought.

'If you stop now,' Frost said, 'you can be with your daughter again. You think she wants to see you behind bars the rest of your life?'

'Who are you?'

'DS Frost.'

'Well, DS Frost, it's too late for me now. If I'm caught – I won't ever see her again.'

Riddick felt his stomach turn. 'What do you mean?'

'It means what it means, and I have to make peace with her. And that means I have to leave...'

'Graham!' Riddick heard footsteps stumbling away. 'Graham!'

Nothing.

'Stand back,' he told Frost, then drove his shoulder into the door. Pain exploded through his chest, the morning's biopsy site screaming. The door barely shuddered.

'Armed response should be here any second,' Frost said. 'Be careful, Paul.'

He backed up for another run. 'But we're losing him now.'

Outside, distant but approaching fast, the wail of sirens grew louder.

36

Graham slipped into Lucy's room and ran his hand over the crisp sheets.

How long, baby? How long has it been since you last slept here?

He picked up Stripes – a stuffed zebra he'd had as a child. He'd gifted it to Lucy and she used to cling to it while he read to her in this very room. She'd also taken it to her early dialysis sessions, back when they still had hope her kidneys might recover.

One day, after she'd gone to live with Samantha, he'd told her how lonely he was without her. She'd pressed Stripes into his arms and told him that he could cuddle it at night when he was lonely and think about her.

She was kind like that; selfless. Always thinking of others.

Unlike her mother, Lou said.

'I didn't say that.'

Detective Inspector Riddick's muffled shouts echoed from the locked bedroom. Graham clutched Stripes to his chest and stumbled towards the back door. His legs nearly buckled as he crossed the garden – eight hours of fever finally demanding payment. The fence loomed impossibly high.

You won't make it, Lou whispered.

He dragged a wheelie bin to the fence, climbed onto it with trembling limbs, and hauled himself over. He landed hard on the other side, knees buckling, chest heaving. Each breath rattled with phlegm.

After the warning about armed response, he expected to take a bullet. But they weren't here yet – though the helicopter throbbed much closer now, somewhere above the rooftops.

His time was short. He needed to get Stripes to Lucy at Samantha's in Gillygate. A taxi was his only option.

All I ever wanted was to love and be loved in return.

Don't we all? Lou said.

He clung tight to Stripes as he stumbled forward, using garden walls for support. Behind him, sirens wailed. Above, the helicopter circled like the crows from his grandmother's stories.

Whatever would be, would be.

But Lucy would have Stripes. She'd know he'd tried.

She'd know he'd loved her.

37

Riddick collided with the door a fourth time.

The oak barely moved, but his heart did.

Not metaphorically; it actually lurched – a violent skip-thud-thud-skip that made him gasp. Despite his chest tightening, he drew back to charge again.

Frost grabbed his shoulder. 'Listen…'

The sirens were so close now. Right outside.

His heart stuttered: skip-thud-thud-skip.

'Shit.' The word came out breathless.

'Are you okay?'

Wire seemed to tighten around his chest. His balance wavered, and he staggered backwards.

'Paul!'

His palm pressed against his chest, trying to steady the erratic rhythm.

'Need to…' Another stutter. 'Need to calm down.'

'Paul?' Frost held his arm. 'Talk to me.'

'My meds. Tacrolimus.' The words came between gasps. 'Missed… the afternoon dose.'

'Where are they?' She thrust her hands into his jacket pockets.

'Shit... The car. My bag.'

His legs gave out – not dramatically, just a slow slide down the wall until he was sitting on the floor. Frost went down with him, supporting his weight.

The memory hit him: in the car with Frost, deep in conversation about their dead children, the phone reminder chirping. He'd silenced it, promised himself he'd take them when they stopped. But they'd arrived at Graham's house, and everything had moved too fast.

Silly boy.

'Okay.' Her voice stayed steady. Professional. 'Slow breaths. In through the nose.'

In. Hold. Out.

The drill was familiar from grief counselling days.

In. Hold. Out.

'I'll be fine.' Eyes closed, he willed his borrowed heart into submission. 'Just need to—'

The arrhythmia answered with another violent skip. But the pain was sharp and real.

In. Hold. Out.

Behind closed eyes, another scene emerged:

Lightning illuminated the tent. Eighteen years old, lying beside his father in that leaking tent. The storm raging outside while they talked about love and home and dreams of families not yet lost.

'Dad, how did you first know you were in love with Mum?'

'You just feel, you know, *better*.'

Reality crashed back. *Better*. Christ, he'd give anything to feel better right now. The transplanted heart stuttered again.

His palm pressed harder against it, trying to hold steady this gift – this borrowed life – that was failing him.

Pounding erupted at the bedroom door.

'Armed police! Open up!'

Frost's voice pitched to carry: 'Police officers in here! The door's locked from outside!'

Heavy footsteps thundered on the front path. Multiple officers. The response they'd waited for, finally here.

'This is Mike Seven,' a gruff voice called through wood. 'Identify yourselves.'

'DS Frost, badge number 4812. I'm with DI Riddick. We're locked in the suspect's bedroom. Suspect has fled. My partner is down – cardiac event. We need immediate medical assistance.'

'We're clearing the property first.'

Standard procedure. Armed response assumed threats until proven otherwise.

'DI Riddick needs urgent medical attention,' Frost repeated.

'They have to go room by room,' Riddick managed weakly. 'It's protocol.'

In. Hold. Out.

Riddick's eyes closed again, and he was back with his father again.

'I had this dream. In it, I'd a wife and two daughters.'

Lightning illuminated his father's tear-streaked face. Why was he crying?

'It sounds like a nice dream, son.'

'Yes, it was... there was this indescribable warmth.'

Back to reality. No warmth remained, just biting cold spreading through his chest.

God, how he missed them. Kissing Lucy's and Molly's foreheads before school. Warm and alive and—

Frost squeezed his shoulder. 'Paul?'

'Still here.' But was he? The edges kept blurring. The tent and the room covered in newspaper headlines. His father's tears and his own pain.

From beyond the door: 'Clear!'

Then another voice at their door: 'Are there weapons in there?'

'Negative,' Frost said. 'We're both on the floor. No threats.'

'Keep hands visible.'

'DI Riddick can't – he's having a cardiac event. He's sitting against the wall, needs immediate medical attention.'

A pause. Muffled discussion.

'Right then. For everyone's safety, you need to get on the floor, ma'am. Hands behind your head. Your colleague stays still, no sudden movements.'

'Understood.'

'I'll be fine,' Riddick whispered, though doubt crept in.

Frost's warmth moved away.

Focus returned to breathing. In. Hold. Out.

'Stand clear of the door!'

'Down and ready,' Frost confirmed.

Wood splintered as the frame cracked. A Halligan bar wedged into the frame, leveraging with precision. Less dramatic than ramming, more effective. The door broke open.

Two officers entered in rapid succession, weapons raised but not aimed. The distinctive shuffle-step of tactical entry, each covering their sector. Checking corners in segments. No blind spots. No surprises.

'Clear left!'

'Clear right!'

'Room clear!'

Weapons lowered but not holstered.

One officer moved to Frost, checking her warrant card

before helping her sit up while maintaining visual on Riddick. The other – sergeant's stripes visible – crouched beside him. With trembling fingers, Riddick extracted his ID and let it drop.

The sergeant examined it. 'DI Riddick, you're the one who needs medical?'

'Heart transplant,' Riddick managed. 'Missed... immuno-suppressants. Need medication.'

The sergeant keyed his radio. 'Mike Seven to Control. Scene secure. Need immediate medical response. Officer down with cardiac issues. Heart transplant patient.'

'Roger, Mike Seven. Paramedics holding at cordon. Releasing them now.'

The sergeant studied him with concern. 'You were locked in?'

'Suspect... Graham Blanks. He fled... Back garden...'

'We'll find him. Let's focus on you.' The sergeant's expression softened. 'Your medication. Where is it exactly?'

'My bag. In the car.'

Frost started to stand. 'I'll get it—'

'Hold on,' the sergeant said. 'Need to verify your details first, ma'am. Standard procedure.'

'Are you fucking kidding me?'

'Ma'am—'

'My partner needs his medication *now*!'

'And he'll get it. Soon as we confirm your badge number with Control. Twenty seconds.'

Through the haze, Riddick heard more radio chatter – something about a pursuit three streets over, helicopter support, suspect on foot. They'd lost sight of him.

He closed his eyes and was dragged under again:

'Remember, son, that love, real love, is as much about the pain as it is about the joy.'

His father's words in the storm. Understanding now what he'd meant. The pain of loss was the price of love. You couldn't have one without risking the other.

If only I'd been smarter, if only I'd found Graham in time, then I could have helped him understand too...

The sergeant's face swam back into focus. Behind him, paramedics pushed through the doorway. Green uniforms. Equipment bags. The cavalry's cavalry.

'There we go,' the sergeant said. 'Help's here, sir.'

They descended on him with practised efficiency.

38

The taxi driver, a burly sixty-something Yorkshireman, accepted £10 and drove him off the metre.

The pine air freshener hung thick in the cab. The driver must have been a smoker. Good. It might mask the stench coming off his clothing.

Two minutes into the journey, it became clear it hadn't when the driver cracked the window.

The helicopter's thump-thump-thump overhead intensified through the gap.

Was it following him? Had he managed to get into the taxi undetected? Graham knew the chances were against him.

'Rough night?' The driver's eyes flicked to the rear-view mirror.

His reflection stared back – Christ. Hair plastered to his skull, skin grey as old dishwater. He clutched Stripes tighter to his chest.

'I wish,' Graham croaked. 'Flu – worst I've had in years.'

'Where you been?'

'Helping a friend with some moving in Tang Hall. Sorry

about the smell. Put a shift in before' – a violent cough doubled him over – 'this ambushed me.'

'Aye, you should be in bed, mate.' Another glance in the mirror, longer this time. Assessing.

'That was the plan...'

Those eyes again. Examining. Curious. Suspicious.

'Hope it passes, fella. It's a shitshow getting a GP appointment these days. Three weeks I waited last time.'

He's on your favourite subject! Lou said. *Why don't you fill him in on your crusade?*

'Not now,' he hissed under his breath.

'Sorry?'

Graham shook his head. 'My daughter,' he said louder now, forcing focus. 'She's all I need. Always makes me feel better.' He held up Stripes. 'For her.'

The driver laughed, tension easing slightly. 'Kids, eh? Great, aren't they... Of course, mine are all grown up now. How old is yours?'

'Eight.'

'Ha! Who'd have thought? Same as my granddaughter. Our Lisa. She's a bloody handful like, but aren't they all a handful at that age, yeah? All attitude and eye-rolling.'

A smile took enormous effort – not just from flagging energy and fever, but because Lucy had never been like that. Too sick for normal childhood rebellion. Too grateful for every good day to waste them on sulking.

'Beans on toast,' he said suddenly.

The driver glanced back. 'Sorry?'

'Her favourite food... Lucy. It was beans on toast.' The fever was making him ramble. Making him remember. 'Has to be triangles though. Never squares. And no crusts.'

'Fussy eaters.' The driver laughed. 'Lisa's the same. Everything has to be just so. Won't eat if foods are touching on the plate.' He indicated to turn, then added, 'Beans on toast though – can't go wrong. Bit of butter, lovely. Though have you seen the price of beans now? Paid over a quid for a tin yesterday! Used to be half that.'

'Lucy's not fussy. She just... knows what she likes.'

Get a grip, Lou said. *Next you'll be telling him about the special diet. The medications that make food taste wrong. The constant nausea.*

'Bloody hell.' The old man craned to look up through the windscreen. 'They only bring out the chopper for proper stuff. Terrorism, has to be. Though the way things are going, wouldn't surprise me.'

He switched on the radio. MP Marcus Crist's voice filled the cab: '...this senseless act of violence on Micklegate is an attack on our entire community. We will not rest until this dangerous individual is apprehended. I urge anyone with information to contact police immediately. In these difficult times, we must stand together against those who would tear apart the fabric of—'

'Can we turn it off please?' The sound of Crist made Graham's blood boil. 'I've a headache.'

'Of course. Not a fan either. Bloody politicians; especially this one. Religious nut, you know? Neighbour sometimes goes along to where he preaches... can you believe it? Need more than religion to bail us out in these trying times.' He looked at him in the rear-view mirror. 'Eh? Sorry, yer not religious, are you?'

Graham shook his head.

'Been a stabbing today, too. A doctor... Poor bloke. It's mental health, you see. Everybody's mental health is skew-whiff these days.' He shook his head. 'The system's buggered.

My daughter waited two years for help with her anxiety. Two years! And that was after I voted for that useless prick, Crist! Promised to help fix the NHS, didn't he? Do you remember all that?'

How could I forget? Graham thought and nodded.

'Then he ended up voting for more cuts... Useless, the lot of them. Always lying. Can barely afford to heat the house, and the NHS is on its knees. My own bloody fault for believing them! They best be careful – everyone snaps eventually.'

Isn't that the truth? Lou said.

'Yes,' Graham agreed.

'The system just pushes and pushes until something breaks,' the driver continued.

Like our daughter's kidneys, Lou said.

Graham closed his eyes and rubbed his forehead.

Or Dennis Hartley. But he wasn't just broken, was he? For the want of a better word, he was pulped.

'No.'

'Sorry, are you all right back there?' The driver's eyes narrowed. 'You're mumbling.'

'The flu,' Graham repeated. 'Just need to get home. See my daughter.'

'She sounds a princess.'

'Yes... she is.'

They turned onto Gillygate. Bootham Bar loomed ahead, the ancient stone gateway with its medieval walls stretching away on either side. Tourists walked the wall-top path even now, taking photos of the city lights beginning to flicker on.

'Just here,' Graham said, pointing to a row of Victorian terraces. 'Number 23.'

The taxi pulled over. 'You take care now.'

'I will.'

'Get yourself tucked up in bed. You look like death warmed up.'

Graham's legs nearly buckled as he climbed out. Eight hours of fever had hollowed him out, left him running on fumes and desperation. He stumbled towards the house, aware of the taxi idling behind him.

The driver was still watching – waiting to see if the sick man made it to the door or checking if he was the lunatic the helicopter was hunting?

39

Blood pressure cuff tightening on his arm, oxygen mask over his face, ECG leads pulled through his shirt, while his mind drifted between his father's tent and Graham's hallway.

'Irregular rhythm,' one said. 'Rate's all over the place.'

'What meds is he on?'

'Beta blockers.' Frost's voice. She was back, must have been cleared. 'Bisoprolol... tacrolimus...'

'How long post-transplant?'

'About a year.'

'Right, let's get a line in. Get him stable for transport.'

The sharp prick of a needle finding the vein. Cold fluid rushing in. His heart stuttered once, twice, then settled into something approaching normal rhythm. The relief was immediate, like a fist unclenching in his chest.

'Sir? What's your pain level?'

'Improving.'

'One to ten?'

'Four.' More like six or seven, but that would mean morphine, and another blow to his clarity.

He had a crazed man on the loose, and he was still clueless about what was happening with Gardner. Clarity was a precious commodity.

'You feeling calmer?'

'Yes,' Riddick said. Surprising, really, when lying in a house where a desperate father had built a shrine to systemic rage. Where newspaper clippings screamed about failures. Where they'd been locked in like naughty children while Graham went hunting.

'Laura?'

'I'm here.'

'Graham Blanks. Someone needs to—'

'Half of North Yorkshire Police is responding now.'

'Someone's died, haven't they?'

'Don't worry about that—'

'Haven't they?'

A pause. Then: 'Yes, at Micklegate.'

'Who?'

But they were already moving him, the gurney wheels clattering over the threshold. His heart responded to the movement with a warning flutter – not quite arrhythmia, but close enough to make the paramedic frown at the monitor.

Outside, the circus was in full swing. More police cars, more uniforms. Somewhere above, the helicopter circled, hunting a father who'd run out of options. A man who'd crossed lines because he believed every other path had been blocked.

Maybe he was right.

'We'll be at York in ten minutes,' the paramedic said. 'You're going to be fine.'

Frost leaned in, pressing Riddick's mobile into the younger paramedic's hand. 'His phone. He'll want it.'

The paramedic placed it on the side shelf while hooking

him up to another monitor. The screen showed his heart's erratic patterns – occasional PVCs, nothing immediately dangerous but enough to warrant watching.

'Find him,' Riddick said to Frost.

She nodded, and the doors closed.

The ambulance pulled away, siren wailing.

'You're stable now,' the paramedic said, checking the IV drip rate.

'I know... Can I sit up?'

'Not just yet.' The paramedic adjusted the oxygen flow. 'Your heart's been through enough for one day.'

Riddick eyed his phone on the side shelf. As soon as they looked away, he'd check it. Gardner. Graham. Both situations spiralling while he lay here, useless.

Behind them, the hunt continued. Graham Blanks against the world. Most would think it was a foregone conclusion. The smart money would only go one way.

Except the smart money had never watched their daughter dying. Had never been told the rules mattered more than lives. Had never been pushed past every breaking point until only rage remained.

Riddick closed his eyes and took a deep breath, feeling his borrowed heart skip once before settling. His father's tears in the lightning. His daughters' warmth in the morning. Graham's newspaper wall screaming truth.

All of it circling like the helicopter above.

All of it coming to an ending nobody would win.

40

Graham reached Samantha's door. It was painted a cheerful blue; the kind of colour people chose when they wanted to seem welcoming. In fairness, Samantha had always been welcoming.

In your case, Lou, the apple did fall far from the tree, he thought.

Window boxes held dead winter plants.

A welcome mat worn thin by feet that belonged here.

You don't belong here, Lou said.

I belong anywhere my daughter is.

He knocked, each impact sending shockwaves through his fevered body.

Movement inside. Footsteps. The chain being taken off, then Samantha opened the door. She looked exhausted; grey-faced, hollow-eyed, wearing a cardigan that had seen better days.

Something was wrong. Very wrong.

'You look sick,' she said.

'Is the taxi still there, behind me?'

'Yes.'

He pushed past her.

'What are you doing?' Samantha said.

'Coming in. Taxi driver needs to see it's my home.'

'Why?'

'He knows something's off.' He closed the door behind him, turned and faced his ex-mother-in-law, coughing violently into his hand. When the fit passed, he steadied himself against the closed door.

'Graham, what's happened?'

He noticed a cigarette in her hand. His vision tunnelled as his eyes fixed on the cigarette. 'Why? Why are you smoking?'

'Sorry?'

'What the fuck are you doing?' The shout tore from his throat. Couldn't stop. 'Don't you understand how bad that is?'

'Graham, please, you're scaring me. Calm down.'

'*Calm down?* You're killing her. You're all killing her. The whole world is killing my daughter!'

When had he moved so close? He was in her face now, fever-bright eyes wild.

'Graham...' She quivered against the wall. 'Stop... you're not well... Please...' The cigarette dropped as she slid down the wall.

His foot slammed down on the cigarette. 'Do you have any idea,' he hissed, 'how sick that can make her? How dare you, Samantha...'

And now my mother? Lou said. *Are you going to hurt her too?*

If that's what it takes!

God... how far you've fallen.

41

Riddick was on the mend. He'd told the paramedics to stop the ambulance.

The request, of course, was ridiculous.

When the paramedics started to freak out, Riddick said he would stay if he could sit up, and that they take the sirens off and slow down. He agreed to keep the ECG on. He also requested they fill him in on what had happened on Micklegate.

They told him that Graham had stolen a car and run someone down.

That was some escalation – what next?

And he'd come so close – been within two metres of him!

Could he have pounced before Graham slammed that door and locked them in?

Gardner was firmly on his mind too. Surely Yorke would have an update for him by now. Riddick picked up his phone. It was switched off.

Jamie, the paramedic said, 'Phones can interfere with the equipment.'

'Is my rhythm and blood pressure okay?'

'Yes,' Jamie said. 'But—'

Riddick switched on the phone. 'I've had my meds now.'

'Yes, but we'll need to run some more tests at the hospital. Make sure there's no damage.'

'I'm fine.'

'A heart transplant patient, having arrhythmias after missing medication? You're a lot of things, but fine isn't one of them,' the older paramedic said.

His phone glowed as it came to life.

'Fair point,' Riddick said. 'But I'm not resting while it's still a shitshow out there.' *And while I have no clue what's happening in Wiltshire...*

The older paramedic sighed. 'Been there, done that. Just pace yourself, yeah?'

Riddick assumed he was talking about times he'd worked when severely compromised... the pandemic perhaps.

His phone buzzed.

Three missed calls from Control.

Two from Yorke.

A number he didn't recognise.

And a data packet from Intelligence.

Christ – where to start?

Yorke.

'Shit.' The bastard hadn't left messages.

The call went straight through to voicemail. 'Shit... Phone me, Mike.'

The data packet came next.

SUBJECT: Graham Blanks – Requested Information URGENT

The file loaded slowly, 3G struggling with the data.

Come on. He shook his phone as if that would actually make a difference.

When they turned a corner, they must have hit a better reception area.

The folders appeared: Health history. Employment history. Universal Credit claims.

A folder on Lucy Blanks caught his eye. He opened it.

'Sir?' Jamie was watching the monitor. 'Your heart rate's climbing.'

Riddick forced himself to breathe steadily. In through the nose. Hold. Out through the mouth.

Frost's number was busy when he tried it.

The intelligence packet began forwarding to her. The progress bar crawled across the screen: 15 per cent, 23 per cent, 41 per cent.

'We're nearly there,' Jamie said. 'A&E's been notified. They'll fast-track you through.'

'Great.' But Riddick wasn't thinking about hospitals. His mind was on Graham Blanks. On his own children, and how loss could twist into something monstrous. The system had failed Graham, and Graham was breaking.

The screen showed 67 per cent, 78 per cent, 89 per cent.

Finally: 100 per cent. Message sent.

Another attempt to reach Frost. Still no connection.

She was probably still in the dead zone at Tang Hall.

They wheeled Riddick out into the grey February afternoon.

Above, a police helicopter circled, its searchlight already probing the gathering dusk. Still hunting.

Gardner came to mind again.

Yorke's assurances about remedying the situation echoed hollowly. Riddick had always struggled with trust – but Gardner had always spoken so highly of Yorke.

But if that promised update didn't come soon... what choice did he have?

Gardner had been there for him. Not to mention his feelings for her.

There was no chance he wouldn't be there for her if she needed him now.

42

Samantha was sitting on the floor now, crying and covering her head.

She's never been anything but kind to you, Lou said.

'Please...'

He pointed down at her, his finger trembling. 'Where is she?'

'You're doing it again.'

Graham turned and thrust a clenched fist into the plasterboard, leaving a crater of white dust and broken edges. 'Where is she?'

'You know – deep down, you know.'

'Just shut the fuck up!'

You'll do well to listen to her, Lou said.

'And you can fuck off, too.'

'Who are you talking to?'

'Where. Is. She?'

Well, if she was here, Lou hissed, *she'd be terrified now, listening to you ranting and raving!*

Samantha was crying too hard to speak now.

Graham stumbled into the lounge. The sofa drew him first. The same sofa where they'd watched Disney films together... Lucy curled up close to him under a blanket. His fingers ran over a framed photo on the mantelpiece.

Lucy's sixth birthday. Before the ordeal had begun.

Her gap-toothed grin as she blew out candles. Him and Lou on either side.

I remember that, Lou whispered. *We still believed in forever.*

'Liar.'

Another photo caught his eye: Christmas morning, Lucy maybe five, surrounded by wrapping paper. Lou in her dressing gown, coffee in hand. Laughing.

It seemed like so long ago.

'I... I...'

We laughed together in this room, Lou reminisced. *In our bungalow back in Tang Hall, so many times...*

'You're tricking me?'

Am I? Remember those evenings watching Strictly *while Lucy practised her dance moves?*

He closed his eyes and saw Lucy there. Her little feet spinning on this same carpet, her giggles filling the air.

Samantha appeared at the door to the lounge, sobbing. 'I'm sorry, Graham. You're not well. You don't deserve—'

'Don't.' He turned and pointed at her. 'Just don't.'

I don't know what you're trying to achieve, Graham, Lou said.

His voice rose, spit flying – his finger trembling as he continued to point at Samantha. 'The doctors. The council. Lou. And now you, Samantha. How could you? Keeping her from me. Thinking I'm not worth it. I thought we were on the same side.' Graham thrust a finger into his chest, hard enough to bruise. 'I decide, okay? I decide whether I see her. No one else.'

Samantha took a deep breath, steeling herself.

'Graham, Lucy's gone.' Her voice steadied. She took a step forward. 'You know this. Deep down, you know this.'

He doesn't know shit any more, Mother, Lou snorted.

'You're unwell and—'

Graham swept his arm across the coffee table. Magazines scattered. A mug shattered against the wall. Lou's favourite, the one Lucy had painted at pottery class. 'No, you're lying. She had an appointment today... It's my fault... yes... but she's here... she should be here.'

Samantha approached with a determined look on her face. 'She died, Graham. Six months ago, she died. You were there with her. I was, too. It was peaceful. She didn't suffer and—'

'No!' Graham lurched forward. 'Stop!' His hands grabbed her tightly by the arms. 'Lying.'

She squeezed her eyes closed.

'Look at me, you lying old bitch! *Look at me!* You know what I've done today?' He shook her. 'Have you seen the news... seen what's happening... what I'm capable of? Tell me where my daughter is. This is your last chance.'

The rhythmic thump-thump-thump of a helicopter filled the silence.

'Hear it? That's looking for me. Have you not seen the news?'

She shook her head. 'What have you done?'

'Put it on. I've finally stood up for what's right... for my daughter.'

Samantha was crying again. 'I don't want to.'

'I don't care what you want! I don't care what anyone wants, apart from Lucy... apart from my daughter.'

'This isn't you any more, Graham. This isn't you.'

I've been trying to tell him, Mother, Lou said.

Samantha gulped, squeezed her eyes closed, tears leaking from the corners, and spoke again, each word deliberate and heavy. 'Graham, Lucy died. Six months ago. You know this. You really do know this.'

'*Liar!*'

He threw her against the wall and charged out of the lounge. The stairs flew beneath him, two at a time. Second door on the left. Pink nameplate: LUCY'S ROOM. Unicorn stickers. He'd helped her put those up. She'd been so precise about the placement. Everything had to be perfect.

'See...' he shouted down. 'You're lying... See! Her room is perfect...' A glance back over his shoulder. 'Perfect... You said six months!'

Samantha's footsteps came up the stairs, slower, each step heavy with dread. She reached the top of the stairs and looked at him with her tear-streaked face. 'Because I clean it. All the time. Just like you clean her room at your place.'

'Don't say that.'

'Graham, I'm sorry.'

His finger shook as he pointed at her. 'Don't you fucking dare. Don't you say that...' He walked in. 'But I can smell her?'

Samantha said, 'I still hear her, see her... smell her... every single day.' She gulped. 'Every single day.'

Graham looked around the empty room, perfectly organised... crystallised in time. 'This doesn't make sense... This is wrong... Where is she?' Samantha's hands touched his back. He brushed her off. 'Don't.'

It's not just you... It isn't just you, Lou said. *You're not the only one drowning in this, Graham. You're not the only one who wakes up expecting to hear her voice.*

He clutched his head. 'Shut up. You weren't even here. You weren't here when she...' The words died in his throat.

So, you remember now? Lou asked.

* * *

August 14th.

Stiflingly hot.

He came to see Lucy at Samantha's armed with sugar-free ice cream.

She wasn't well enough to go to the cinema. He'd promised her two movies, back to back, to make up for it.

Dialysis had been tough. Her body had been weakening lately.

His heart almost stopped when he saw the ambulance outside Samantha's home. He tried to steady his breathing, reassuring himself that the scene was calm. The blue lights were off. The back doors stood open, but no one was rushing.

The lack of urgency made his head spin.

There was a terrible, final calm, and he very nearly dropped the ice cream.

When Samantha opened the door, he couldn't see tears. But there was something else. Something far deeper. She reached out. She tried to speak but couldn't.

'What's happened?'

She took her hands from him and stepped aside.

'Please...'

'I tried to phone,' she finally said.

Graham reached into his pocket, saw he'd had his phone on silent, and he'd missed several calls.

He ran up the stairs. Towards what he loved the most in the world. Towards what he feared the most.

Lucy's door was open. A paramedic stood there taking vitals. Another paramedic stood back, observing. She turned her eyes on Graham. Kind, sympathetic eyes – the worst kind of eyes because of what they meant.

'What's happened?' he asked.

Samantha touched his back. He turned. 'Samantha?'

'She's going, Graham. She's—'

'No... no...' He turned back.

'I found her like this. She hasn't woken... She's pale... Her breaths are slowing...'

'Why aren't they taking her to hospital?'

He turned and looked at those kind, sympathetic eyes. 'Why?'

The paramedic stepped forward and put a hand on his arm. 'Go and be with your daughter.'

Lucy was on the bed. So small. So still. Eyes closed. Short shallow breaths.

'Your favourite pyjamas,' Graham said. Tears ran down his face. He looked back at the paramedics and smiled. 'Unicorns.'

He turned back and knelt. He took her cold hand.

'Lucy isn't in pain, but she's weak... too weak to move.'

Graham looked back again. 'Please help her.'

The paramedic gave a gentle nod. 'Be with her.'

Her face was peaceful. No pain. No struggle. Just... absent. Empty. He could barely hear her breaths now.

'I don't understand. She had her dialysis.'

But he did understand. He'd been warned about this moment. Deterioration recently had been rapid. He'd been told that her body might give up.

He'd refused to believe it.

Until now.

'I brought you ice cream.'

He leaned in so he could feel the faint breath on his face.

'What films do you want to watch?'

He kissed her forehead. Cold lips on cold skin.

He closed his eyes and enjoyed the gentle breath on his cheek.

'I love you, Lucy.'

They allowed him to stay a while even when the gentle breaths had stopped.

* * *

Graham's legs buckled. He stumbled and fell forward onto the empty bed. He reached into his pocket and pulled out Stripes. 'I brought this to you, Luce... I brought you Stripes.' He closed his eyes and tried to imagine that gentle breath on his cheek again. But there was nothing. Just the empty room and the echo of his own breathing. She was gone. Really gone. Had been for six months.

And none of what I've done today, he thought, *has brought her back.*

'I love you, Lucy.'

43

The muted colours and the gentle lighting in the cardiac ward at York Hospital felt very deliberate. Forcing calm on all those with rebellious hearts.

It was turning out that the young heart supplied to Riddick by that unfortunate motorcyclist was not failing him after all. The medication in his blood levels was back at optimum levels. Rhythm and blood pressure were back to normal. Dr Mitchell expected him to stay for 'a couple of hours' observation'.

He'd reluctantly accepted, knowing deep down that he'd be bolting for the exit with any change of circumstances.

Still no update from Yorke.

He stared at his phone, willing a message.

The phone kept transitioning between two and three bars of reception.

Was this the reason?

Eventually, a message:

> Still no word on Emma. Wiltshire police
> expanding search. Will update in an hour.

Riddick sighed and tried Yorke so he could elaborate. He hit voicemail, left him an abrasive message, threatening him with a visit, and then took some deep breaths, not wanting to raise his blood pressure again.

It was a hard one though. There was no one left in Riddick's life that meant more to him than Gardner. If anything were to happen to her...

With a taxi, he could be on the M1 in thirty minutes. Head to the airport, get a flight.

Surely sitting here twiddling his thumbs was worse for him? Acting on stress was better than drowning in it. Surely?

But it could end up being even worse. Yorke was keeping him at arm's length. Down there, he would push back even harder. And who would blame the DCI? By forcing himself into that situation – a situation he knew little about – Riddick could end up putting Gardner in even more danger.

To distract himself, he resumed his research into Graham Blanks again, despite knowing that he was now well and truly out of the picture where that was concerned.

Graham Blanks. Forty-three. Former NHS IT administrator at this very hospital. Probably walked these same corridors thousands of times, fixing computers, updating systems, keeping the digital infrastructure running so doctors could save lives.

A necessary cog until the restructuring and efficiency savings decided otherwise.

Graham and forty others had been let go. Non-clinical staff. Expendable.

And then there was his deceased daughter, Lucy Blanks.

Eight years old. A little girl with a body that had turned against her. An immune system that had attacked her kidneys after a simple throat infection.

Chronic kidney disease secondary to post-streptococcal glomerulonephritis. The medical terms were cold, clinical. Two years of dialysis and special diets; watching other children play while she sat hooked to machines. A childhood measured in blood tests and creatinine levels. She'd been on the transplant list, waiting.

Riddick thought about the loss of his own daughters.

Gone with a click of the fingers – hitting him like a wrecking ball.

Lucy Blanks's death, however, had dragged.

Just as damaging, but in a different way. A weary, soul-sapping kind of damage. One interrupted by brief moments of hope. Having it ripped away again.

And the fact that they'd found a match and had been unable to contact Graham!

What that must have done to him.

Riddick read the notes twice to make sure he understood. The transplant coordinators had tried to reach Graham for six hours. Called his mobile – number out of service. Called his landline – disconnected for non-payment. Even sent someone to his listed address – but he'd moved and hadn't updated the system.

By the time they'd tracked him down through Samantha, Lucy's grandmother, the kidney had gone to the next person on the list. A forty-year-old teacher from Hull. She was doing well, apparently.

Lucy Blanks never got a second chance.

Or, looked at another way, Graham Blanks never got a second chance to save his daughter.

How do you live with that?

But Riddick knew the answer already.

You don't.

Riddick closed his eyes. He knew about self-blame; about the weight of 'if only'. If only he hadn't investigated Ronnie Haller. If only he'd been more careful. If only he'd seen the threat coming. Then Lucy and Molly would still be alive. Still sliding down banisters and bruising their chins.

Riddick had turned to substance abuse, hiding in a self-imposed fog from the pain.

Still, it always found you, eventually.

Seemed Graham had opted for something different. Something outwards, rather than inwards.

Violence and aggression.

There'd been a pattern of escalating incidents. Three months after Lucy's death, there'd been a verbal altercation at the Jobcentre. He'd called the advisor, the now-dead Dennis Hartley, a 'murderer' for sanctioning his benefits. No charges had been pressed.

Four months after her death, he'd been removed from council offices after screaming about rats and how they carried disease... about how his daughter's immunity had been low, and that she'd had to live with her grandmother for the last year. That their failure to do anything had robbed him of precious time with her.

A month after that, he'd been barred from York Hospital after confronting a transplant coordinator and demanding to know if 'rich kids' got organs first. He'd had to be sedated then.

Each time, no charges. Each time, people understanding his grief, making allowances. The system trying to be kind. But kindness without help was not kindness. Not really.

You could argue that it was just a brush-off.

Graham's medical records revealed more. Severe depression. PTSD. And then, two months ago, the first recorded incident of dissociative amnesia. Graham had been found at Lucy's school, waiting to pick her up. Had become angry when told she wasn't a student there any more and couldn't remember she'd died.

The psychiatrist's assessment was textbook: 'Patient exhibiting signs of dissociative amnesia likely triggered by severe psychological trauma. Episodes appear to involve complete repression of daughter's death, with patient reverting to established behavioural patterns from when child was alive. Prescribed sertraline 100 mg daily and quetiapine 25 mg for acute episodes. Referred for trauma-focused CBT.'

Maybe he hadn't taken the medication? Maybe it just hadn't worked?

Groundhog day, Riddick thought. Like that film where Bill Murray kept reliving the same day, trying to get it right. Except Murray's character had been trying to win love. Graham was trying to save his daughter, waking up thinking today was the day. Today he'd get her to the hospital; today the doctors would fix her. Today everything would be okay.

Until reality crashed in. Until someone reminded him. Until he had to lose her all over again.

How many times could a mind take that? How many times could you wake up with hope and then go to bed destroyed?

The more he thought about how unstable Graham was, the more anxious Riddick began to feel. After all, Frost was still out there, likely pursuing Graham after the murder on Micklegate. She'd be following protocol, coordinating the search, maybe even closing in on him right now.

And Graham was dangerous. Desperate. Armed with nothing but rage and grief.

Riddick was now regretting not being there with her.

44

Graham paced the room.

Pink walls, stuffed animals arranged with military precision, books alphabetised. Medicine bottles in neat rows. Everything perfect, exactly as it should be. All of it waiting for a girl who would never come back.

My girl.

'Have you not been taking your medication?' Samantha asked.

Graham shook his head.

'But surely you want this to stop happening?'

Graham opened Lucy's bedside drawer and rummaged through hair ties, lip balm, bracelets. His fingers found a small silver locket.

'Sometimes, when I take them, I worry I'm going to forget what she looks like. I start to panic.' He tapped his temple. 'What if I forget? What if I never see her again? In here?'

You can't think straight when you don't take them, Lou said.

He opened the locket. Inside, a photo – him and Lucy at the hospital, but not a sad photo. She was laughing, holding up a bottle of juice in triumph. He was making bunny ears behind her head.

Graham coughed into the back of his hand. 'I need water. I've sweated buckets.'

'Let me call someone,' Samantha said. 'An ambulance? You need help—'

Graham's head snapped towards her. 'Do you not get it?'

Samantha looked away. 'You're sick. Physically sick.'

'As well as mentally?'

She didn't respond.

'Those sirens, Samantha, the helicopter – they're for me. Didn't I tell you that?'

'You said, but—'

'You didn't believe me?'

'Graham, you were having an episode. You thought Lucy was—'

He stepped forward, twirling the locket between his fingers. 'I just killed the idiot from the Jobcentre, Samantha.'

Her face drained of colour and she grabbed the doorframe for support.

'I can't blame that on dissociative amnesia.' His voice was flat, matter-of-fact. 'I ran him over. Twice. I wanted to do it.'

'No.' Samantha's voice came out as a whisper. 'That's not – I don't believe you.'

'It's true.'

'You believe in what's right. You've always – you wouldn't hurt someone.'

Graham nodded slowly. 'Before him, I stabbed a doctor. More of an accident, that one, but still...'

Samantha shook her head, backing away. 'How do you know it was all real? How can you be sure?'

'Listen to the sirens. The helicopters.' He crossed to the bed and sat down heavily. 'Dissociative amnesia, eh? The brain protecting itself. All that trauma, shock, guilt... protecting.' He laughed – bitter and broken. 'Protecting who?'

It certainly hadn't protected Hartley and Dr Phillips.

Looking into the locket again, he studied Lucy's smile, frozen in time. Perfect. Unchanging. Unlike the reality of what she'd become in those final months.

He looked up at Samantha. 'Maybe I should stop.'

'Yes, you should—'

A knock at the front door cut through the moment. Samantha was already heading downstairs.

'Don't,' he called out.

At the top of the stairs, he watched her look back up at him.

'Please,' he said. 'They'll make me take those pills. I'll spend the rest of my life in prison, dosed up on God knows what.'

'I won't,' she said as the knock sounded again.

'I don't want to forget her face.'

'I promise,' Samantha said. But he saw the lie in her eyes. She knew he needed to be stopped. Samantha would do what was right.

She opened the door.

'DS Laura Frost. Sorry to disturb you—'

The policewoman who had found his other home.

Graham retreated into Lucy's room.

So this was it.

Maybe it was time to stop running. To stop forgetting. To stop the cycle of remembering and losing her again and again. Looking into the locket one more time, he saw their faces smiling up at him. That perfect moment when everything had seemed possible. When treatments were working; when hope was real. When 'forever' didn't seem like a lie.

His hands trembled.

Everything trembled.

The past and present.

Love and violence.

Memory and madness.

He heard the door close downstairs. The DS's voice carried up, closer now.

Inside the house.

And then Graham knew what he was going to do next.

45

Riddick's phone buzzed with a text message. Finally, a text from Frost:

> En route to Samantha's house. She needs to be warned.

Riddick called her. Straight to voicemail.

He left a message:

> DO NOT APPROACH. Lucy had been living with Samantha for almost a year before she died. If he's suffering from dissociative amnesia, he might still think she's there. Stand down!

Yeah, like he would have done that himself.

Riddick rubbed his temples. Shit!

How could he lie in bed, listening to that bloody machine beep, while she was out there? He'd led her into this rampage. She was supposed to be sitting at a desk researching store robberies – gathering intelligence!

Pulling the wires off his chest, he stood. The machine made some unhappy sounds.

Riddick dressed quickly. A nurse appeared in the doorway. 'DI Riddick? You need to—'

'I'm discharging myself.'

'The doctor wants to observe you.'

'I've had enough observing to last me a lifetime!'

'We must insist.'

'Me too,' Riddick said, trying the phone again. Voicemail.

'Sir, you've had a cardiac event. You can't—'

But he was already brushing past her, moving slowly down the corridor. Christ, when had walking become so hard? He followed the signs towards the exit.

His phone buzzed. Another text from Frost:

> Don't worry. Already here. Samantha is fetching me tea. Graham hasn't been.

He texted back:

> How do you know that? He could be bloody hiding upstairs.

He reached the hospital exit. Riddick hoped that Frost didn't run into the man trying to save someone who couldn't be saved.

What would happen when Graham finally realised he had nothing left to lose?

Riddick hadn't suffered amnesia himself, but he'd suffered visions. Seen his lost children, had even talked to them. He'd been in a similar situation, clinging to these falsehoods.

Graham Blanks had lost his daughter six months ago. But in his mind, she was still alive, still waiting to be saved. When reality hit and the dream unravelled, he might collapse. It might just end, like it had, in some fashion, for Riddick.

But what if he didn't?

What if it went the other way?

The sudden cessation of all hope was a powerful trigger.

And he didn't want Frost anywhere near a cornered animal.

Climbing into the taxi, he gave the address from the data file on his phone. 'As fast as you can, please.'

46

Graham listened to Samantha lying to DS Frost.

He was surprised; he knew she would think that his capture would be for the best, that he could get help and no one else would get hurt. Maybe she worried that he would hurt the police officer? Or maybe his fear that he would forget his daughter's face if he was drugged up to the eyeballs had made her sympathetic.

Samantha was currently in the kitchen getting a cup of tea for the visitor.

He waited until he heard DS Frost come out of the living room to meet Samantha returning via the hallway. 'I'd like to check upstairs.'

Graham sighed, swung back towards Lucy's room, and went for the window he'd already opened. He managed to climb out, hang down from the sill and drop down to the back of the house.

His fever-weak legs buckled, sending him sprawling onto the garden. He got to his feet. Nothing broken. The buckling probably helped prevent an injury.

He glanced up. DS Frost's face appeared at the open window. 'Graham!' She leaned out, hands gripping the sill he'd just hung from. 'There's nowhere to go. I know this isn't you.'

'You don't know anything about me.'

'I know you're confused. I know you're putting your own life in danger.'

'Do you think I care about my life?' He turned and ran.

Behind him, the officer's voice carried on the wind: 'Graham, stop! Let me help!'

Help?

Now that would be a first.

Where was help when Lucy was dying?

Where was help when my landline and mobile were cut off and I didn't get that message?

And don't you work for the same government that Hartley worked for?

He crashed through the back gate, stumbling into the alley behind Victoria Terrace. His chest burned, each breath felt like drowning from the inside.

Every time he coughed, his mouth filled, and he spat out gunk.

Left onto Gillygate. The medieval street stretched before him. It was quieter now, but tourists and evening shoppers still created an obstacle course. He weaved between them. It was darkening but there were streetlights.

At one point, it became too busy for him to spit without hitting someone, and when he accidentally swallowed a mouthful of phlegm, he had to veer off into a doorway, bend over and vomit.

Nothing solid.

A stream of mucus.

When was the last time he'd eaten?

He was falling apart, but if they caught him that would be the least of his problems...

Health tourism, son. Plain and simple, Lou said.

Eh? he thought. *You never said that... That was... Williamson... Yes... blaming waiting times on all those...*

He rubbed his temples. *What am I doing?* 'Get out my fucking head,' Graham hissed, pushing himself onwards.

When he took a glance behind him, he was certain he sighted DS Frost in the crowd.

I understand your situation is difficult, Mr Blanks... but the rules apply equally to everyone.

'Get...'

Look, no offence, but round here, if it's not the tourists trying to get one over on us, it's the desperate people. There's a lot of both. We have our policies and, well, that's the way it is.

'Out...'

I could be your kid's daddy for a couple of hours.

'My...'

A consultation starts at two hundred pounds, before any tests or treatment.

'Head!'

A crow perched on a lamppost, watching him.

Another on a shop sign.

A third prowling along the gutter.

Bootham Bar loomed ahead. The medieval gatehouse, four storeys of limestone and centuries. The entrance to the walls. The high ground.

'Graham! Stop!'

DS Frost! Behind him.

It's over, Lou said.

The stone steps were worn smooth by tourists' feet. He took them two at a time, hand clutching the metal rail. His legs screamed in protest and his chest felt like it might explode, but up was the only direction left.

The Walls walkway stretched before him. Six feet wide. Stone paved. A ribbon of medieval defence now reduced to a tourist attraction. To his left, the drop to the street. To his right—

Twenty feet down to gardens. No fence. No barrier. Just gravity and consequence.

He staggered forward, each step an effort. The wind hit harder up here, cutting through his sweat-soaked clothes.

'Graham, stop!'

The crowds moved away, opening up space.

He made it another fifty yards before his legs gave out and he dropped to his knees on the cold stone.

He listened to Frost approaching from behind. 'It's over, Graham. Put your hands behind your head.'

Over. Yes. It has been over for months. Since Lucy died. Since before that, maybe. Since the first diagnosis. Since the world decided some people mattered more than others.

He linked his fingers behind his head.

'Thank you, Graham. I'm going to get help.'

He looked up into the sky at the circling birds.

Crows?

How many?

He listened to her calling. 'Control, this is DS Frost. I have Graham Blanks on the city walls near Bootham Bar. Suspect is compliant. Requesting backup.'

Compliant. Like a package.

She lowered her voice, stepping away slightly. 'Subject appears to be in mental health crisis. Maintaining visual contact. Will not approach further unless necessary.'

They're speaking about you like a wild animal, Lou said.

I'm a father. I loved my daughter.

Wild animals love their young, too.

I'm not a wild animal.

Frost moved closer again. 'Help is on the way, Graham. Just stay calm.'

'Help for who?'

Help for her, you fool! Lou hissed. *Protection from the wild animal.*

'No one helped my daughter.'

He looked around. People watched on, clutching loved ones, whispering...

Frost came alongside his right, keeping her distance. 'I'm sorry about Lucy, Graham. I truly am.'

They're always sorry, aren't they? Lou said.

'You said before that you didn't think this was me,' Graham said.

'That's right. I believe you're ill. You need medical attention.'

'Ill?' He unlocked his fingers and dropped his hands.

'Graham, please keep your hands where I can see them—'

He stood.

Some of the onlookers gasped. He turned to his right to look at her.

Her eyes widened. She took a step back. 'Graham, let's talk about this.'

'I am not a problem to be managed,' he said.

'I never said you were.'

'But that's what I am to you, isn't it? To all of you? Has it ever occurred to you that maybe I'm not the problem here?'

'Graham, I understand you're angry—'

He raised his voice and thumbed his chest. 'How could you possibly understand?'

'Because I lost someone too—'

'When are you going to realise that people like you *are* the problem?'

Frost took another step back, phone already at her ear. 'Suspect is becoming agitated. I need that backup now.'

'A suspect!' The words tore from his raw throat. 'I paid my taxes! Worked for the NHS for twenty years! Can't you at least use my name?'

His ex-wife laughed deep in his head.

Frost held out her free hand, trying to calm him. 'Graham, please. Let's just wait for—'

'Reference number YRK-3847-GDB!'

'What?' She shook her head, confused.

'Reference number YRK-3847-GDB!'

'Graham, I don't understand what—'

'Reference number YRK-3847-GDB!' He took a step forward. 'That's all I am now! Not a person, not a father – just a fucking reference number!'

She backed away further, closer to the unfenced edge. 'Graham, please stay back—'

'I... am... a... *father*!'

He darted forward. She lurched back instinctively. Her heel caught on uneven stone. Arms windmilling. Phone flying from her hand. Her mouth opening in shock as her weight shifted backward towards the drop...

He reached out—

Too late.

She was gone. People were screaming, running.

The phone lay on the stone where it had fallen, screen lit up. He picked it up. The emergency call was still connected, but another call was coming through: DI Riddick. He pressed to switch calls.

'Laura? Thank God. Where are you?'

Graham said nothing.

'Laura? What's happening? Talk to me!'

Graham stood at the edge, looking down. She lay twisted in the gardens, one leg bent wrong.

'I'm sorry.' The words came out quiet. Calm. 'I didn't mean for that to happen.'

A sharp intake of breath. 'Graham? Graham Blanks?'

'Yes.'

'What's happened? Where's Laura? Where's DS Frost?'

'An accident.'

'If you've hurt her – tell me where you are. Tell me she's okay.'

He looked down at Frost's still form. Had she meant well?

'*Graham!* Talk to me! Where are you?'

'Bootham Bar walls.'

'Where is DS Frost? Can you see her?'

'Yes... She's not moving.'

'Is she okay?'

'I don't know.'

'Graham, listen to me. Stay there. Don't run. Paramedics are coming—'

'Can you hear them, DI Riddick? The lies?' He cut across the panic. '"The system will catch you when you fall." But it doesn't catch anyone. Not really. MPs like Marcus Crist, voting to let you drop while promising otherwise.' He looked down at DS Frost again and sighed. 'Him, Hartley, all of them... just watching us fall.'

'Graham, please—'

He hung up.

And ran. Along the walls, away from the screams, from what he'd done, but not from what he'd become.

The crows followed.

Behind him, York carried on. Ancient city. Eternal city. Built on bones and blood and all the accumulated cruelties of centuries.

Nothing new under this old sun.

Nothing new at all.

Agitated, Riddick demanded the taxi driver get closer.

'It's chaos. I'll get trapped, pal,' the driver said, nodding forward to where blue lights strobed the medieval walls.

Riddick considered ordering the driver to do as he asked, but he was right, and the other officers wouldn't thank him for clogging a crime scene with an unnecessary vehicle.

Having already paid for the ride on the app, he jumped out without a word.

His legs felt borrowed. Wobbly. Unreliable.

For once, it wasn't his heart, or the medication; it came from sheer dread.

Pushing past the usual crowd of ghouls, he noticed their raised phones everywhere. One young man turned his phone camera on Riddick himself – bright-eyed, excited, some kind of influencer. Riddick brushed past him.

'Watch it, mate!' the man protested.

'Police!' Dipshit, Riddick thought.

Another spectator was really getting into it, her partner filming while she used the chaos as a background.

'Police. You're interfering,' Riddick hissed, wading between them.

Behind him, the spectator condemned him for whoever her audience was. 'Here comes the strong arm of the law, bulldozing us little people out.'

Idiots.

Two ambulances sat ahead. The rear doors of the first were open. Three patrol cars stood at odd angles, suggesting a fast arrival and a fast stop. All around, officers moved with purpose but not panic. He envied that control and purpose.

Right now, with the fates of two of his friends in the air, it felt completely elusive to him, but he had to keep himself together, or he would render himself useless again. In a hospital bed.

And that was the reason that this whole bloody mess with Laura had—

He caught a glimpse of the stretcher being wheeled over to the ambulance.

Blonde hair visible despite the neck brace. An IV line already established.

'Sir, you can't—'

Riddick's badge cut off a uniformed officer. 'That's my colleague.' He kept his eyes on Frost and the paramedics. 'How is she?'

'I don't know much.'

Abandoning the useless officer, Riddick approached the stretcher.

Frost's face was pale beneath the oxygen mask, a dark stain spreading through the dressing on her head. Her eyes were closed. Her chest rose and fell. Still breathing. Still fighting.

'Laura?'

She didn't stir.

One of the paramedics looked up. 'We're doing what we can. Need to get her to hospital now.'

'What's your assessment?'

'Until we know the extent of the head trauma, it's too early to say. We need to move.'

Riddick took her hand. Cold but not ice-cold. He squeezed gently.

'You're going to be all right.'

Nothing. No return squeeze, no flutter of eyelids.

Shit!

He backed away so she could be loaded into the ambulance. The stretcher locked into place with metallic clicks. An older paramedic climbed in beside her, already adjusting drip rates.

The doors were closing. In seconds, she'd be gone, racing through York's streets with sirens clearing the path.

Looking down, he caught sight of his own hospital bracelet – ironic, she was now heading to the place that had taken him from her side, initially.

Christ! If he hadn't forgotten his tablet... if he hadn't tried to barge that door down like a maniac... none of them would have ended up here.

He was such a bloody idiot!

'Sir?' A new voice. A wide, suited individual approached – full-faced and full of colour. Unlike Riddick with his dicky internal system, and now Frost too, who faced God knows what challenges. 'DS Greg Morrison. I was first response.'

Behind Morrison, the ambulance wailed away. Riddick waited for the sound to diminish as it carried Frost into the distance. He took several deeper breaths, had to fight to be calm. His hand touched his chest, wondering if his heart was

going to start doing things again that would alarm his cardiologist.

'Are you all right, sir?' Morrison asked. 'Must be a shock. You
look like you could do with sitting down.'

'I always look like that these days. Just tell me what
happened here.' The words came out harder than intended.

Morrison glanced at the growing crowd of phone-wielding
gawkers, then gestured towards one of the patrol cars. 'Let's talk
over there. Away from the audience.'

They walked together, Riddick's legs operating on a two-
second delay.

Morrison opened the patrol car's rear door. 'Sit. Please.'

Riddick nodded and did as he was asked, and Morrison
positioned himself alongside. 'DS Frost fell from the walls.' He
pointed towards Bootham Bar, its medieval bulk visible beyond
the emergency vehicles.

A couple of SOCOs worked at the foot of the wall, gathered
around a pool of blood.

Riddick rubbed his temples.

'She was with Graham Blanks,' Morrison continued. 'The
man responsible for—'

'I know who he is, son. I spoke to him on her phone... just
after she fell.'

'Jesus. What did he say?'

Riddick explained the conversation. 'You recover her
phone?'

Morrison shook his head.

'Right, track it. Let's hope he was stupid enough to keep it.
Look, this is my fault. I sent her the information and was...
otherwise engaged. I should have been with her. She shouldn't
have gone to the mother-in-law's alone.'

'Don't be too hard on yourself – she made the decision to go alone.'

Riddick sighed. As would he have done. After all, it'd been obvious for a while now that they'd been cut from the same cloth.

'I've spoken to witnesses,' Morrison said. 'She'd chased him onto the walls, had him down on his knees while she called for backup. Then it all went wrong. He lost his temper, started squaring up to her. It's unclear whether he actually pushed her or she fell backing away. He got close, though. Witnesses say he was shouting about being a father, shouting about reference numbers.'

'It's twenty feet,' Riddick said, eyeing the wall.

'Could have been worse. She landed partly on a raised flower bed – soft earth instead of pure stone. She's hit her head hard, but hopefully that spared her worse damage.'

A brief moment of hope and relief was ended by a sudden crash of guilt.

But she was still broken, still lying in a hospital bed because he'd been too sick, too slow, too caught up in his own spiral to be there with her. Another colleague hurt on his watch. Another person paying the price for his failures.

'Any idea where he's gone?'

'Not yet.'

'Christ! He's desperate, sick, his face is all over the news, and yet he's vanished again. What is this man – smoke?' Riddick pointed up at the helicopter. 'Surely that should—'

'The thing is, sir, these medieval streets make it harder—'

'Save it.' Riddick knew already. Tiny alleys, narrow roads, shadowy courtyards. The place was a maze, squashed and concentrated. To a helicopter, it probably just looked like a mass of incoherent lines.

And Graham Blanks would have intimate knowledge of York's labyrinthine geography. Despite illness and madness, there was something about a desperate fugitive with nothing left to lose. It gave you focus.

Riddick didn't know Graham well enough to work out his next move, but he knew someone who did.

And she wasn't too far from here.

48

Graham followed Bootham's long stretch northwards.

He was encountering a run of expensive Georgian proper-ties. The insulated, camouflaged by elegant facades. He wondered what it was like to never have to worry about Universal Credit or about losing a phone connection. Or of living in squalor so unhealthy that you had to move your child away...

But most importantly, about not getting the medical help you so desperately needed.

The insulated. Alive and healthy.

Unlike his daughter.

He reached Clifton, and the city surrendered to countryside. First came scattered cottages, then hedgerows, then the stench of manure and open fields.

Behind him, somewhere in the distance, helicopter blades chopped the air. Still hunting. Still circling the medieval streets.

They wouldn't come over the farmland.

With capture inevitable, he'd determined now to finish what he'd started.

He wouldn't go into custody alive. He would never allow them to force-feed drugs that took away his memory, and his love for Lucy...

Her face.

And you still think all this is a good idea now, do you? Lou asked.

Like I'd ever care what your opinion is – a mother who abandoned her daughter like that? You're no mother at all.

In my defence, I did always tell you that I didn't want to be a mother. It was you who made me.

That's just not true.

I'd sooner have been rid of her.

Why are you so cold?

I'm honest. You should try it. You think you're achieving something with all this but just look at you! Roaming the dirt and manure.

He followed a public footpath towards the Stray, leaving the road for a muddy track between hawthorn hedges.

The path opened onto vast grassland dotted with cattle. In the middle distance, farm buildings clustered. Graham turned away from them, following a lesser track that branched west. This wasn't marked on any tourist map. This was the kind of path only locals knew – or those who'd spent their childhoods exploring these margins.

The track deteriorated with each step. Tarmac gave way to gravel, gravel to mud, mud to something that was more water than earth. His feet squelched. Trees leaned over the path like twisted, drunken spirits.

You still know the way? Lou asked.

'Yes, of course.'

Even after all this time?

'Not easy to forget.'

Running towards Hell.

'Except I'm not running.' He smirked. 'I'm just... walking... stumbling.'

And you think this will help in some way?

'It can't hurt.'

The cottages appeared through a gap in the hawthorn. Not the pretty stone cottages that featured in *Yorkshire Life*. These were the ones the tourists never saw. Rendered walls with the render falling off in sheets. Roofs patched with corrugated iron and blue tarpaulin. Gardens that had surrendered to nature decades ago.

One stood apart from the others, at the end of a track that was more suggestion than road. Smaller. Meaner. Smoke trickling from a tilted chimney.

Graham's legs trembled as he approached. The fever... the exhaustion...

The fear of seeing him? Lou asked.

I'm not scared of him.

You keep telling yourself that.

The door had been blue once. Now it was the colour of a fading bruise.

A sign reading 'NO COLD CALLERS' hung at an angle, the text barely visible through accumulated grime. Graham raised his fist and knocked.

He heard shuffling inside; a chain being fumbled with.

The door cracked open.

Graham heard the wheeze and hiss of medical equipment. It made him think of Lucy attached to her dialysis machine.

The door opened wider.

And he stared at a ghost.

'Hello, Father,' Graham said.

49

Samantha Whitfield sat in the corner chair, a box of tissues on her lap. Riddick clocked the brown tea stain up the wall. Graham had brought his rampage to this room and left his ex-mother-in-law in a terrified state.

Samantha's eyes were red-rimmed. She regarded Riddick sadly. 'I'm so sorry about your colleague.'

Riddick nodded. 'She's in good hands.'

'I wanted to warn her that he was upstairs, but...' She twisted the tissue in her hands. 'I was worried he'd come down and hurt her. I didn't know what to do.'

'It must have been scary.' His gaze travelled the room. Photos crowded the mantelpiece – years of family history in mismatched frames.

'He was always on edge,' Samantha said, pressing a fresh tissue between her hands. 'Always complaining the world was against them. But it got worse after he lost his job and then Lucy got sick. He became angrier, more withdrawn.' She paused. 'My daughter ran off to Australia with some bloke while Lucy was dying. That was gross and unacceptable.'

'Are you in touch with your daughter?'

'Lou showed for the funeral. I told her what I thought of her for abandoning Lucy.' Samantha's voice hardened. 'I doubt we'll ever speak again.'

'That must be tough.'

She stared off into space for a moment, contemplating something. 'One thing you could never fault Graham for though was his devotion.' She stood and picked up a photograph from the mantelpiece. 'He adored Lucy. He's never been the most settled' – she touched her head – 'up here. I guess you couldn't be if you wanted to be with my daughter! This was Lucy's sixth birthday. Just before she got sick. Look how he's watching her.'

The photo showed Lucy blowing out candles, Graham beside her with an adoring expression on his face.

'She lived with me for the last year, you know. He wouldn't have her in his bungalow any more – too damp. He worried for her health. I offered him a room here, but he didn't want to crowd the place.' Her voice softened. 'He came all the time though. Every day. Taking her to appointments, sitting through dialysis. Like I said, he was a good father. It breaks my heart. Losing a child... and someone as special as Lucy... it was always going to hurt him badly. But this...' She looked at Riddick. 'Is it true? Did he kill that man?'

Riddick nodded. 'I'm afraid so. And now two other people are fighting for their lives. Which is why the sooner I find him, the better. Before anyone else gets hurt, including him.'

She picked up another photo – a family beach holiday. Graham throwing Lucy in the air, her face split with joy. Samantha's daughter was also in the image.

'They look happy,' Riddick said.

'They were. But Lou... she could never settle. She struggled

with fidelity. Had affairs when Lucy was young.' Samantha set
the photo down carefully. 'I knew about some of them; Graham
did too, but he never challenged her. Never threatened to leave.
He didn't want Lucy to lose her mother.'

A police siren wailed in the distance. Both of them froze,
listening until it faded.

'But after the job loss and Lucy getting sick,' Samantha
continued, 'he just got angrier and angrier. Then Lou left with
this other man.'

Samantha turned to face Riddick. Tears ran down her face.
'I felt more like a mother to Lucy than a grandmother.' She
pressed the tissue to her eyes. 'It ripped out my heart.' She sat
down again, and Riddick gave her a moment to compose
herself.

'I saw a wall of newspaper clippings at his place. Do you
know about that?'

'Yes.'

'When did it start?'

'About a year ago. After the missed kidney match.' She
waved her hand dismissively. 'You probably know all about that
– how he blamed himself, blamed the system. That's when he
became obsessive.'

Riddick's phone buzzed. A text from Control:

No sightings. Search continuing.

He pocketed it.

'Obsessive how?'

'Researching all the time. Statistics on other children who
died waiting. Money spent on private healthcare.' She pulled a
fresh tissue from the box. 'He worked in IT. He knew how to
find things.'

The floorboards creaked above them. Samantha's eyes darted upward.

'Just the house settling,' she said, but her voice shook. 'I keep thinking he's still up there.'

But Riddick knew that couldn't be the case. The area immediately around her house was now swarming with officers.

'The way he talked,' she continued after a moment, 'it was like he understood how all the systems connected. How one department's decision rippled through others.'

Riddick shifted in his chair. His chest was tightening – he needed his medication soon.

'But even with everything that's happened – the bad moments, those other incidents of amnesia – nothing was like today. I barely recognised him. The Graham I knew, who sang Lucy silly songs during dialysis, who learned to braid her hair...'

Her voice broke. She stood abruptly, walked to the window.

'There was always some of that Graham there. Today, though, it had all gone. Every last drop. And he looked terrible – feverish, coughing.'

Riddick looked at the photos again. Years of love documented, archived, proven. He had his own collection of photos, of course, but Riddick couldn't bring himself to look at them. The possibility of unravelling again followed him like a dark shadow.

He still didn't have anything concrete to help him find Graham.

'Tell me more about the amnesia. It's happened before, according to his medical reports.'

'Started several months back. He'd wake up thinking she was still alive, still needed him.' She turned from the window. 'The doctor said it was his mind's protection against unbearable pain.'

Another siren, closer this time. Riddick tensed.

'This wasn't the first time he's come here looking for her,' Samantha said quickly. 'But today was the worst. The other times were just moments – fleeting confusion – then he'd realise.'

She moved back to her chair, sat heavily. 'Each time shattered him, but I could pull him back. Today was different. Complete bewilderment. He truly believed she was still alive and needed saving. He was desperate.' She met Riddick's eyes. 'He's completely coming apart. The anger and the amnesia are at war inside him.'

Riddick stood, restless. A child's drawing on the wall – stick figures labelled 'Me, Daddy, Granny'. Lucy's careful handwriting.

'Where will he go, Samantha? When the running stops, when he can't flee any more – where?'

'Depends. If the amnesia returns, maybe the hospital. Here again.'

'Those places are being watched.'

'What about the bridge?'

'What bridge?'

'Lendal Bridge. He used to take Lucy there to feed the ducks when she was small. After she died, he'd go back and stand at the rail, looking down at the water. Once I found him there, helped talk him down. He might go there.'

It was better than nothing.

Riddick checked his phone. There were updates from search teams, but no sightings. Graham Blanks, invisible in his grief, could be anywhere.

Lendal Bridge it was.

'He won't stop,' Samantha said quietly. 'His eyes today... they seemed dead. I think he's gone or going. What's left is just

momentum. Rage and memory pushing him forward until...'
She didn't finish.

Riddick looked around the room one more time at photos of
a man who gave everything for his daughter and had nothing
left when she was gone.

Riddick understood that loss. The kind that burned your
world down. And pushed you until there was nothing left but
the actual breaking.

'I'll find him.' He stood. 'I'll stop him.'

'Don't hurt him.'

'I'm a police officer, Samantha. That's not what I want.'

'No. Really. I understand your anger, your pain about your
friend.'

Riddick took a deep breath and lowered his head. Graham
had hurt Laura, but revenge wasn't what he wanted. This was
different; this man was lost and had suffered the worst loss.

A loss that hit so close to home.

Riddick lifted his head before a tear could form.

'It really is the opposite of what I want.'

She nodded. 'Thank you.'

'I'm going to try my best, okay?'

He wouldn't promise – they were too far down a dangerous
road to be making promises like that.

'You're not how I remember you, Patrick,' Graham said.

His father's skin was like parchment stretched over a skull. Eyes rheumy above the clear plastic tubing that fed oxygen to his nostrils. He rested one hand on the portable oxygen tank which sat alongside him like a faithful dog.

And you thought you were feeling like shit, Lou said. *Look at him. This is your future. This is where you end up.*

I don't plan to last that long, Lou, he thought, collapsing onto the sofa opposite the single chair his father occupied. The room swam for a moment, and he had to grip the armrest to steady himself.

Each of Patrick's inhalations sounded like an old washing machine. Wet, laboured, mechanical. Strangely soothing in its rhythm. Graham felt his own breathing synchronise with it. Father and son, both struggling for air. Both circling the drain. He felt himself drifting. His head snapped forward. No. Not yet. He shook himself and sat up. 'How long do you have left?'

The old man didn't reply immediately; instead, he adjusted

his oxygen tube with trembling fingers. 'They want me in a home, so not long if I have anything to do with it.'

Graham's weary eyes rose to the ceiling. Damp stains spread across it like disease, dark blooms of rot eating the plaster. The whole house was dying with its occupant.

He coughed violently into his arm, tasting copper, and slumped back.

Patrick wheezed – his attempt at a laugh. 'You look as bad as me. Death warmed up.' The old man's voice was like gravel in a cement mixer. 'I saw your face on the news.'

'Did you now?' Graham's vision blurred. He closed his eyes briefly. 'Did they catch my good side?'

'They say you killed someone. Hurt a doctor, too.'

Tell him about the tin of beans, Lou whispered. *Tell him about the car. Tell him how Dennis Hartley crawled. Make him proud.*

Graham couldn't help laughing over Lou's sarcasm.

'I always knew you'd come to a bad end.' He broke off to cough. 'You always looked like a wrong 'un to me.'

Graham opened his eyes. 'Strange thing to say... you barely ever saw me.'

Patrick fiddled with the oxygen adjustment again.

'I prefer you when you're making jokes,' Graham said. 'Look, if I was a wrong 'un, well, I could have... could have appreciated a father figure in my life maybe.' The words came out jumbled. Graham wasn't sure they made sense.

'I gave your mother a hell of a lot of money.'

Graham rubbed his forehead. When had the room gotten so hot? Or was that the fever climbing again? He looked at his hand. The sweat on his palm glistened, and for a moment he saw Lucy's hand in his. Small. Cold. No, that was at the hospital. No, that was – when? Yesterday? Six months ago?

Focus! Lou snapped. *He's talking about money.*

'Money and love aren't the same thing.'

Patrick laughed, coughed and drew deep on his oxygen. The tank hissed as it worked harder. 'Some would disagree, regardless. We make the best of what is. People make do with less than what you received. You should have been grateful.'

Grateful!

Graham wanted to laugh. Grateful for being paid to disappear.

Graham snorted, triggering another coughing fit. This one went on and on, his chest burning, vision spotting black at the edges.

'I'd suggest a doctor,' the old man wheezed. 'If you weren't England's most wanted.' He grinned. 'So, why are you here? Is this some kind of reckoning before they put you away?'

Good question, Lou said. *What are you doing here? Lucy's dead. You killed a man. The police are coming. And you're sitting here with Daddy? A daddy who probably can't recall your name, incidentally.*

'I don't know, for sure...' Graham's mind kept drifting. He was in the car hitting Dennis. No, he was at Lucy's bedside. The satisfying thump. No, he was at Lucy's bedside, watching monitors. No, he was ten years old at this very gate, mud on his face, dogs barking that didn't exist. When was now? Where was now?

God, he was exhausted; the fever was making time fold in on itself.

'Well, you best get thinking... I'm sure they'll eventually work out who your father is, and they'll be coming through the door...'

'Ha,' Graham said weakly. 'I'm not so sure. You were very good at keeping it secret.' Graham's words slurred slightly. 'And, well, if they find me here then so be it. We weren't together at the beginning, nor most of my life, but I guess we will be at the end.'

Poetic, Lou mocked. *The abandoned son returns to die at Daddy's feet.*

Patrick grunted and shifted in his chair. The oxygen tank's wheels squeaked. 'You were never a full shilling. Even as a baby.'

'So you keep saying.' Or had he said it before? Graham couldn't remember.

'You never cried.'

'Maybe I was happy.'

'Looked at folk funny.'

'I was a baby.'

'Huh...' Patrick sucked on his oxygen.

Graham coughed again, and this time blood splattered across his palm – bright red against his fever-pale skin. He wiped it absently on the sofa, adding his stain to the farmhouse's collection. 'So this is your excuse for abandoning me? That I didn't cry and looked at folk funny?'

He's making excuses, Lou whispered. *Just like you make excuses. Lucy's dead because of you. Because you couldn't keep track of a phone number.*

'Hard to say I abandoned you. I gave your mother a lot of money.'

'And we're back there. Money isn't love. Besides, you gave my mother money so she never told anyone.'

Patrick looked away, sucked hard on his oxygen for a while, then said, 'Well, long time ago now. Water under the bridge.'

'Whose bridge, Patrick?' Graham's mind flashed to Lendal Bridge. The iron railings, the dark water below. He'd jumped from there once. Or thought about jumping. Or Lucy had asked about jumping. Or was that today? Yesterday? Was Lucy still alive then? Which memory was real?

'You screwed up your own life.'

'I married. Had a daughter...' Graham's voice cracked. Lucy's face swam before him. Eight years old. No, six. No, she was dead.

Six months dead, Lou reminded him. *Today, you've been chasing ghosts.*

'And you let it all go,' Patrick said.

Graham's eyes widened, fury cutting through the fever fog. 'What the hell do you mean? You think I chose for my wife to leave, for my daughter to get sick?'

Patrick shrugged. 'A man takes care of business.'

Listen to him, Lou said. *Even your dying father thinks you're pathetic.*

'I've watched from afar, son. A man doesn't let his woman walk away like you did. And a man protects his children.'

The oxygen hissed between them. Patrick's chest rose and fell with effort.

'Ha... like you protected me?'

'I provided.'

The words hung there, obscene in their inadequacy. Provided money. Not time. Not presence. Not love. Just money, as if Graham were a bill to be paid.

'You've lost your mind. You think a man can control everything?'

'I managed.'

Graham looked around the decaying farmhouse, but the walls kept subtly shifting, breathing in and out like something alive. Or like Lucy's chest in those final moments, so shallow he'd had to lean close to see if she was still there. He gripped the sofa arm harder. *Stay present. Stay here.* 'You're dying alone.'

'Everyone dies alone, and in misery.'

'My daughter didn't.' The words came out before Graham could stop them. But had she? He'd been there, hadn't he? Or was that another dream?

You were there, Lou confirmed. *Holding her hand while she died. August fourteenth. The hottest day. Remember?*

Patrick nodded but didn't say anything.

'Nothing to say?'

'I'm sorry for her. I'm sorry she didn't get the life she deserved.'

'But you're not sorry I didn't get the life I deserved?'

'You're a man. You make your own destiny.'

Graham's head was pounding. When had he last taken the flu remedy? Hours ago? Days?

The farmhouse smelled of trapped time – old cooking grease, damp wool, the sweet-sick smell of approaching death. The old man shifted in his chair, the oxygen tank squeaking on its wheels as it moved closer. The sound made Graham think of Lucy's wheelchair, also squeaking, also following her everywhere like a faithful dog.

'You used to be wealthy,' Graham said, grasping for something solid in the conversation, something that wasn't memory or fever dream.

'Well, the farming industry isn't what it was. The government turning its back on what's important.'

Sound familiar? Lou taunted. *Like father, like son. Both abandoned by the system. Both failures.*

Graham snorted. 'I thought you were a man making his own destiny.'

'Well, I never scavenged. Always knew how to work. They said on the news that you were on benefits... then, when you didn't get your handout, you killed the person responsible. To think!'

Graham sneered, but the expression hurt his face. Everything hurt. 'I'm not sure you've had it explained clearly enough to you.'

He knows exactly what you did, Lou said. *Everyone knows. You're a murderer. A failure. A man who couldn't save his own daughter.*

'Oh, I understand well enough. Look. Life's hard for everyone. Everyone suffers. Has setbacks. You pick yourself back up. It's only when you get to my state that it's time to call it a day.' Patrick tapped the oxygen tank for emphasis, as if it proved his point rather than undermining it.

'Easy to say when you're born with opportunities – you certainly were.'

'I gave your mother money.'

'How many other mothers did you give money to?'

Patrick smiled. 'I took responsibility.'

'Do you know how old I was the last time I saw you?'

'I recall coming to you when you were eighteen and giving you money to help you set up a life.'

'Five thousand pounds. I remember.' The exact amount. He'd counted it so many times that first night, spread across his single bed in the bedsit. Blood money. Silence money. 'Came with conditions, didn't it?'

Patrick's eyes slid away. The oxygen hissed louder, as if objecting on his behalf.

'Never contact you again. Never darken your door.'

'It was your chance. Five thousand pounds. You should have been more careful.'

More careful, Lou echoed. *Like you were careful to change the emergency contact for the hospital?*

Graham's jaw clenched. He gripped the sofa harder. 'My mother had just died. I had nothing. No family. No connections. Just a father who wanted me to disappear. So I took your money and I tried to disappear, to become someone else. Someone worth knowing. Someone who mattered.'

'And you did. You found a career. A family. You could say I helped in the end. It was you who chose to throw it away.'

Graham closed his eyes, and immediately the room began to spin. The farmhouse, Patrick, the oxygen, the decay – all of it whirling like water down a drain. He felt himself falling backward through time, through all the versions of himself: the abandoned boy, the hopeful husband, the desperate father.

You're losing it, Lou whispered. *The fever's taking you. Maybe that's for the best.*

He fumbled in his pocket with clumsy fingers, found the flu tablets, punched two out. They stuck to his dry tongue as he tried to swallow them. The bitterness made him gag, but he forced them down.

After a few moments, Patrick said, 'Are you asleep?'

'No.' Graham's voice sounded far away, even to himself. 'But I was hoping I could have a sleep. Just for a short while.' Just close his eyes. Just for a moment. Maybe when he woke, Lucy would be alive again. Maybe when he woke, none of this would have happened.

The old man wheezed. 'The bedroom's through there if you want—'

But Graham was already drifting, Patrick's voice fading, the oxygen's hiss becoming the sound of waves, the farmhouse dissolving around him...

* * *

He was thirteen again, in the shadow of York Minster. Another stone hit him.

He gritted his teeth against the pain. The bullies laughed.

They're still laughing, Lou said from somewhere far away.

He saw Dennis Hartley laughing. And Dr Phillips.

There was Clive from the shop, too... and Williamson for the hospital waiting room...

One missing.

There he was. The Viking from the home counties.

All of them laughing.

He waited for it to stop, to go quiet, then opened his eyes.

They were leaving.

He didn't get to his feet just yet, was content to stare at the Gothic towers spearing into a blood-red sky.

Was this a dream or was this real?

Does it matter? Lou asked. *You're dying either way.*

The bullies were real. Always had been. Always would be.

Crows circled now. A few at first, though they quickly multiplied. Suddenly, there were hundreds, descending from the Minster's towers like a black avalanche.

Always.

He closed his eyes, willing them to leave, but when he opened them again, they were all around him. Hopping. Cocking heads. Eyes locked somewhere between life and death.

He thought of his Irish gran, dead for almost five years. No, longer. Time kept slipping. The only person who had ever really seemed to have time for him.

Until Lucy, Lou reminded him. *And look how that turned out.*

She'd once told him a story of battlefield crows. 'The ones that would choose who lived and who died.'

There was the Morrigan, though he'd thought it sounded

more like 'Morgan' when he was younger. 'A queen who became a crow.'

Or maybe she was always a crow?

Three crows came close.

Three sisters?

The first pecked at his hands where the stones had cut. The second at his cheek where tears mixed with blood.

The third watched. But that was so much worse.

Like Patrick watched, Lou said. *Like everyone watched while you fell apart. While Lucy died.*

Those that watch. That allow this. That somehow relish this.

'Washer at the ford,' his gran's voice echoed. 'She washes the blood from your clothes before you die.'

But there was no water. Only Lucy's face in the fever dream, asking why he hadn't saved her. Why the kidney went to someone else, why he'd let her die.

Then there were more beaks and feathers. Brothers and sisters. A thousand tiny wounds opening across his skin.

But it didn't hurt any more.

There was only release.

Yes... he lay still, encouraging them on. Peck deeper.

Find the poison in my veins. The fever in my brain. Make me clean. Making me empty.

Take away the grief in my heart...

But the grief remained. It always remained. Lucy's face appeared among the crows, and she was smiling.

She's not smiling, Lou corrected. *She's dead. Six months dead. And you've been running from it ever since.*

* * *

Graham opened his eyes, gasping.

The farmhouse solidified around him. How long had he been unconscious? Minutes? Hours?

Patrick had moved his chair closer. He had a shotgun straddled across his lap.

'I see,' Graham said, his voice barely a whisper. 'You couldn't even let me sleep.'

He's going to kill you, Lou said with something like satisfaction. *Your own father is going to put you down like a sick dog.*

Patrick took aim.

51

Riddick crossed Station Road.

He lumbered, slow and heavy, weighted down by ghosts again. And not just the ghosts of those from before. But the ghosts of those which may come.

Frost, Gardner... Graham.

Strange, to feel this weight of responsibility for a killer who'd put his colleague in intensive care.

But wasn't he a killer, too? One pushed by the same desperation as Blanks.

Okay, Dennis Hartley had not been Ronnie Haller, but a life was a life.

For better or worse, Riddick shared a bond with Graham. And with that came an inevitable sense of responsibility. In the same way someone who is a sponsor in AA might feel responsible for someone's drinking. Or like a parole officer who feels accountable when someone they vouched for falls back into old patterns – even when they know they can't control another person's choices.

He approached the Gothic iron bridge that Samantha had

identified: 'Lendal Bridge. He used to take Lucy there to feed the ducks when she was small. After she died, he'd go back. Standing at the rail, looking down at the water.'

The white roses of York adorned the painted railings, interspersed with crossed keys and English lions. His footsteps echoed hollow on the bridge's surface as he joined the flow of tourists and locals crossing between the medieval towers.

He walked it several times but there was no sign of Graham.

On the final pass, he paused halfway across, gripping the cold metal railing. Below, the River Ouse moved sluggish and brown, swollen with winter rain. On the embankment near Lendal Tower, a young mother knelt with two children – a boy, maybe seven, a girl no more than five. They were tossing bread to the mallards that bobbed in the calmer water near the bank.

The girl's delighted squeal carried up to him: 'Look, Mummy! That one's got a green head!'

He was suddenly back in the past:

'Daddy, why do boy ducks have prettier feathers than girl ducks?'

Lucy, six years old, hanging over this same railing on tiptoes while he kept a protective hand on her coat. Molly beside her, already knowing the answer but letting her sister ask.

Rachel said, 'The males need to attract the females, so they evolved brighter colours.'

'Like peacocks!' Molly added.

'Exactly like peacocks.' Rachel smiled at him over their daughters' heads.

'Can we feed them?' Lucy asked.

'We've been through this,' Riddick said, looking left at a family who had a whole loaf of Warburtons. 'It's not good for them.'

Rachel's hand found his, warm despite the October chill.

Work always intruded on his thoughts. How often had he admonished himself for not appreciating these moments more? He'd reassured himself that there would always be more Sundays.

Until there weren't.

The children below on the embankment by Lendal Tower had run out of bread. Their mother led them away, the little girl waving goodbye to the ducks. 'See you next time!' she called out, absolute in her certainty that there would be a next time.

Never take that next time for granted, he thought.

Riddick's hands tightened on the railing until his knuckles went white. Graham had stood here with Lucy. Fed these same ducks. Made the same promises about next time. Watched his daughter fade away week by week, dialysis by dialysis, until there were no more next times.

Two fathers. Both destroyed by loss.

As the last of the daylight died away, Riddick struggled to keep himself together.

He felt a desperation he'd never felt before.

The most peculiar yet.

The desperation to help a killer.

52

'Nice way to welcome me home,' Graham said. He coughed. His throat stung, but nothing came up this time.

'This was never your home.' Patrick paused, sucking in air. 'And you're not my son... not really.'

'Believing that makes it easier for you to pull that trigger.'

'Nah. I don't want any trouble. I just want you to go.'

Graham nodded. He sat up. He felt a little clearer – his last dose must be lowering his temperature. 'What are you afraid of? Look at the state of you. You haven't got long left anyway.'

Patrick shook his head. 'I just prefer natural causes.'

Tell him about how Dennis slipped from the bonnet of that Astra, Lou whispered, *and how you ran him over again.*

'Was there ever any regret?' Graham asked. He studied his father's face, looking for something – recognition, regret, anything human. Finding only the stubborn set of a Yorkshire farmer's jaw.

Outside, he heard crows calling.

He noticed the opened box of shells on the floor. The shotgun was loaded, then.

'There was a boy who followed his mother to this house one day,' Graham said.

'Save it,' Patrick said. 'I just want you to leave.'

'He was curious, you see. She'd been sneaking off, telling him she was going to work extra shifts. But he knew she was lying. Kids always know.'

Just like Lucy knew you were lying about everything being okay, Lou said.

Graham nodded to himself. 'Yes. Kids always know.'

Patrick narrowed his eyes. The shotgun trembled in his grip. 'I don't want to hear this.'

'Maybe not, but I think you need to. The boy was ten, skinny thing. He followed her all the way from their council flat to this cottage. Not as rundown then, was it? This place, almost respectable. Paint on the door. Garden actually had flowers instead of weeds.'

The gun barrel wavered. 'I don't care.'

'The boy waited outside while she went in. Waited in the bushes like a little spy. Could hear voices through the window. His mother crying. A man's voice, gruff. Yorkshire farmer through and through. And another voice. A woman.'

Patrick's face tightened.

'Margaret. The wife that looked away.'

Just like everyone has looked away ever since, Lou said.

'And when the mother came out – always crying after these visits, clutching a handful of notes – the bare minimum to live on – the little boy stayed behind, knocked on the door.'

Patrick had to lower the shotgun with one hand to press his oxygen mask to his face and suck desperately at the air. He closed his eyes and shook his head.

Graham had the opportunity to rush him, but the pills

hadn't completely worked their magic yet. Better to bide his time.

Patrick's eyes flew open. 'For fuck's sake, give it a rest. Stop talking about yourself like that.'

'Why? It almost doesn't feel real. It was the first time I ever saw you, Patrick. I could also see Margaret through the doorway. Blonde hair in curlers. Pink housecoat. Just standing there, looking away. As if your little problem didn't exist. As if I didn't exist.'

'Maggie had nothing to do with—'

'She stood there washing dishes while her husband dealt with his bastard at the door.'

'She's dead. Be respectful.'

Dead like Lucy, Lou said. *Dead like your mother. Dead like Hartley.*

'You'll be joining her soon enough.'

His father's face went grey. He put both hands back on the shotgun.

'It's the same look then that you have now – trapped animal figuring out how to bite.'

'Nonsense.'

'I knew you were my father. Mum had a photo hidden in her jewellery box. You were younger in it, but I knew. Do you remember?' Graham paused to cough, leaning back in the sofa. 'Do you?'

'Vaguely.'

'Does this help: "Are you my dad? Are you my dad?" I must have asked twenty times.'

Patrick shook his head. 'It was a long—'

'"Please, mister. I just want to know. Are you my dad?" You know what you said? "Go home, boy. Go home to your mother."

But I wouldn't go. I thought you'd crack under the pressure. You cracked, but not in the right way.'

The old man flinched.

'So you do remember!'

'I don't know what you mean.'

'You grabbed me by the shirt. Lifted me clean off the ground. I was so shocked I stopped talking. Then you slapped me. Again, and again... I was ten!'

Silence. Outside, the crows called again. Closer now.

'And Margaret stood in that kitchen, washing her clean dishes.'

'Leave her out of this.'

'I could barely see on the way home through all the tears.'

Patrick shook his head. 'It gave me no pleasure.'

He's lying, Lou said. *They always lie.*

Graham closed his eyes and took a few deep breaths. He was feeling a little better, but he still needed to take a moment. He opened his eyes. 'You remember dragging me to the gate? Throwing me in the mud and telling me you'd set the dogs on me if I came back. Except you didn't have dogs, did you? Just empty threats and a woman who'd learned not to see.'

'She was innocent.'

'She knew.'

'She had no choice.'

'Everyone has a choice. You chose your reputation over your son. And she chose you over morality. She watched you beat the shit out of me, Father.'

'What do you want from me? An apology? Fine. I'm sorry. There. Happy?'

'Your acknowledgement is enough.'

'I had to make sure you never came back.' Patrick's breath

rattled worse now, the oxygen not enough. 'Just fuck off, will
you? Let me die in peace. That's all I want.'

'Peace? Lucy wanted peace from the pain. I wanted peace
from watching her die. You want peace from your past. We have
more in common than you realise.'

Graham stood slowly, joints protesting, black spots dancing
at the edges of his vision. 'I only want one thing from you and
then I'll leave. I promise.'

'What? Money?'

'No... that didn't work last time, did it? Not going to work
again. I want some petrol.'

'Eh?'

'Petrol. I know you keep it for your tractor. Some in a jerry
can, somewhere?'

The old man's eyes narrowed. 'What for?'

Time to burn it all down, Lou said with satisfaction.

'Don't worry, it's not for this place.'

'Are you going to hurt more people?'

'Do you care?'

He thought about it and didn't respond. A long moment
passed. Then Patrick gestured with the gun towards the back
door. 'In the shed. Take it and go.'

Graham walked through the kitchen, through the smell of
gas and damp. His hand slipped on the door handle – sweat or
weakness, he couldn't tell. The back door stuck, needed shoul-
dering open, which sent pain shooting through his fevered
body.

The shed lurked in the overgrown garden like a guilty
secret.

Inside, the detritus of agricultural life: rotting feed sacks,
rusted tools. And there, beneath a workbench – a red jerry can.
Half full by the weight of it, though lifting it made his arms

shake. The smell of petrol sharp and sweet. He scoured the shelves until he found a box of matches and pocketed them.

The petrol fumes mixed with the memory of leaking gas from the kitchen was a dangerous combination. One spark...

He carried the jerry can back through, having to stop twice to catch his breath. Patrick's eyes were closed. The shotgun lay across his lap.

At first, Graham thought he was dead.

He went closer and saw his chest moving.

Setting the jerry can down quietly – carefully with the petrol near that hissing oxygen – Graham reached for the shotgun with trembling hands. Patrick didn't stir as he lifted it from the old man's lap.

The weight almost made him drop it. So heavy. His arms shook with the effort.

He cracked it open. Both barrels loaded.

Several steps back, nearly stumbling, then he raised the gun. It wavered in his grip.

His father's eyes were closed.

Should I wake him?

He deserves to know it's coming, Lou said. *Like Lucy knew.*

'Please, Lou.'

She did know.

'She was everything to me.'

And yet you were nothing to this man in front of you.

'Yes... Let him see,' Graham said. 'Let him know.' He raised his voice. 'Oi!'

Patrick's eyes snapped open.

They widened. 'What the—'

Over Patrick's shoulder, Graham saw three black shapes reflected through the glass by dying light. Watching. Always watching.

'The Morrigan's sisters,' his grandmother's voice echoed. 'They come for the dying.'

'You think this solves anything?'

'No. It's too late for that ten-year-old boy.'

Graham braced himself and pulled the trigger.

The blast took the old man in the chest, throwing him back in the chair. The oxygen tank clattered over, its valve hissing louder now, mixing with the smell of gunpowder and blood.

The recoil sent Graham stumbling backward. He hit the wall hard, slid down it, but somehow kept his footing. His ears rang. His vision blurred.

He staggered forward and looked down at his father.

Still alive. Eyes wide with shock more than pain. His mouth moved, trying to form words. Maybe an apology, maybe a curse. Graham would never know.

Their eyes met – properly met – maybe for the first time in Graham's life.

Patrick's hand twitched, reaching for something. His son? The gun? The oxygen?

Graham didn't move closer.

'Water under the bridge,' Graham said.

The old man's chest hitched. A wet sound.

'Water under the bridge.' Quieter now, almost gentle.

Patrick's eyes began to glaze, but they stayed on Graham's face. Looking. Finally looking. A final exhale, rattling through blood.

The cottage fell silent except for the dangerous hiss of escaping oxygen, filling the room with its invisible threat.

The black shapes at the window were gone, but he could hear their cries fading into the February dusk.

Keeping the shotgun in one hand, Graham picked up the petrol can with the other, matches heavy in his pocket. The petrol sloshed inside, and he was acutely aware of the oxygen still hissing behind him. One spark and this whole place would go up.

But not yet. Not here.

He headed for the door.

One more bridge to cross.

53

The taxi smelled of pine air freshener and stale cigarettes, despite the NO SMOKING stickers plastered across the dashboard.

MP Marcus Crist's voice filled the taxi – that particular brand of political smoothness that could make even genuine emotion sound rehearsed. 'This is a dark day for our city. What should have been a celebration of York's rich Viking heritage has been marred by senseless violence.'

Riddick's phone rang. His hands shook as he fumbled for it. Was it about Gardner, Frost or Graham Blanks? Take your pick.

The taxi driver killed the radio.

Reading the name, Riddick took a deep breath and answered. 'Mike?'

'Paul. Where are you?' The voice was measured, professional, but Riddick saw through it to the stress and anxiety.

'In a taxi, heading to the hospital, I have a colleague injured...'

'I'm sorry to hear that—'

'Mike, what is it?'

'I have an update, but I need you to hang tight, Paul... not panic... I need you to stay in control... I need you to keep the promise to stay put.'

'What. Is. It?'

'CCTV footage,' Yorke said. 'From a service station just outside Salisbury. Some people attached to Article SE, an organised crime outfit with tendrils in many major corporations in the South East of England, accompanied her to use the toilet. It was these three men who must have collected her from her home.'

'Okay, that's good, isn't it? You know where she is?'

Yorke paused. 'Not exactly. They seemed to be treating her respectfully. They've stopped to allow her to use the toilet. They've accompanied her, but she isn't struggling. She may have gone with them without a fight from her home – this may turn out to be her intention, but...'

'But?'

'We've lost track of the vehicle.'

'Shit.'

'It's an old trick. They change vehicles, licence plates. Throws ANPR off.'

'But you know who they are?'

'Not by name – they've been sighted with members of Article SE, but not identified.'

'So, you still don't know where she is?'

'No.'

'And when was she in the service station?'

'Last night about nine.'

'Jesus, so she's been gone overnight?'

'Afraid so.'

Riddick squeezed his eyes closed and gritted his teeth – it

was all he could do to stop himself from screaming at the top of his lungs.

'Paul.'

Riddick leaned forward and pressed his forehead to the back of the headrest of the passenger seat. 'She's been gone over twenty hours,' he managed.

'I know.'

'Anything could have happened to her. What if she's hurt?' His heart, unsurprisingly, was pounding beyond safe levels again. 'Or dead?'

'I remain confident we'll get her back,' Yorke said. 'Firstly, she may know what she's doing...'

'Three men accompanying her to the toilet?'

'Well, maybe she's got herself into something that she knew was risky. She could still be in some kind of control. Every resource is being deployed. We'll find her.'

Will you?

Forgive me for not being confident.

Everything around him was in the process of turning to shit.

Frost... His heart... a maniac on the loose... and Gardner in God-knows-what trouble...

'You need to stay put. Coming down here won't help anyone.'

'Sorry, but that ship has sailed.'

'As I said before, worst-case scenario is that they're posturing,' Yorke continued. 'They'll have her back by midnight, if we haven't located her by then. They won't want the heat if they can avoid it. This'll be Article SE warning her off. I know how they work. And if you trust me, Paul, when I have her back, enough is enough. I'm putting a stop to this vendetta. It's out of control. You have my word.'

'It's not enough,' Riddick said. He hung up. He leaned

forward and asked the taxi driver how much he would charge to drive him to Salisbury.

'I'm not sure her indoors would appreciate that all that much – however, I could phone someone to help you.'

After phoning, and speaking to someone, he said, 'He's just finding out if he can use the vehicle this evening – he and his brother share.'

'Thanks,' Riddick said, rubbing his temples.

The radio came back on. MP Marcus Crist was still at it, paying tribute to those affected by Graham's rampage. He was calling, as he always did, for community and unity.

'It's an opportunity to understand,' Crist continued. 'We must ask ourselves how someone could slip through the cracks of our support systems. How a father could become so desperate, so lost, that violence seemed his only recourse.'

And something occurred to Riddick.

Pulling out his phone, he scrolled through the photos he'd taken at Graham's house. The wall of rage, the desperate mathematics of benefits calculations...

In the background, Crist carried on. 'The Viking Festival will continue. We won't let one troubled individual destroy our celebrations. York is stronger than that. We've survived Vikings, we've survived civil wars, we'll survive this.'

He stopped at one image. It was partially hidden behind a newspaper clipping about NHS waiting lists. But there, in the corner of the frame...

A flyer. Bright yellow, the kind pushed through letterboxes during election season.

MARCUS CRIST – WORKING FOR YOU

And below that, in smaller text, a schedule of constituency

surgeries. Every second Saturday at the community centre, every fourth Tuesday at the library. Regular as clockwork.

And at the bottom:

> For pastoral care and spiritual guidance, join me and my wife alternate Friday evenings from 7 p.m. at Questions of Faith at Stonegate Common Hall, Water End, Clifton Moor.

'Turn the car round, please,' Riddick said.

'Okay, where to?' the driver said, slowing. 'I'm still waiting on my mate regarding the Salisbury journey.'

Riddick gave the address of the Stonegate Common Hall.

'Yeah, I know it. Didn't figure you for the type,' he said, turning the vehicle around.

'What, religious?'

'Aye.'

He wasn't. Any hope there was a god had disappeared the day his family had died. Still, he felt like praying.

Praying for his two close friends.

And for a man destroyed by loss.

54

Graham stood at the edge of the gravel car park, petrol can heavy in his left hand, shotgun in his right.

The Stonegate Common Hall was a modest wooden structure. The kind of place where good people gathered to pretend the world wasn't burning down around them.

So, you bring the fire to them? Lou asked.

'It's half past six,' Graham said. 'The good people aren't here yet.'

He approached, the petrol sloshing with each laboured breath. He coughed several times, and spat on the gravel.

The medicine had helped with the fever, but his exhaustion was at the point where reality seemed to shimmer at the edges.

You want to watch out for that, Lou said. *The boundary between what is and what might be is wearing really thin...*

'It's never been clearer.'

A Bentley Continental GT sat alone in the car park. Two hundred thousand pounds of engineered arrogance. Crist was a man who believed in hierarchies. In the natural order of things where some rose and others were crushed beneath the wheels.

Tonight's lesson would be simple: everything burns, and everything turns to dust.

The great equaliser.

Three crows perched on the centre's roof like gargoyles. Watching. Waiting.

Do you believe that they're really there? Lou asked.

'In the same way that I believe you are really there.'

The community centre's door stood open, yellow light spilling onto the wooden steps. Voices drifted from inside.

He paused at the threshold, peering into the hallway. Pine-panelled walls adorned with notices about coffee mornings and food bank donations. A coat rack holding two expensive over-coats. The smell of furniture polish and righteousness.

Through an internal door, he listened to them.

A husband and wife.

Or rather two people who'd never had to wonder where their next meal would come from, he thought. Who'd never watched their child fade while the system ground on indifferently.

Pushing through the door, he entered the main hall – rows of wooden chairs facing a modest altar, evening light streaming through tall windows. And there, at the front, arranging papers at a lectern, readying his service, stood Marcus Crist.

Going through the motions of faith while the world outside haemorrhaged hope.

Marcus looked up, squinted but didn't look concerned. Maybe the distance between them was still large enough to mask Graham's fever-wild state. He clearly hadn't recognised him from the images circulating the media.

'We're not beginning for another thirty minutes,' Marcus said.

'I'm cold,' Graham said. 'And this is my last stop of the day. Can I come in?'

'I haven't seen you before.' Crist's eyes were narrowing. He was doing the calculation now – potential voter, potential donor, potential problem. 'What's that in your hands? Sorry...' He rustled around on his lectern. 'Misplaced my glasses.'

Graham put down the petrol can, turned and closed the door.

'Sorry... if you could just wait in the hallway – we need to prepare the room. Then you can join us for prayer.'

'I'm not here for prayer,' he said, his back still to the MP. 'I'm here for truth.'

He could hear Marcus approaching down the aisle between the arranged chairs now. Graham waited until he was very close before turning.

Marcus stopped dead. His eyes widened, then he focused on the shotgun.

'It's you, isn't it?'

The butt of the shotgun caught the MP across the face. Marcus stumbled backward, hands flying to his nose. Blood immediately began streaming through his fingers.

Graham pointed the shotgun at him. 'Get down on your knees.'

Marcus, who could have been crying or merely suffering the effects of a broken nose, made no sense in his response.

'Now,' Graham repeated.

Marcus went to his knees the exact same moment a woman's scream split the air.

Looking up, Graham saw Rowena Crist at the rear door of the community centre. Her hands covered her mouth.

Is she guilty, too? Lou asked.

He didn't know the answer to that – but she wasn't who he was here for, anyway. 'Leave.'

'Call the police!' Marcus managed, more clearly now. He'd taken his hands from his face.

Graham hit him again, a short, vicious swing that sent him sprawling onto his back.

Rowena screamed a second time.

The politician groaned, trying to curl into himself.

'Why are you doing this?' Her voice trembled, but there was steel beneath. A politician's wife knew how to face crisis. That was probably why she hadn't run yet.

That was something Graham needed to rectify quickly, before she got hurt too.

'We have children. Grandchildren,' Rowena said.

He stared at her. 'I had a daughter, Lucy. She was eight years old.'

'Then you can understand—'

'I understand that Lucy loved to draw, animals mostly. Said she'd paint the whole world when she got better.' His voice cracked and he looked down at Marcus. 'But she never got better. The system your husband voted to cut couldn't save her in time.'

The politician was shaking his head on the floor now. 'I don't know what you mean.'

'You voted for every cut, every reduction in NHS funding. Every reform that put profit before people.' Graham raised the shotgun and pointed it down at Marcus. 'I'm here for everyone who ever suffered because of those cuts.'

Rowena had her phone out.

He turned the gun in her direction. 'Go. Now. Last chance.'

'Just do it, Ro...' Marcus gasped.

Graham started coughing and was forced to spit onto the floor.

'You're not well.'

'Go!' Graham shouted.

Rowena disappeared out the back.

To call the police, Lou warned.

'This will be over before then.'

'Who are you talking to?' Marcus asked.

'Not you.'

A noise behind him. He swung, shotgun extended. The door had simply clattered open in the wind and was banging back and forth. He'd not shut it properly. Moving forward, he closed it. When he turned, Marcus was bearing down on him.

He fired.

The MP's hand exploded in a spray of blood and bone. He staggered and dropped to his knees, his scream primal – the sound of a man discovering pain existed beyond his carefully controlled world.

Graham reeled backward from the force of the discharge but was stopped by the door he'd just closed.

If only your daughter could see you now, Lou said.

'Shut the fuck up!' Graham shouted, kicking out at one of the wooden chairs. It flew over onto its back.

How proud she would be.

Marcus knelt in a spreading pool of his own blood, weeping and shaking, cradling the ruin of his hand. He stared at it, face grey, eyes wide with shock.

Graham walked to where Marcus knelt and pressed the barrel against his forehead.

The politician was too shocked to respond clearly; he managed only a wet mumble. This wasn't what Graham had wanted. He'd wanted him clear-headed before the end, confessing and apologising for his mistakes.

'I wrote to you, called your office. Begged for help when they sanctioned my benefits while my daughter was dying. Don't recall you mentioning any of that on the radio earlier.'

'I... didn't... know...'

'I signed it Graham Blanks, but I guess you get a lot of letters. I tried phoning once when time was running out for Lucy. Your secretary said you were too busy. Important votes coming up. Had to make the hard choices about spending.'

'What... do... you... want?' The MP looked on the verge of passing out.

'Truth. Like I said before. And not your religious truth. You promised to fight the good fight for the NHS. I voted for you, believed you. Told Lucy things would get better because good people like Marcus Crist were fighting for us.'

'I tried—'

Graham shoved his head backwards with the barrel. 'Don't fucking lie to me.'

Do you take pleasure from his terror? Lou said. *Scaring him like that?*

Everyone's scared when it's their turn, he thought in response. *I remember how scared our daughter was.*

Marcus closed his eyes, rocking on his knees.

Graham wasn't going to get the apology he craved. Turning away, Graham marched to the petrol can. He placed the shotgun on a chair, knelt and unscrewed the cap. The smell of petrol filled the air, sharp and promising. He began splashing it over the wooden chairs, down the aisle.

'You know what your last vote was?' Graham didn't wait for an answer. 'Privatisation of NHS services. Selling off dialysis units to companies that could run them more "efficiently".' He laughed, a sound like breaking glass. 'Efficiently, like they're manufacturing car parts instead of keeping children alive.'

Some of the petrol splashed from the floor onto Marcus's hand and he screamed in agony.

Listen to him scream, Lou whispered. *The pain... it's real... and he's feeling it.*

Does it hurt as much as watching our daughter's kidney's fail? Graham thought. *Is it more agonising than counting down the days until her body poisons itself?*

'Please... please... talk to me...'

'Talk to you now? I wanted you to listen. That's all I ever wanted. For any of you to really listen.'

Graham continued to pour.

55

Riddick stepped from the taxi, and the unmistakable boom of a shotgun discharge made him flinch.

'Jesus, what's that?' the taxi driver said.

'What it sounds like. Call the police,' Riddick said, swinging back. 'Tell them—'

He was cut off by a crying woman running up to him. 'My husband...'

He faced her as she clutched his arms. 'Help my husband.'

'Mrs Crist? My name is DI Riddick. Can you tell me what's happening?'

She nodded frantically. 'It's the man from earlier in York, the one the police are looking for. He just came in the front waving that shotgun, and told me to leave.'

'Have you phoned the police?'

'Yes,' she gasped.

'Okay. Wait in the taxi.' He leaned in, addressing the driver. 'Both of you, out of harm's way – please.'

He waited until she was in the taxi and the door was shut before jogging over the gravel path. It was hard to keep his mind from the borrowed heart when it beat so heavily in his chest, but right now, a man was spiralling and more lives were at stake.

And the person responsible had experienced unimaginable loss, not unlike his own.

He heard the taxi driving away, which gave him some relief, and then he looked through the community centre window.

He saw Marcus Crist on the floor on his knees covered in blood. He was clutching the remains of his hand to his chest.

He spotted Graham carrying a red petrol can – the kind people keep in garden sheds for lawnmowers. He still looked ill with his shaky movements and regularly had to steady himself against furniture.

But despite that, there was a methodical, peaceful air to his movements. Had he moved beyond desperation into something quieter, more dangerous?

Riddick realised that this wasn't rage any more. It was a conclusion.

The liquid glinted in the light as it spread across the wooden floor, pooling around chair legs, seeping into the grain.

Riddick's phone buzzed. Text from Control:

Armed response ETA 5 minutes.

In five minutes, this building could be an inferno. Marcus dead. Graham dead.

And him, Riddick? If he went in there, would he die too?

Graham moved closer to Marcus as he poured.

Some of it must have caught the MP's open wound, because he tilted his head back and wailed like nothing Riddick had ever heard before.

It propelled Riddick towards the entrance. The door was unlocked, and he burst into the hallway, before thrusting open the door to the hall. Graham stood in a pool of petrol with a box of matches. His head was lowered. He mumbled, 'I'm sorry I let you down.'

He noticed Riddick and lifted his head.

'Who are you talking to?' Riddick asked.

Graham reached for the shotgun. He lifted it and aimed at Riddick. 'None of your business.' Graham's eyes remained strangely peaceful, and Riddick wondered if they were the eyes of someone who'd already gone.

'Your daughter?'

Graham took a deep breath.

'Lucy?'

'Why do you want to know that?'

'Because I know all about ghosts, too,' Riddick said, trying to stay focused and ignore the fear that came from having a shotgun pointed at his chest.

56

'Ghosts? I'll tell you about ghosts, DI Riddick. The Welfare Reform Bill. Cutting housing benefit for families with disabled children. That still haunts me to this day.' Graham glanced behind at the MP swaying in his blood. 'That sixty-four pounds a week they cut? That was our food budget.' Turning back to Riddick, he continued. 'The Benefit Sanction Reform. Another ghost. Excluded medical appointments from sanctions. Oh, and let's not forget the Emergency Services Communications Act. Centralising NHS contact systems, for efficiency. That one was a real poltergeist. Changed how transplant notifications worked. When Lucy's kidney came available, the call went to a dead number. My fault, apparently, but I did update it – it just got lost in the new systems. The ghost in the machine, eh? I wasn't the only one it happened to, and isn't it strange that those with the right postcodes experienced nothing of the sort?' He shrugged. 'It's almost as if extra special care was taken...'

'What... do... you... want?' the MP managed through his broken teeth.

Graham swung around. 'I want my daughter to live!' The
scream tore from his throat. 'I want her to go to big school!
Learn to drive! Fall in love! Have her own children! Normal
things that normal people get to want! But the things you voted
for made sure that can never happen now.

'It's not just me, though, is it?' Graham asked, turning back
to Riddick now. 'Ghosts like these haunt every family like mine.
Fill up food banks and hospital wards and graveyards. Invisible
to men like Marcus Crist because they never have to see what
they've done. I want you to leave now, DI Riddick. As far as I'm
aware, you've done nothing wrong. But I can't live with those
ghosts any more, and neither should he.'

The shotgun went down on a chair as Graham took the
matches from his pocket. He readied one.

Daddy.

'Not now, Sweetpea.' He struck a match.

Daddy, please—

In that small blue flame, Graham saw Lucy's face.

This isn't what I want.

'I know, Lucy, but—'

'You should listen to her,' Riddick said, his voice strange,
distant.

'And what would you know about it?'

'A lot more than you realise. Would you like to hear?'

'But what's the point?'

'It's either that or you burn us. All three of us.'

The match flame flickered, casting dancing shadows on the
walls where pictures of Jesus watched this terrible passion play.
Graham looked at this detective with his empty hands and
haunted eyes and recognised something...

He understands, Daddy, Lucy said. *He really does understand.*

Graham blew out the match, cast it aside and lit another. 'You have until the flame burns my fingers and I have to drop it.'

And so Riddick started talking.

57

'One moment I had a wife and two daughters,' Riddick said. 'Then I had nothing, so if you want to die now, Graham, I can die with you.' The words came easier than they should have. Part of him had been ready since that day of the explosion. Ready to stop fighting, to let go, to join Rachel and the girls in whatever waited.

Still, another part, smaller and quieter, whispered Emma's name. If she needed him, and there was even the slightest chance he could see her again, could he really throw that away?

The fever gave the man's face a waxy sheen, but his gaze was sharp, calculating. 'What were your children's names?'

'Molly and Lucy... My wife... Rachel.'

Riddick felt the intensity of Graham's eyes. Grief was suddenly a currency. And Graham was willing to accept it. 'Lucy? Same as my Lucy?'

Riddick nodded. 'Yes, that's why I wanted to find you. I think I understand.'

Graham coughed. For a terrible second, Riddick thought he would lose his grip on the match – however, his coughing merely blew the match out. He immediately lit another. 'How did your family die?'

'Car bomb.' The words came automatically now, worn smooth by repetition. How many times had he told this story? To therapists, to colleagues, to bottles of whisky in the dark?

'Why?'

Riddick felt the walls of the community centre closing in. Had he misjudged? Had he believed he could control such a powerful memory? Taking a deep breath, he tried to stabilise himself. He'd been in this uncomfortable moment millions of times. The school run he'd missed because of paperwork, Rachel taking the girls instead. The explosion that had turned a normal Tuesday morning into the end of everything.

He needed to be here now.

'I did my job, put the bad guy away – but he took revenge.'

'It's one of the worst things I've ever heard,' Graham said, and there was something almost like awe in his voice. The recognition of a fellow member of the world's worst club.

'I know you blame yourself for Lucy,' Riddick said.

Graham narrowed his eyes. 'How do you know that?'

'Because I blame myself for what happened to my family.'

'We are not the same.'

'No, but tell me, who else is there really to blame?'

'Try the man on his knees behind—'

'No,' Riddick said. 'It doesn't work like that. It won't work. It'll always come back to you. You think once he's gone, it's over? It won't be. Your mind will just go back to that missed call.'

Graham flinched and closed his eyes.

Riddick considered the opportunity to jump him, but he felt confident he could talk him down now.

Graham opened his eyes. 'You know a lot, DI Riddick. So, in your case, why do you blame yourself?'

'Smugness.' Riddick forced himself to continue, though each word felt like swallowing glass. 'I baited the bastard in custody. Revelled in locking him up more than I needed to. You don't aggravate a poisonous snake.'

The silence stretched between them, two fathers separated by eight feet of petrol-soaked floor and an infinity of loss.

Graham looked confused. 'How can you live knowing the man that did this is alive?'

'The truth is, I couldn't.'

Graham blew the match out and lit another. There was fascination in those red-rimmed eyes. 'So?'

'Well, he died...'

'How?'

It was best not to share the circumstances of his death with people who could still walk away. 'In prison. In a fight.'

'Did you feel relief?'

'Not really.' And it was the truth that still haunted him. He'd thought he would feel closure... peace. Instead, when he'd heard about the death, he'd felt nothing. Empty. The man's death hadn't brought his children back. Revenge was supposed to mean something. But it had turned out to be hollow.

'I don't believe it.'

'Well, you should, it's the truth. I could tell you what you want to hear, Graham. That burning everything down makes sense when they take your children, but I would be lying.'

'But at least he paid. That man behind me... he hasn't. And he's no different to the thug who did that to you. He's worse. He sits in parliament. In a suit. He's supposed to be the best of us.'

Riddick edged forward, looking down at the match that was almost burning Graham's fingers. 'The satisfaction lasts about as long as a match flame. Then you're alone again with the same ghosts.'

Graham blew out the match, his hands shaking now, barely able to hold it steady. The tremor wasn't just from fever. It came from exhaustion. The adrenaline was finally bleeding out of him. He lit another, but it took two tries, his fingers fumbling with the matchbox. 'I guess the difference is, I won't be here. I hope I no longer have to feel anything.'

'I could have taken the easy way out, and now, a day doesn't go past when I'm not grateful I didn't.'

Even as he said it, he doubted it, but it was true. There was gratitude. For the time he'd spent with Gardner, for the children he'd saved from being trafficked, for the borrowed heart someone had died to give him. And spite, of course. His refusal to let the bastards win. To let grief have the final word.

'Yet you're willing to die now for some problem that isn't yours?'

'If that's what it takes. To make you listen, like I listened to others before it was too late.'

'And who did you listen to?'

'I used to see them all the time. All of them – my wife and kids. Ghosts. I lived with them. Talked to them. Slept with them even... until I met someone who changed things.'

'Who?'

He thought of Emma holding his hand in the hospital. Emma refusing to give up on him even when he'd given up on himself. Emma who was now—

No. Think about that later. Not now.

'To you, that's not important. What is important is that I know, and you should know, that one day you won't live under the spell of these ghosts. They will never leave, but eventually, they start to live under your spell.'

'I wish I could believe that.'

'It's true. Why don't you ask your daughter what she wants?'

The question hung in the air. Riddick saw Graham's face twist, saw the exact moment the words hit home. 'No.'

'Okay, why not?'

'Because...' Graham's voice cracked like ice. 'Because...'

'Go on,' Riddick said, edging forward. 'Because...'

'I already know what she wants.' He squeezed his eyes against the pain of the match which had now burned down, but he didn't drop it.

'Tell me.'

'You already know!'

'Still... say it.'

'She wants me to stop!' Taking a deep breath, he opened his eyes. The match had burned out against his fingers. Tears filled his eyes. 'Okay? She wants me to stop!'

Riddick nodded. 'Okay... so, listen to her.'

'I did. I held her while she cried from the pain. While she grew thinner, weaker, greyer. I listened to her breathing stop.' Graham's words were blades, and Riddick felt every cut. He hadn't been there when his girls had died.

'I would give anything to hold my girls again,' Riddick said, and his voice cracked now. 'Anything...'

Graham readied another match to strike.

'Put the match down, Graham. We'll walk out of here together. You can tell your story. Make them listen.'

'Who listens to a convicted murderer?'

'They will. This time I think they will.'

'Rubbish! No one ever listened to me. I tried everything. Filled out forms in triplicate. Made complaints to departments that didn't exist any more. Wrote letters to MPs who sent back form responses about "difficult decisions" and "fiscal responsibility". Called helplines that put me on hold until they closed. Proper channels got me here... why should I bother with them again? Now I have their attention – what makes them worthy of my time of day?'

'Because it may help someone else. It may help their child. And at the end of the day, that's all we've got, isn't it? Small, tiny opportunities to make things better – or the alternative...' He looked around the room. 'Small opportunities to make things worse. Sometimes you've just got to ask yourself – what would they want?'

'But what do I do with all this pain?'

'Is it pain, or is it love?'

'It feels like the same thing.'

'Maybe it is.'

'So what do you do with it?'

'I carry it day by day. Breath by breath. Hour by hour. Because that's what love demands.' The words felt raw coming out, like he'd peeled back skin to show Graham something he rarely showed anyone. But if opening himself up, making himself vulnerable, could save this man's life and stop more bloodshed, then it was worth it. Sometimes the only way through was to bleed together.

'She used to sing. In the hospital. Even with the tubes and the pain. Little voice like a bird. Kept the other kids' spirits up. I wish I was as strong as that.'

Graham's voice was softer now. The memory was pulling him back towards who he'd been before grief had broken him. Riddick could see it in his eyes: the father was resurfacing, the killer receding.

Riddick would be foolish to think that the desire for revenge was gone. He knew, more than anyone, that this would be wishful thinking. But the hate was now competing with something older and deeper – and far more precious. 'What did she sing?'

'Everything. Nursery rhymes. Pop songs. Made-up nonsense.' A ghost of a smile crossed Graham's face, and for a moment he looked younger, like the father he'd been before grief carved him hollow. 'There was one about a dinosaur who loved strawberry laces. Complete gibberish. But it made the other kids laugh, and even the nurses would stop to listen.'

'Tell me more about her.'

And Graham did. Real memories now, not fever dreams or accusations. Her first day of school in her too-big uniform. Teaching her to ride a bike in the park, running behind with one hand on the seat, terrified and proud in equal measure.

Graham paused to cough.

After he stopped, Riddick asked, 'Let me help. Will you give me the matches?'

Graham looked down and closed his eyes. Eventually, he said, 'Yes.' He handed them over.

Riddick took them and thrust them into his pocket, relief flooding through him. He'd seen the chance to end this without more death and had taken it, and now his borrowed heart steadied its rhythm. 'Now, please let's go outside.'

'Thank you...' Graham said.

'You're welcome.'

'...for being one of the only people that truly understands.' Graham reached for the shotgun.

'Graham, don't—'

A tiny red dot appeared on the side of Graham's head.

'Stop!' Riddick shouted.

But Graham raised the weapon and the window exploded inward. The sound of the shot came a microsecond later. Graham's head snapped to the side, and as he fell he turned slightly, looking right at Riddick.

Tasting bile, Riddick lurched and went down to the shot man's side.

Graham's eyes fluttered, still somehow there, clinging to the last seconds of a life that had become unbearable. His lips moved, trying to form words through the bubbling blood.

Leaning close, Riddick cradled the dying man's head in his lap. He could hear boots on gravel outside, radios crackling, the machinery of law and order finally catching up to chaos.

Riddick couldn't make out the last word that whispered out on his dying breath, but he could hazard a guess.

'Lucy's waiting,' Riddick whispered. 'She's waiting for you, and she's not hurting any more. She knows that you tried and she's singing that song about the dinosaur.'

For a moment, Riddick held the hand of the father destroyed by loss, seeing himself in that face. How close had he come? Different circumstances, different choices, and he could have been lying here.

Riddick knew that the line between him and Graham Blanks was thinner than anyone would ever admit. Just luck and timing, nothing more.

Then he closed his own eyes and saw his children feeding the ducks at Rowntree Park. He wept for every parent who'd ever lied to their child and told them that everything would be okay.

Kneeling there in the petrol and blood, holding a dead man who'd loved his daughter into madness, he wept for a world that could break people so completely and then act surprised when they broke things in return.

58

Riddick looked through the observation window at his colleague.

It was pleasantly disorientating to not be the one in the hospital bed for once.

Still, he'd swap places with her in a heartbeat.

Her head was bandaged, and one side of her face was swollen. Both her arms were in casts.

She'd fractured her skull, broken both wrists, shattered her left shoulder and suffered internal bleeding that had required emergency surgery. She was alive, though – against the odds.

Unlike Riddick, she wasn't from Yorkshire, but she clung to life with the same stubbornness.

The doctor had been as positive as they could have been considering it was still early days. She was responding to stimuli and her pupils were reactive. The swelling in her brain was reducing faster than they'd expected.

There was no denying the long road ahead though. Months of rehabilitation. But there was hope.

Although, how often had hope let him down? He was

certain he'd talked Graham Blanks down. He'd been wrong, and then he'd been too late to seal the deal.

'I couldn't save him,' he said out loud. No one was near to hear him, but he felt foolish for speaking.

Maybe he just couldn't be saved, he thought.

But as much as he wanted to believe that, he just couldn't.

After all, Emma saved me, didn't she?

59

Riddick went home with the intention of packing for Salisbury. However, once back in his flat, he was so overwhelmed with exhaustion and needed to lie down. As he reached for his ringing phone, he saw on his alarm clock that it was now the early afternoon of the following day.

'Bollocks.'

He'd slept for eighteen hours.

He answered his phone. 'Mike?'

There was a moment of silence.

Not good.

'Mike?'

'Yes, Paul. Are you at home? In York?'

'Yes, I'd have been down last night, but a nap turned into anything but... Anyway, why?'

'I don't know how to tell you this.' Yorke sounded close to tears.

Riddick tasted bile. Please God... don't... just don't...

'Is there someone you can be with... someone you can call?'

'Mike, I'm not a fucking child. What's happened?'

'We've found a body.'

Riddick's vision blurred.

'Paul...'

Riddick swung his legs out of bed, leaned over and started to cough.

60

Coughing, Riddick sat in the Fox and Hounds.

His throat was like sandpaper, and he had an escalating temperature.

Not that he cared.

On the table in front of him sat a double whisky on ice.

His fingers traced up and down the side of the misty glass.

It'd been like this for thirty minutes – he was yet to take a sip.

In between coughs, and the temptation of the whisky, he checked the time. It wasn't long until his train to Salisbury.

Taking hold of the glass, he swirled the whisky around, catching the smell. A welcoming smell. A smell like coming home.

A trick... a trap... It offered oblivion... annihilation. Problem was, right now, he was struggling to care.

The phone call from Yorke was on a loop in his head:

'Burned remains were found in the woodland in the early hours.'

'Burned... It might not be her.'

'Gardner's belongings were there with the body.'

'That doesn't prove anything.'

'Article SE have accepted responsibility.'

'They're lying.'

'I need you to prepare yourself.'

'Fuck you, Mike.'

Riddick lifted the whisky from the scarred wood.

How many times had he been in this position? How many glasses between him and the car bomb, between him and his daughters' graves? In his mind's eye, he saw Graham opening a box of matches.

He coughed again and ripples spread over the amber liquid.

Emma.

He could feel her hand in his.

Emma.

Why did you have to go hunting monsters without me?

Worse even: why did I let you?

He pressed the glass to his lips, closed his eyes...

'Don't... Don't...'

He heard her demands.

He put the glass down, folded over and cried.

He coughed and cried, until it grew dark, and then in his mind's eye, he saw Graham dropping a match.

And this time it was lit.

61

Riddick woke in a place that was familiar to him.

Machines beeped around him, and tubes ran into his body.

He felt like he'd been hit by a bus. His vision was cloudy and his mouth dry.

He took a deep breath and then started to cough; he turned and threw up over the side of the bed.

The machine started to beep wildly.

* * *

After he was cleaned up, the doctor explained what had happened to him.

'You've been fighting a severe respiratory infection – pneumonia,' Dr Mitchell said, checking his chart. 'Your immunosuppressed state made it critical. You've been unconscious for four days, Mr Riddick.'

Four days. Christ.

'The IV antibiotics are working, but you'll need more time before we can consider discharge. You may experience some memory gaps – that's normal with the high fever you've been running. Some patients remember fragments, like dreams; others have complete blackouts.'

Riddick's chest ached with each breath. His limbs felt like they belonged to someone else.

He started to plead for his phone, trying to sit up. 'I need to go to Salisbury—'

'Paul, you're in no condition—'

'Emma... There's a body!' His voice cracked, sending him into another coughing fit. The panic was rising, making his heart monitor accelerate. 'I have to—'

The doctor signalled to a nurse, who prepared a syringe.

'This will help you rest.'

'No—'

But the sedative was already entering his IV line. The world tilted and went dark.

* * *

He didn't know how long he slept, but when he woke, he felt marginally better. Well enough to think clearly, at least.

Weak legs barely held him as he stumbled out of bed to retrieve his phone from the bedside cabinet. Five days since Yorke's call about the body. His hands shook as he scrolled through messages – two from Yorke, one from the chief constable.

But he was drawn to one voicemail from an unknown number. He couldn't say why – just felt compelled to listen to it first.

Static. Background noise like wind or traffic. Then, someone said his name, gently. 'Paul.'

The monitor registered an increase in his heart rate.

It had to be.

He listened again. 'Paul...'

That voice. Even through static and distance and whatever hell she'd been through, he knew that voice.

'Emma?' He pressed the phone harder against his ear. 'Emma, is that you?'

But of course, it was a voicemail and there was no response.

He stared at the phone while the monitor beeped frantically. A seventeen-second call. His name. It was all it took for hope to be reborn.

A nurse came in. 'Mr Riddick, you really need—'

'She's alive,' he said, cutting the young man off. His legs gave out and he sank back onto the bed, still clutching the phone. Relief and hope and fear all crashed over him at once, and for the first time in months, he felt the weight lift just slightly. Not gone – never gone – but lighter. Bearable. She was alive.

62

Graham Blanks was buried beneath a grey Yorkshire sky.

Samantha Whitfield stood alone by the graveside, her black coat inadequate against the February wind, holding an umbrella in case the drizzle turned to rain.

Samantha had hoped that Lou would return from Australia for the funeral. She hadn't and there'd been no former colleagues from his NHS days, or friends of sorts who had made an appearance.

Not that she could really blame anyone – considering the circumstances around Graham's final actions and death.

She had hoped the kind DI would make an appearance, but he was sick in hospital with pneumonia – she wondered if it was connected to the same illness that had run Graham into the ground on that final day.

The vicar spoke in practised generalities about loss and redemption, words worn smooth from overuse. He mentioned Graham's love for Lucy at Samantha's request, but it wasn't much more than just another service to get through before lunch, another name in the register, another soul commended to God's mercy with minimal fuss.

Afterwards, she went to visit a small headstone, already weathered by six months of Yorkshire rain.

LUCY BLANKS, BELOVED DAUGHTER, 2015–2024

She kissed her fingers and touched the stone.

'Before all this, your father was a good man,' Samantha said. 'That matters, even if people say otherwise.'

Sudden movement above caught Samantha's eye – dark shapes circling against the grey sky.

Crows.

Three of them landed on nearby headstones, heads cocked, watching, as if bearing witness. As if remembering what others chose to forget.

63

Several days later, DI Paul Riddick came to visit Samantha. She welcomed him in. 'How are you feeling?'

'Much better, thank you,' he said, proffering a bunch of flowers.

'They're lovely, thank you. Would you like a drink?'

'No, it's a flying visit, I'm afraid. I have a train to catch.'

'Anywhere nice?'

'To hopefully see an old friend in Salisbury,' he said and smiled.

They talked about the service that Riddick had missed due to his illness, and then Samantha felt tears in her eyes. 'I saw one headline, the day after, and I can't shake it.'

Riddick nodded. 'I know it's hard, but it's best to try and shut out the outside noise.'

'"Benefits Scrounger Goes on Killing Spree",' Samantha said, ignoring his suggestion. 'They don't mention Lucy. Don't mention the sanctions or the missed transplant call. Don't mention twenty years of public service. Just another dangerous man who needed putting down. They even refer to you as the hero that put him down.'

Riddick sighed. 'Precisely. They write what they want. We know the truth, don't we?' He recalled phoning her immediately after Graham's death. He'd wanted her to hear the truth from him, rather than any other fictional nonsense the press chose to run with. 'Shut it out, Samantha. The news suits certain people. Making Graham into a convenient caricature of working-class rage. It's the system fighting back, rewriting history, giving him no values.'

'He isn't the only one with blood on his hands.'

'I know,' Riddick said. 'And the government has promised a review,' he offered, knowing how hollow it sounded. 'Into the benefits system. How it handles families with sick children.'

Samantha scowled. 'Reviews and reforms and lessons learned. Soon forgotten about when the press move on to something else.'

Riddick sighed.

'You know what he'd say now? Graham?' Samantha asked. 'He'd say it was nonsense. That changes are always too expensive to implement, too complex to navigate. Much easier to add more security to Jobcentres, hire more guards for MPs, build the walls higher between those who decide and those who suffer.'

'Do you know what?' Riddick said. 'I will stay for that drink if that's okay.'

'Your train?'

'I can get the later one.'

She smiled. 'That would be nice.'

64

Riddick never caught that train.

On his way to the station, he received another unknown call.

His hands trembled so much, he almost dropped the phone while answering. 'Emma?'

Static.

'Emma? Please talk to me.'

More static.

'For the love of God, please...'

'Paul.'

He had tears in his eyes. 'Yes... God... yes, it is you. Where are you?'

And static resumed.

'Emma?'

'Paul...' She spoke so quietly. 'I...'

He jammed his finger into one ear, fearful he might miss a whisper.

'I need you to stay away.'

His throat tightened. 'Why? Where are you?'

'Please.' He was certain he heard fear in her voice. Or, God forbid, was it resignation? He couldn't tell through the static and his own desperate need to understand.

'But I can't. Are you in danger? Let me help.'

'You can't.'

She was alive and asking him to abandon her. How could she expect that? After Molly, after Lucy, after Rachel, after everyone he'd failed to save, how could she ask him to walk away when he finally had a chance to help someone he loved? Because that's what this was, wasn't it? Love. And it may be inconvenient, but it couldn't be ignored.

'Trust me,' she said.

And then she really was gone.

65

So, Riddick sat on his hands, and it was the hardest thing he'd ever done.

Over the next two weeks, he touched base with Yorke regularly, but SEROCU were none the wiser. DNA had already confirmed that the body wasn't Gardner's before Riddick had even listened to that message from her, but he'd been unconscious in a hospital bed.

The body was a Jane Doe.

But a small organised crime outfit, connected to Article SE, had claimed responsibility for killing Gardner. 'She'd been too close, and this is what happens' was the only message they'd delivered. Members of this crime outfit had since disappeared, so they couldn't be questioned over the false claim.

Yorke had received similar messages from Gardner to back off, and so, despite throwing resources at it, he was working on keeping an extremely low profile.

Over that fortnight, MP Marcus Crist resigned. The official statement cited mental health grounds – the trauma of the attack, the need to 'heal privately with family'. He gave one carefully managed interview from his townhouse, speaking earnestly about forgiveness and the importance of moving forward. Rowena sat beside him holding his remaining hand. They never mentioned the votes that had started it all, nor did they acknowledge the policies that had drawn a desperate father out of the woodwork for a reckoning.

Less than a week later, Crist had a consulting position with Pharmatech Solutions, one of the companies bidding for NHS contracts. Senior advisory role, healthcare policy expertise required. Six figures to help private companies navigate public sector opportunities. The announcement came the same week Universal Credit sanctions were quietly extended from three to six months for missed appointments. No fanfare, no debate. Just another adjustment buried in the small print of a broader bill.

Riddick thought about Graham turning in his grave.

Frost remained in a coma. Riddick visited every day, sitting in the same plastic chair, watching the machines breathe for her. Sometimes he talked – about the Hurren case, about Emma, and his desperation to go to Salisbury and find her, about the weather, about nothing. Sometimes he just sat in silence, two broken people in a room full of mechanical hope.

'Oh, and Crist got a new job,' he told her still form. 'Pharmaceutical consulting. Probably got a sympathy bonus in the salary negotiations. Survivor of extremist violence.'

The ventilator wheezed its response.

'While Graham's daughter stays dead. While the next Lucy is already getting sick somewhere, starting down the same path.'

He leaned back in the uncomfortable chair.

Makes you wonder if he had a point, he thought.

But then he admonished himself. Violence could never be the answer. If it was, then the world was most certainly doomed.

Deep down, he heard Graham's voice. *Then the world is doomed.*

But then Frost woke up, and everything seemed a little brighter for a short time... until it wasn't.

66

'Today, she thought I was her father,' Riddick said.

Dr Rhinds nodded.

'Better than yesterday, I guess, when she thought I was Graham Blanks.'

'But she recognised you three days ago?'

Riddick nodded. 'So, is she regressing?'

'Traumatic brain injury isn't linear, Detective. There will be good days and bad days. The fact that she's having more good days is encouraging.'

'She won't be coming back to the job, will she?' Laura Frost – sharp, capable, driven – would never wear a badge again. The woman in room 314 looked like her, sounded like her, but something essential had broken in that twenty-foot fall. Not just skull and spine, but the ineffable quality that made someone a detective.

'It's far too early—'

'She had good instincts. Now she can't remember what she had for breakfast. Can't follow a conversation for more than five minutes without drifting.'

'If she can't go back to the job, then she'll find a different path,' Rhinds said carefully, using the tone medical professionals reserved for difficult truths. 'Many TBI patients go on to fulfilling lives. Different from what they'd planned, perhaps.'

Riddick's chest ached. Laura Frost, who'd arrived in York looking for a fresh start, who'd been sharp and capable. Now reduced to 'adaptation and acceptance'. Another person broken on his watch. He smiled, said thank you and left before the doctor could offer more platitudes.

67

The Danny Hurren case was wrapped up five days later. At long bloody last!

The cash-in-transit job had gone ahead as planned – professional crew from Manchester, inside man at the security firm, everything lined up perfectly. Except this time, North Yorkshire Police were waiting. Armed response units in position, helicopter support, the full machinery of law enforcement ready to pounce.

They took down seven men without a shot being fired. The crew surrendered the moment they realised they were surrounded, professionals who knew when the game was up. Danny Hurren himself had tried to run, made it all of fifty yards before a police dog brought him down in a pub car park.

'Good work, Paul,' the chief constable said after the press conference. 'Textbook intelligence-led policing.'

Textbook?

Was he making a point?

After all, no one had been too pleased with his gallivanting around York after Graham – even if he was the one that eventually found him.

Riddick stood at the back, watching Hurren being led to the transport van in cuffs. Their eyes met briefly. Riddick made a point of not sneering – when he'd done that to Haller, it'd ruined his life.

Hurren spat on the ground and narrowed his eyes.

Riddick then realised the irrelevance of a sneer.

The hate was still there.

And if the incident with Graham Blanks had shown him anything, it was that if and when you started to hate, anything was possible.

Haller had killed Riddick's family from hate, not because of Riddick's arrogance.

He wasn't worried about Hurren though.

Riddick had no family left to take.

68

Riddick had hoped for some satisfaction from the Hurren case, but he took none.

Just another arrest, another file closed, another criminal heading to prison while the machine that created them ground on unchanged.

Jamie Morrison was still in witness protection and would probably never return home to York. The shop owners who'd been burgled would get their insurance payouts eventually. The security firm would tighten procedures until the next inside man saw an opportunity. And somewhere, another Danny Hurren was already planning, already desperate, already willing to take what the system wouldn't give.

He struggled to switch his mind from cold hard facts:

Lucy and Graham Blanks were dead.

Frost was learning to walk again.

Gardner remained missing, having warned him off.

And Riddick was still going through the motions, playing detective while feeling nothing but the numb weight of under-standing that nothing really changed, nothing really mattered, and the best they could do was clean up the mess while waiting for the next one.

He filed his report, closed the case and went home to his empty flat and his prescribed medications, another day done in a life that had become about endurance rather than purpose.

69

Riddick's new heart was starting to play ball. His latest tests showed improvement – the new heart settling into its rhythm, rejection markers down, his body finally accepting this borrowed gift. 'Remarkable progress,' Dr Mitchell had said.

Someone else was experiencing remarkable progress according to Dr Rhinds, too.

Not that Riddick needed to be told – he visited his colleague daily and saw it for himself.

Frost could sit up properly now, track conversations, remember his name every day. There were whispers she might even return to some form of duty, though these came from her rather than any medical professional.

Still, optimism was welcome.

He sat beside Frost's bed, both of them watching the small television mounted on the wall. On screen, the BBC News anchor delivered the day's tragedy with practised neutrality. Another benefits-related suicide, this time in Leeds. Father of two, sanctioned for missing appointments while his wife was undergoing chemotherapy. Eight weeks without payments. The note he'd left spoke of failing his family, of being worth more dead than alive.

'Turn it off if you want,' Frost, who was now well enough to pick up on his discomfort, said. Her voice was clearer now, the slur almost gone.

Riddick watched to the end. The victim's photo filled the screen – an ordinary man caught in extraordinary desperation. Thin face, nervous smile, the look of someone trying to hold it together for the camera. Then came the family photos. Two boys, maybe eight and ten, who'd now grow up wondering if they could have saved their father. Another widow left to navigate the same system that had broken her husband.

Tomorrow's Graham Blanks being forged in today's institutional cruelty.

'System's fucked,' Frost observed. 'What do we do?'

Riddick had no answer. He thought of Graham's wall of newspaper cuttings – all those documented failures. Some would be press blather, but some would be evidence based. Evidence of systematic cruelty.

North Yorkshire Police had photographed every inch for evidence, catalogued each article, filed it all away in boxes that would gather dust in storage.

Truth documented but ignored.

'We do what we've always done,' he said finally. 'Show up. Bear witness. Try to catch people before they fall completely.'

'So, we're the sticking plaster?'

'Better than nothing.'

On screen, the news had moved on. A nationalist rally, a celebrity scandal, tomorrow's weather. The dead father already forgotten, reduced to a statistic that might feature in some future government review that would change nothing.

Frost reached for the remote with still-shaky hands and

switched it off. In the silence that followed, they could hear the everyday sounds of the hospital – trolleys in corridors, distant conversations, machines keeping people alive. The grinding machinery of care overwhelmed and underfunded but still trying.

'We can't ever think that Graham Blanks made the right choices,' Riddick said.

'But did he have the right choices available?'

Riddick shrugged, said goodbye to Frost and headed home.

April rain began to fall, washing York's ancient stones clean for another day of the same old struggles, the same old failures, the same old desperate people pushed past their breaking points. He was tired. Bone-deep tired. Tired of bearing witness to suffering he couldn't prevent. Tired of showing up too late, of picking up pieces that could never be put back together.

70

After several fitful nights of dreams about Gardner with still no word from her, Riddick decided enough was enough.

He wasn't familiar with Salisbury, so after an early morning drive, he spent the afternoon in the presence of the cathedral, gathering his thoughts.

He looked up to where the spire was puncturing the darkening clouds, and when the rain bled through, he felt contented that he'd made the right choice.

* * *

Yorke opened the door before he could knock. He regarded Riddick with a sigh. 'Surprised it took you this long.'

'I don't know. Maybe I just wasn't ready. I'm feeling better. Fitter.'

'So, her warning to stay away means nothing?'

'No, not nothing. I just don't trust it.'

Yorke led him through to the kitchen, put the kettle on with movements that suggested this conversation had been inevitable. 'First question, do you still genuinely believe it was her that phoned?' Yorke's expression was carefully neutral, but Riddick caught the sadness underneath. The doubt.

'Yes. It was her.' And there really was no doubt in Riddick's voice.

Yorke looked at him and gave a contented, sharp nod. 'And you still want to go against her explicit wishes?' He raised an eyebrow.

'It's been two months. Neither of us has heard from her again.'

'Two months is a long time. Do you suspect the worst?'

Riddick shook his head. 'No. She's alive.'

'How can you know?'

He touched the centre of his jacket, beneath which was the transplanted heart that was feeling more and more like his own every day. 'I know. And I'm not waiting any longer. Like I said outside, how can we trust what she said? She could have been forced to say it. Also, whatever these things are could have changed. Two months is a long time...'

Yorke nodded. 'I don't disagree. So what exactly do you plan to do?'

'I want to speak to Fairweather.'

'He's the most untouchable man I know. Wrapped in legal protection so thick we can't even interview him without a battalion of solicitors present. You don't speak to him – he speaks to you.'

'With all due respect, Mike, he hasn't met me yet.'

Yorke smiled and nodded. 'No, he has not.'

They moved to the living room. They sat across from each other like chess players considering their next move.

'The bodies,' Riddick said quietly. 'Tell me more about those bodies.'

Yorke sighed. 'Three bodies found in properties connected to Fairweather's shell companies. Then, the fourth, the one in the woods, the one with Emma's belongings. No paper trails, no missing person reports that match. They were people who wouldn't be missed. But every property had been sold on, every connection severed through intermediaries. The bodies could have been placed there by anyone. There is no real link to Fairweather other than the coincidence that he formerly owned those three properties.'

'And the organised group, the one that claimed responsibility for Emma's supposed death?'

'Gone. Disappeared.'

'And what did they do before they took responsibility and then suddenly disappeared?'

'Too much to explain now – maybe you'd like to see the file.'

Riddick took a deep breath, feeling a sudden growth of trust for Yorke.

'Emma loves you.'

This made Riddick flinch.

'Oh, don't act surprised. You know.'

'I'm not surprised... just didn't expect you to say it.'

'Because of that, I thought her judgements regarding your instincts and capabilities were compromised.'

'And now?'

'Now, I don't know. I'd like to say I sense something, something that suggests I was wrong, but I don't know if that's wishful thinking.' He leaned forward. 'But listen, I'm desperate, too. She's one of my closest friends. And I agree with you, we've been sitting on our hands for too long. So, you're in, but Paul...'

'Yes?'

'I've made some kind of peace with the fact that we may have lost her. Fragile peace, but peace all the same. You haven't.

I don't know whether that's a good or a bad thing moving forward, but I really hope you can control yourself should the situation change in a way none of us like or want to imagine.'

'Mike.' Riddick fixed him with a stare that had seen too much to be surprised by anything. 'I've buried my family. Survived alcoholism and substance abuse. Been stabbed, survived a heart infection and then a transplant that is only now starting to settle. Recently, I watched a good man die because he couldn't save his daughter and went mad. I held him after a sniper's bullet ended his pain. I have the credentials to stay in control.'

Yorke nodded.

Riddick thought it best not to mention his hands around a glass of whisky following the phone call. A momentary lapse. He wondered now if he'd have come through it if not for the sudden onset of flu.

'However, I will warn you, Mike... until I see her body – until I can touch her face and know beyond doubt that she's gone – I am never giving up on her. Never.'

Yorke nodded slowly. 'Okay.'

'So when do we start?'

'We start when you finally call me boss.'

'Very alpha.'

'Not really,' Yorke said, smiling, 'but if I'm taking you to HQ, I don't want anyone else getting ideas.'

'Favouritism?'

Yorke snorted. 'I think we're a way off that, don't you?'

And then Riddick felt something shifting in his chest. For once, it wasn't his heart.

Here he was in Emma's territory. Traces and echoes of her everywhere.

It felt intimate, intrusive even.

This was the world she'd returned to when she'd shut him out.

He was here without permission. It felt wrong, somehow, but how could he respect boundaries in such a situation?

After meeting Yorke, Riddick returned to the cathedral.

Somewhere, out there, in this world of spires and secrets, Emma was alive.

He knew that Yorke would expect him to play by the rules.

Of course, he would try his best to honour that trust, but Emma came first.

And if and when it came to it, he would ditch any rules that protected the predators and abandoned the prey.

* * *

MORE FROM WES MARKIN

The next instalment in Wes Markin's gripping, gritty Yorkshire Murders series is available to order now here:

https://mybook.to/YorkshireMurder8BackAd